DOUBLE EXPOSURE

DOUBLE EXPOSURE

BARBARA TAYLOR McCAFFERTY
and BEVERLY TAYLOR HERALD

𝆎

Kensington Books
http://www.kensingtonbooks.com

KENSINGTON BOOKS are published by

Kensington Publishing Corp.
850 Third Avenue
New York, NY 10022

Library of Congress Card Catalog Number: 96-80344
ISBN 1-57566-207-8

First Kensington Hardcover Printing: September, 1997
10   9   8   7   6   5   4   3   2   1

Printed in the United States of America

Acknowledgments

Special thanks again go to Bill Love for sharing his thirty-plus years of radio expertise and advice. Mr. Love is currently afternoon disc jockey for WKDQ-FM, Evansville, Indiana, and has been Program Director or morning announcer in such cities as Chattanooga, Louisville, Cleveland, Orlando, and Knoxville. Thanks, Bill, from both of us, for all the inside information.

Chapter 1

•

NAN

I suppose I've always known that it would be pretty difficult to get away with murder. I had no idea, however, that it might be equally difficult to get away *from* murder. Otherwise, I would never have agreed to emcee that stupid telethon at the mall. No matter what Charlie said.

Charlie Belcher is the program director at WCKI, Country Kentucky Indiana, the premier country music radio station in Louisville, Kentucky. I'm not quite sure what *premier* means in reference to country music radio stations, but this is how I've been told to say the station ID, so I don't argue with it. What it does not mean, without a doubt, is that we're number one in the market. If we were, I'm sure I'd have been told to come right out and say so, oh, about a million times a day. I'm Nan Tatum, CKI's midday disc jockey, playing the hits during the ten-to-three time slot.

My job, believe me, sounds a lot more terrific than it really is.

It especially sounds terrific if you're listening to my twin sister, Bert. To hear Bert talk, you'd think that I was a cross between Wolfman Jack (only without the beard) and Madonna (only without the figure, the face, the voice, the fame, and the money).

Bert also seems to have the idiotic idea that, because I'm off the air at three, I get off work the very second I turn off my mike. That almost never happens. Mainly because good old Charlie keeps coming up with some harebrained thing or another that I'm supposed to do to promote the station after my shift.

In the past, Charlie has arranged for me to climb flagpoles, milk cows at the state fair, and judge greasy barbecue contests. He has even arranged for me to appear at Churchill Downs being led around the track, mounted on a skittish thoroughbred. This last had been a compromise. Charlie had wanted me to ride the brute in a mock race, but when I'd casually mentioned WCKI's skyrocketing health insurance rates and the distinct possibility of my having to undergo years of physical and psychological therapy if I sustained any injuries whatsoever, he'd finally relented.

Now Charlie was at it again. On a beautiful Monday in April, when warm breezes and spring flowers were all but beckoning to everybody in Louisville to take the afternoon off and spend it in a park somewhere, Charlie had come up with a gig indoors. He'd stopped me in the hallway this morning just as my first newscast at eleven was starting.

Newscasts are something that disc jockeys look forward to. It's during this time that a newsperson takes over the mike for a few minutes, and you get to duck out for a bathroom break and maybe grab a Coke. Those were certainly my intentions this morning. Dale Stewart, the newsguy at WCKI, had just started his newscast when I made for the door. Unfortunately, as soon as I set foot in the hall, Charlie was waiting for me. "Come on, Nan, say you'll emcee this telethon, OK? The telethon is for a good cause," he'd said, giving the sheaf of papers in his hand a little shake for emphasis.

I just looked at him. "Oh? What good cause would that be?"

Charlie is about fifty pounds overweight, and he evidently thinks if he wears clothes too big, it'll make him look thinner. He's wrong. It makes him look as if he's wearing hand-me-downs. From Orson Welles. Charles gave the waistband of his baggy trousers a little hitch over his beer belly, and then he said, "Well, let me see, the good cause is—" He gave the papers in his hand a long look, obviously searching for a name, but he must not have found it. "—well, it's a *charity*," he finally said. "I can't remember which one offhand, but I think it's one of the biggies. You know, diabetes, cancer, Lou Gehrig's disease, something like that." He shrugged his meaty shoulders and hurried on. "Besides, who cares? It's good exposure."

Now we were getting down to the nitty-gritty. I'd known, of course, that this was the one and only reason he wanted me to do this thing. Charlie could not have cared less if every man, woman, and child in Kentucky came down with diabetes, cancer, *and* Lou Gehrig's disease, all rolled into one. Unless, of course, the illnesses hampered their ability to tune into WCKI. Nope, what Charlie mainly cared about was getting WCKI's name in front of as many people as many times a day as possible.

It didn't matter to Charlie that in the last few months I'd had more *exposure*, as he put it, than I'd ever had in my entire life. How had I managed to generate all this publicity? Looking back, it hadn't been all that hard. First, I'd managed to be born with a twin sister. Not exactly something I'd set out to do.

And second, my twin sister and I had managed to put a killer behind bars who'd eluded the police for over twenty-five years. Come to think of it, Bert and I had not set out to do this one either. We hadn't had a whole lot of choice. It was either catch the killer or have the killer catch us.

You might've thought, however, from the way the local media jumped on this thing that Bert and I had suddenly donned matching capes and started scouring the night skies in the hopes that Commissioner Gordon would send up a bat signal.

This is not to imply that Bert and I actually believe that it was our astounding crime-solving skills that got us so much media attention. Hardly. It was, without a doubt, because we were twins. As one local television anchorwoman told me, "You two are a very visual story."

We were visual all right. For a while there, I thought if I saw one more photo of Bert and me with the caption, "Double Trouble," I might actually throw up. *Twice.*

The *Courier-Journal*, the main newspaper here in Louisville, even made a big deal about our being named after the Bobbsey twins. As if maybe Bert and I had planned our mutual crime-fighting career from the day we were born.

I hated to break it to the *Courier*, but neither Bert nor I have ever been terribly thrilled about our having the same names as the older set of twins in the Bobbsey books. For one thing, we couldn't help but notice that the Bobbseys were boy and girl twins.

Mom, however, had evidently made up her mind to name her twins after the Bobbseys, and she wasn't about to change it. When her babies turned out to be two little girls instead of the boy and girl twins she'd been so sure she was going to have, Mom had simply lengthened the name *Bert* to *Ber-*

trice. And then, she'd gone around telling everybody she knew to call Bertrice *Bert* for short.

Like I said, the *Courier-Journal* ate the whole Bobbsey twin thing up. "You know, I've had so much exposure lately," I'd told Charlie this morning, "I wonder if I really need any more right now. I mean, isn't there such a thing as overkill?" Even now, I can't believe I used that particular word. Without missing a beat or anything. So much for the theory that twins have a heightened sense of intuition. "Isn't it possible," I went on, "to be in the public eye a little too much?"

Charlie certainly gave that little suggestion thoughtful consideration. He burst out laughing. "Are you *nuts?*" he said. "Can't you see what all this publicity has done for your career?"

I hate to be talked to as if I'm still in kindergarten. Of course, I could see what the publicity had done. After Bert and I became the local Bobbsey batgirls, my ratings—which had been on an unmistakable downhill slide the past few years—had suddenly taken a substantial leap in the fall book. *Book*, by the way, is radio-ese for the Arbitron ratings book. The fall book had shown that a significant portion of the Louisville TSA—total survey area—had switched to WCKI— otherwise known as me—for middays. So many, in fact, that right after the book came out, I actually began to worry about whether WCKI was going to move me to another time slot.

That's the way it works in television and radio. TV execs really aren't trying to drive you crazy by hiding your favorite show when the new season opens. Some yahoo in a board room really does have a plan. When a network or station finds itself with a winner, they often move that winner around to boost the time slots they're losing in. Or to provide competition for a winner another network may have.

The good news for me had been that the sagging time slot to which CKI might've moved me had been mine, so I'd stayed right where I was. Thank God, I might add. The next closest ratings loser was nights, the seven-to-midnight shift, and I would've hated to work that one. Not only was it a longer shift, but I could just see myself trying to explain to some guy I'd just met that, at the age of almost-forty, I didn't date on a school night. Or on a Saturday. In fact, Sunday nights were the only nights I had free. Oh yes, that would be fun. Working nights could effectively reduce every date I had to a one-night stand.

Luckily, the only thing that CKI did after my ratings jumped was make a slight change in format. Can you believe it? *More* talk and *less* music. That's what they want. It continues to amaze me, but apparently, a lot of listeners want to chat on-air with a real live person who'd helped solve a real dead murder.

Suddenly, in addition to requests to play "my two-timin' boyfriend a cheatin' song," I started getting calls asking me to help solve every kind of crime from littering to shoplifting.

That, of course, was one of the problems. Because, every once in a while, I've actually had somebody call up to tell me about an unsolved murder. Those calls were the worst. I've had a job in radio for almost twenty years now, and I've pretty much reconciled myself to the harsh reality that my having to take requests makes me a sitting duck for every Tom, Prick, and Hairy (no, those last two names are *not* misspelled) who gets it into his peabrain to make my day with a few obscene remarks.

Lately, though, listening to a few obscenities from Tom, Prick, and Hairy would be a step up. Anything would be better than listening to yet another horrible tale of murder and despair from some poor soul who actually expects me, of all people, to find out whodunit.

This was also why I was getting more and more hesitant to do public appearances. Because, not only did I have people call me at the station, I also had them walk up to me whenever and wherever I showed up in person. I couldn't even go to the grocery anymore without somebody stopping me in the toiletries aisle, or in front of the potatoes, or—even worse— in the checkout lane just when I was starting to think I was home free.

Sure enough, just as I'm breathing a sigh of relief, the lady standing in back of me with the cart full of frozen dinners will say loud enough to echo off the back wall, "Hey, you're one of them twins that solved that there murder, ain't ya?" And then, likely as not, either she—or the woman in front of me, or some guy three aisles over—will have a truly entertaining crime spree to tell me about.

Oh yes, there was definitely a downside to all the publicity Bert and I had been getting.

As well as, I admit, an upside. "Look," I'd told Charlie, "I am well aware how much I've benefited from—"

Charlie was already nodding. "Good, good. Be at the mall in St. Matthews at three-thirty. In the Food Court. You'll be emceeing the announcement of donations. Start the promos that you'll be there."

I just looked at him. *"Start the promos?"* I repeated weakly. He wanted me to start telling all of Louisville exactly where I'd be at three-thirty this afternoon?

Charlie must've sensed another objection coming on, or maybe he caught the look of alarm on my face. "Start the promos," he said again, this time a little more firmly, and then he turned abruptly and walked off. He wasn't about to give me the chance to object again. He moved as fast as he could without actually breaking into a run.

And like an idiot, I just stood there and let him go.

I may have agreed to do the telethon, but I had no intention of driving to the St. Matthews Mall alone. Once Charlie was out of sight, I hurried down the hall to beg a ride from whichever newsguy Charlie had assigned to cover the telethon.

It turned out to be Bob Grayson, wouldn't you know. I believe it goes to show just how anxious I was *not* to drive to the mall all by myself that I didn't hesitate for a second before I asked Bob if he'd give me a ride. Have I mentioned that Bob is twenty-eight, short, balding, has bad teeth, and every time he and I spend more than five minutes together, he complains nonstop about his wife, Edna?

I'm not sure why exactly Bob always does this, but I believe I've narrowed it down to two possibilities. Either Bob is laying the foundation for the Big Move he's going to make on me one day, or else he views me as some kind of mother figure.

And he's telling on Edna.

By the time Bob and I finally got to the mall, of course, I didn't particularly care why Bob felt compelled to enumerate all the ways that his wife was a pain in the neck. I also didn't care that, according to Bob, Edna flirted with every man she met, that she had the vocabulary of a sailor, and that she wore her necklines too low and her hemlines too high. Frankly, all I cared about was getting Bob to shut up, for God's sake.

I'd also begun to wish that I'd simply told Charlie at the outset why I was reluctant to appear in public these days. It wasn't just strangers in general I wanted to avoid. It was one stranger in particular—Looney Tunes.

Looney Tunes was the nickname I'd given the woman who'd been phoning me on a pretty much regular basis ever since the first article about Bert and me had appeared in the *Courier.* The first time she'd phoned, Looney hadn't been too bad. "Nan Tatum, I've got you a murder to solve." Her voice had been raspy, but strong. She'd sounded as if she were presenting me with a gift that should thrill me to no end. "The police," she went on, "all think the murderer's dead, but I know who really did it, and the police are wrong."

I'd told her what the station had told me to say in situations like this. "Ma'am, I'm not a detective. You really ought to call the authorities, and—"

"Are you deaf?" Looney had pronounced it as if it were spelled D-E-E-F. "I *said* the police think the case is closed. They won't listen to me!"

"But, Ma'am, if you have new evidence, you should—" That was all I'd managed to get out before Looney Tunes hung up on me.

Since then she'd called so many times, I'd lost count. The radio station, of course, has always had procedures in place to prevent weirdos from getting through to the disc jockeys. Looney Tunes, however, had been more ingenious than most. Once the receptionist started recognizing her voice, and refusing to put her through to me, Looney had started getting someone else to phone for her. I'd pick up the phone, having been told that there was a male somebody on the other end. And Looney would come on the line.

In the last few days, her voice, always raspy, had grown weaker and weaker. Yesterday it had been little more than a croak. "You're going to help me," she'd said. "You're my last hope. You and your sister. You two are going to help me whether you like it or not."

I'd actually felt a little chilled, she'd sounded so angry. "Ma'am, Bert and I are not professional detectives. We just happened to—"

"Bullshit!" Looney Tunes had said. "This is your kind of case. It's right up your alley. Now say you'll take it on!"

For once, she'd spoken with only a hint of a rasp.

"Ma'am," I'd said, "there are plenty of private detectives in the phone book."

"I don't want them. I want *you!*" She'd coughed then, a choking, phlegmy sound that had made my stomach tighten. Her voice was so faint when she spoke again, I could barely make out what she was saying. "I know I ain't got long, and I want this done before I go."

Judging from the way she sounded, I was pretty sure she wasn't just making a bid for sympathy. And yet, even if she were genuinely ill, what could I possibly do? If she really did have an unsolved murder she needed investigating, she needed a professional. Not me. And not Bert. She needed somebody who knew what they were doing. I started to tell her so.

"Ma'am, you don't understand. You really need to hire someone who—"

This time Looney didn't slam the phone down. She did something even more unsettling. She put the receiver down so gently, it took me a moment to realize that she'd hung up.

OK, so that phone call had rattled me a little. I admit it. Now even with Bob walking right next to me, telling me in vivid detail exactly how his wife Edna had recently flirted shamelessly with the guy who cleaned out their septic tank, I found myself scanning the entire area around me as we walked toward the Food Court. We passed Bacon's, Rode's, Victoria's Secret. I gave each store a searching glance as I went by. Making sure there were no weirdos hanging around just inside the entrance.

I was wearing what I always wear—jeans, denim jacket, and boots—but the sound of my boots as I hurried along seemed a lot louder than usual. And yet, I could still hear my heart pounding. Oh yes, I definitely should've told Charlie that Looney Tunes scared me a little.

Except, of course, I could just hear Charlie. "OK, let me get this straight. You don't want to do this promotion because you're afraid of a little old lady who sounds as if she's dying. Who sounds so weak on the phone, sometimes you can barely hear her. *That's* what you're telling me?"

Even Bert had not completely understood. I'd phoned her this morning right after I'd gotten the ride with Bob. "So," Bert had said, "what is it about this woman on the phone that's so frightening?"

To be honest, I wasn't sure myself. "She doesn't frighten me exactly. She just makes me *uneasy.*"

Bert skipped the details, and went right to the heart of the matter. "Why?"

"Well, for one thing, she sounds like she's nuts. Like maybe grief has driven her mad." I felt like an idiot even saying such a thing.

Bert, no doubt, agreed that I could possibly be an idiot, because she didn't say a word.

"And," I quickly added, "the woman sounds very, *very* angry that we won't help her."

Bert may not have completely understood, but—unlike Charlie—she took my word for it. "If you want me to be at the mall at three-thirty, I'm there," she said. "No problem."

Bert works as an office temporary these days, and I knew she was going to have to beg off early. "Thanks, Bert. I owe you," I said.

"You want to leave as soon as you get done?" Bert asked. "Or do you want me to hang around until you're ready to go, and drive you home then?"

I didn't even have to think about it. "I want to leave right away. I don't want to give this woman—or anybody else— a chance to buttonhole me."

"Don't worry about it. I'll do the usual, OK?"

Bert and I have had some kind of getaway code ever since we were little and being paraded in front of distant relatives during visits as the family oddities. Our current ploy is: If one of us wants to break away, the other one always comes up and says she hopes the getaway twin has not forgotten our dinner date with Mom. And that Mom is now waiting dinner for both of us, and we've got to hurry or everything's going to get cold.

This particular gambit had only one drawback. It can only work on total strangers. Anybody who actually knows Mom would realize immediately that any story involving our mother and the use of a stove was a complete fabrication. Mainly because Mom hasn't cooked a meal since, oh, I guessed, about 1961. Whatever year it was that McDonald's opened up on Dixie Highway, only a few miles from our house. As Mom says even today, "If God had meant for us to eat at home, he wouldn't have made fast food."

"The usual will be fine," I'd told Bert. "But, Bert, don't wait around, OK? Come up and say it the instant I get done. I want to get out of there *right away.*"

I knew I'd sounded like a colossal coward, but I didn't care. I was now almost to the Food Court, only a step or so behind Bob, and I quickened my pace even more. If I had to do this thing, at least I would have safety in numbers.

At least, I *thought* I would. Where exactly was Bert? My clock said three-thirty on the dot, and Bert was nowhere in sight.

Wouldn't you know it, Bert continued to be nowhere in sight for the next half-hour. While I did my bit in front of the mike in the middle of the Food Court, I kept scanning the faces in front of me for one that bore a remarkable resemblance to my own. Bert, however, remained among the missing. By the time I'd finished reading all the names of the donors and the amount each donor had given—and I'd given my standard what-a-thrill-it-was-to-be-a-part-of-this-terrific-cause speech—I was beginning to get a little worried. Where the hell was Bert? I might've thought I'd simply overlooked her in the crowd, except that, to be honest, there wasn't that big a crowd. Charlie's "biggie" charity had turned out to be a drive to raise money for the St. Matthews branch of the Louisville Public Library.

As soon as I learned what the charity was, I wasn't surprised at the low turnout. In recent years, Louisville has had two referendums, asking voters if it would be OK if the powers that be imposed a tax to raise enough money so that the library wouldn't have to start closing branches. Each time the answer has been the same: *No way.* In fact, judging from the percentage of Noes versus Yesses, this last answer was more: *Forget it.*

When I was finally finished with my little spiel, I turned the mike over to somebody or another from the library, who started his own what-a-thrill-it-was-to-be-a-part-of-this-terrific-cause speech. I didn't get the guy's name, and I didn't pay much attention to what he was saying. As soon as I stepped away from the mike, in fact, I was pretty much totally focused on scanning the crowd for Bert. What the hell had happened to her? Bert was, to put the kindest face on it that I could, a bit scatterbrained, but I'd just talked to her, for God's sake. There was no way she could've forgotten this so quickly.

I guess I was looking for Bert so intently, I didn't hear the woman and her companion come up behind me. "Miss Tatum?" the woman said and tapped me on the shoulder.

I must've jumped a foot.

"Oh, I'm sorry," the woman said. "I didn't mean to alarm you."

I turned around, took one quick look, and then my heart began to beat a whole lot faster.

Chapter 2

•

BERT

Nan was going to kill me.

I'd been sitting for the last fifteen minutes in a stupid traffic jam stretching across five lanes of traffic on Shelbyville Road, only a few maddening yards away from my destination—the St. Matthews Mall, a newly renovated shopping center in Louisville's east end. While I was sitting there, boxed in on all sides, I couldn't exactly ignore the little green numbers of the clock on my dashboard getting closer and closer to four o'clock. Even if every one of the cars all around me had miraculously evaporated this very minute, I was still going to be at least a half hour late.

There didn't seem to be anything to do about it either. Other than mentally kick myself for getting into this predicament in the first place. I'd planned to get to the mall early. Nan would probably never believe it, but I'd fully intended to already be there, waiting for her, when she arrived. True, what she'd told me over the phone didn't exactly sound as if her life was on the line or anything; but still, I trusted Nan's instincts. When she got bad vibes, she was usually right on target.

Like, for example, it had been Nan—and Nan alone— who'd warned me not to marry Jake. Mom and Daddy had both thought that Jake Powell was the best thing since sliced bread. Jake was in the top 10% of his class at the University of Louisville, he was handsome, and he didn't call them by their first names. He called them *Mr. and Mrs. Tatum*. That was all it took to win over Mom and Daddy.

Nan, on the other hand, had remained stubbornly unconvinced. "Bert, you're too young to get married," she'd told me. At the time, of course, I'd been convinced that what Nan meant by that was that she herself, at the age of nineteen, felt too young to get married. I, on the other hand, was ten minutes older than Nan, so obviously, she could have no concept just how mature I was in comparison.

When I'd tried to talk to her, though, Nan had held up her hand, signaling me to stop. "OK, OK," she said, "if you must know, it's not just your age, Bert. It's Jake. I've got an uneasy feeling about him."

I'd brushed that one away, too. Nan was a little jealous, that's all. She probably just didn't want to share me with somebody else.

Today, however—twenty years and two children later—Nan isn't the only one with an uneasy feeling about Jake. I've been feeling particularly uneasy about him ever since he left me a year and a half ago to "find himself"—with his twenty-year-old secretary.

Shortly after that, my uneasy feelings grew by leaps and bounds when I realized that I couldn't possibly afford the mortgage payments, so I would have to sell Jake my half of the house in which I'd lived ever since Brian and Emily were born. It also occurred to me that I suddenly needed a job, a pretty scary idea since I hadn't worked outside of the home since my freshman year in college. And I needed a new place to live. This might've been pretty scary, too, except that Nan offered to rent me the other half of the duplex she owns. She'd been living in one half, and renting the other half ever since she bought the place a few years ago.

With all these scary things I was suddenly having to deal with, you'd think that my uneasy feelings regarding Jake would get pushed to a back burner. On the contrary. In fact, my uneasy feelings about Jake have even increased some in the last six months or so. Ever since Jake's child-woman dumped him; and unbelievably, he's been coming around, trying to get *me* to go out with him.

This all goes to say that Nan's hunches have become something that I've learned over the years not to ignore. That's why this morning when she called, I didn't waste any time. As soon as I got off the phone, I took a deep breath, and then I marched right into Mr. Hazlitt's office. I didn't want to give myself even a moment to think it over, because I knew if I did, I'd get even more nervous than I already was.

I do hate asking for favors. It never fails to make me feel like a first grader again, raising my hand in class and asking to be excused to go to the little girls' room. While everybody snickers.

I especially hate asking Mr. Hazlitt for anything. Mainly because every time I look at the man for more than five seconds, I find myself thinking: *Do you know you look just like a lizard?* I try not to, I really do, but I can't help staring at his large, wide mouth, his tiny slit eyes, and his wide, flattened nose. And of course, I have to wonder if he knows what I'm thinking.

It does not make for a stress-free employer-employee relationship.

Of course, why should Mr. Hazlitt care what I think? For a lizard, he has done all right for himself. He's the senior partner in the successful CPA firm of Hazlitt, Horn and McCombs. This firm, in fact, is so successful that it can't handle the load this tax season, and that's why they've hired me. Or rather, that's why they've hired Kentuckiana Temps, the temporary agency I work for.

The nice thing about working at Hazlitt, Horn and McCombs was that their offices weren't located all the way downtown like a lot of the other companies I get sent to. It was on Breckinridge Lane, only a few minutes from Napoleon Boulevard where Nan and I share a duplex. More importantly, though—as far as today was concerned—Breckinridge Lane is even fewer minutes from the mall, where I was supposed to meet Nan.

Now, even as I was tapping on the half-closed door to Mr. Hazlitt's office, I was figuring that if I left right away, I might have time to stop by my house and put on a fresh blouse before I met Nan. Mr. Hazlitt had forgotten to have me type a twenty-page financial statement needed for a client at an eleven-thirty meeting this morning, so I'd spent the morning typing just as fast as my fingers could fly over the keys. With that kind of pressure, I had—as they say in all the deodorant commercials—"lost my freshness." In fact, there was a good chance I might never see my freshness again.

On the upside, I had finished the statement with minutes to spare, and so Mr. Hazlitt should be in a generous frame of mind. On the down side, it *was* April and tax season— not exactly the time of the year that CPAs put up their feet and relax.

My stomach was starting to hurt. "Mr. Hazlitt?" I said again, leaning a little through the open doorway. Not really going in, you understand, but in enough so that I could actually see whom I was talking to.

The lizard sat behind a huge mahogany desk that probably cost more than my Festiva. His bald scaly head was bent over an open manila folder on his desk, and for a moment, I wasn't sure he even knew that I was there. He certainly didn't act like it.

"Excuse me, Mr. Hazlitt?" I said one more time.

Mr. Hazlitt won't admit it, but he's got to be hard of hearing. Like I said, he's the *senior* partner. And when I say senior, I mean *senior*. The other two, Horn and McCombs, were in their seventies, but the lizard had to be ninety if he was a day. He shuffled rather than walked, he'd fallen asleep more than once right in the middle of dictating a letter, and he had more lines crisscrossing his lizard face than a page out of my steno notebook.

That's right, *steno notebook*. In this, the age of word processors, fax machines, and desktop publishing, Hazlitt, Horn and McCombs didn't even use dictaphones. Nope, they still made their poor secretaries troop into their offices, plop down with pen and pad at the ready, and take down their every word. I realize that, having worked so little outside the home until now, I am a bit naive, but I didn't even need Nan to tell me that one of the reasons these three old coots continue to maintain this time-honored tradition was that every one of them enjoyed staring at a pair of female legs on a daily basis.

Mr. Hazlitt was the worst of the lot. His vision doesn't seem to be much better than his hearing, so he apparently has to really squint at your legs to get them into focus. He always ends up looking even more like a lizard. One that's blinking into the sun.

"Mr.—" I began again.

Hazlitt's head shot up that time, and he cut me off, his voice a growl. "What do *you* want?"

His using that tone with me might've really been unnerving, but his eyes were, as usual, on my legs. It seemed as if he were irritated with *them*, not me.

I cleared my throat, and took a tentative step forward.

Nan has been telling me ever since I got my divorce that I need to work on my "assertiveness skills"—her phrase, of course, not mine. I'm not even sure what assertiveness skills are, let alone whether or not mine need work. Apparently, Nan feels that being married for nineteen years to a control freak might've actually beaten me down a little. I suppose she could be right. Nan has made it clear, however, that there's a big, big difference between being aggressive and being assertive, and that I should concentrate on the latter, not the former. Since I don't know enough to concentrate on either one, I usually fall back on what I've always done during times of stress.

I pretend to be Nan.

Nan, you see, has always been the twin with guts. The year we were seven, it was Nan who found every one of our Christmas gifts under Mom's bed two days after Thanksgiving. If I'd ever done such a thing, I'd have been living in terror that Mom would find out. Nan, on the other hand, had a slightly different take on the whole situation. Far from hiding, she'd announced her discovery at the dinner table. "Mom, Daddy," Nan had said, "you two have *got* to find a better hiding place for the presents!" At seven, Nan had managed to sound gently scolding. "You're making it *way* too easy!"

I can still remember how shocked I'd been when Mom and Daddy had responded to Nan's little bulletin by looking chagrined. Mom had actually turned to Daddy and said, "*See,* I told you not to hide that stuff under our bed!"

Since then Nan has been my hero. Or rather, heroine.

Now in Hazlitt's office, pretending to be Nan-the-Fearless, I put a hand on each hip and looked Hazlitt straight in his lizard eyes. "Mr. Hazlitt," I said without so much as a tremor in my voice, "I'm going to be leaving early today. I've cleared off my desk, and there's a personal matter I need to take care of."

Mr. Hazlitt's initial response was dramatic. He scratched his lizard nose. "Personal?" he repeated. His voice sounded like paper rustling, and behind his wire-rimmed trifocals, his tiny slit eyes looked suddenly as if flashlights had gone on behind them. "Are you meeting a boyfriend, Miss Tatum, is that—?"

I immediately shook my head. "Oh, my goodness, no," I said, waving my hand in the air, as if trying to erase the very idea. "I certainly am not. I'd *never* take off work just to go out on a *date.* Good Lord, no, this is a family thing I've got to do. An *obligation.* Something I really can't get out of."

Mr. Hazlitt was still staring at me, but his pale eyebrows looked to me as if they could be moving closer together. I recognized on his bony face an expression I'd seen far too many times on Jake's—it was *pre-frown,* precursor to *full-blown frown,* precursor to *full-blown temper tantrum.*

I took another quick step forward, and began talking very fast. "Look, Mr. Hazlitt," I said, "I'm really terribly sorry to have to do this. I really am. But if you'd please just let me leave early this once, I'll never, ever do it again. I mean it. I'll even come in early and make it up if you like, I really—" Too late I realized I was no longer doing Nan. I had spontaneously reverted to doing me.

Fortunately, Hazlitt cut me off before I began to grovel and plead. "Your *family?*" Hazlitt said. "You mean, you and your twin sister? Well, I do hope you and she aren't off to solve another murder!" Right after the old man said this, something started happening to his mouth. It took me a moment or so to realize that all those grimaces and twitches playing about Hazlitt's thin lips were intended to be a smile. The old geezer was actually *teasing* me. Obviously, he'd read one or more of those dumb articles written about Nan and me, and it had amused him to no end.

I was so relieved I gave him a wide smile. "Oh, my goodness, *no,*" I said, erasing the air again, "Nan and I are *out* of the detecting business. We certainly are. *For good.*"

Yes, I admit it, I actually said this. With a straight face.

Hazlitt's mouth twitched again, his lizard eyes fixed on mine. "Well, now, I'd sure hope so. I'd hate to have anything happen to a pretty little thing like you." His thin smile widened to reveal yellowed back teeth.

My own smile froze.

"You know, Miss Tatum," Hazlitt went on, lowering his voice until it sounded less like paper rustling, and more like cardboard being wadded up, "a woman as attractive as you are should never have to spend an evening alone."

Oh dear.

I tried to keep smiling, but I admit, it was difficult. Because what was suddenly going through my mind was this: *Wouldn't you know it? Nan attracts what my daughter refers to as stud-muffins—hunks half Nan's age, with muscular, tanned physiques, and names like Dillon and Brock. Whom do I attract? Methuselah's granddad.*

"Oh, I don't spend many evenings alone," I lied. "Hardly any, now that I think of it. I'm always running out to the grocery, or the teller machine, or the gas station, or . . ." I was, of course, babbling.

Thank God, Hazlitt interrupted. "I do have a rule against dating an employee, but since you're a temporary, you're not really an—"

I was suddenly so anxious to interrupt him before he could finish what sounded like a pretty awful sentence, that I practically shouted, "*Oh no!*"

Hazlitt looked a little startled.

I lowered my voice. "What I mean to say is, temporaries *are* employees, too," I said. "We certainly are. I mean, you pay us, so that makes us your employees, doesn't it? And your rule is absolutely correct. *Absolutely.*" I was by this time backing out of the room. "It's a terrific rule. Really. A wonderful rule. Yes, indeed."

I guess I might've overdone it a little, because the lizard was now looking unhappy. "Rules," he said, his eyes little more than slits, "were made to be broken."

I just looked at him. "No kidding," I said, my voice unnaturally cheery. "I'll remember that." I'd backed up by then to where I was about two steps from the door. I did a fast about-face, and started through it. Halfway out the door, I stopped and turned to face Mr. Hazlitt. "And thank you so much."

I wasn't quite sure what I was thanking him for, but it seemed as good an exit line as any. I spun on my heel, and I got out of there.

After that little bit of stress, I no longer wondered if I'd lost my freshness. In fact, I'd say any second now my freshness would probably start appearing on the sides of milk cartons.

I headed straight for home, changed my blouse, and was just rolling on another layer of Ban, unscented, intending to follow that up with a spritz of Joy perfume for good measure, when the phone rang.

To this day I'm still not sure why I answered it. I knew I was in a hurry, so why in the world didn't I just let my answering machine get it?

Of course, it did cross my mind at the time that it could be Nan, telling me that I didn't have to show up at the mall after all. That the telethon had been canceled. It also crossed my mind a split second before I reached for the receiver, that it could be Brian or Emily. It *was* Monday, after all.

Monday is the day both my children always seem to call. Brian, nineteen, is at Indiana University and Emily, twenty, is at the University of Kentucky; they're miles apart and yet, oddly enough, if they call at all, they both usually call on Monday, within an hour or so of each other. I'm sure it's purely coincidental that Monday just happens to be the first day after the weekend, and that after doing whatever they've done over the weekend, both my children are usually low on funds. I'm sure they're calling just to hear their sainted mother's voice and not just to beg me for cash, which they invariably do every time they call.

The phone was on its third ring by the time I got to it. I grabbed up the receiver, all but shouted, "Hello!" and then I heard it.

"Is this Bert Tatum? I need to talk to Bert Tatum." The voice was hoarse and raspy, but I was pretty sure it was a woman. For one thing, it sounded as if maybe the speaker had spent the last hour or so crying. Not too many men sound like that.

"I'm Bert Tatum," I said uneasily.

"You're one of them murder twins, right?"

Inwardly, I groaned. Oh dear. This was yet another somebody who'd read one of those idiotic newspaper articles about Nan and me. Would they never stop calling? How long were we going to have to wait until this thing died out? No pun intended.

I cleared my throat. "Murder twins?" I said. "I'm sorry, but I don't know what you—"

I have always prided myself on the way I can act incredibly stupid at a moment's notice, but apparently, I wasn't quite as talented as I thought.

The woman cut me off, now not only sounding sad, but contemptuous. "Come off it, sister, you know what I'm talking about. Don't try to tell me you don't. I know you two are the ones. You and your twin on the radio."

Oh dear.

"I need yours and your sister's help," the woman went right on. "I lost my—my sweet baby seven hundred and forty-eight days ago . . ." Her voice broke at this point, and then she went into a paroxysm of coughing.

Seven hundred and how many days? This woman had actually been counting? And what did she mean by "sweet baby"? Was she talking about an infant—or a lover—or what?

She continued to cough, though, and it didn't seem polite to try to shout a question over that awful sound. Good Lord. The woman really did sound sick.

When she'd finally calmed down, I said before she had a chance to say anything, "Ma'am? Have you had that cough looked at? It doesn't sound good."

Her response was an outright laugh. In fact, the woman laughed almost as long as she'd coughed before. "Doesn't sound good, huh?" she said. "Well, you know, you're right. My cough's been looked at real close, and they tell me it's gonna kill me." At this point she started laughing again. "Which," she rasped, "surely isn't good."

I took a deep breath. It seemed to me that this woman might be suffering from not only a physical illness, but also a mental one.

Which immediately brought another thought to mind. Could this be the woman Nan had just told me about? The lady who'd been hounding Nan at CKI early today? Was this Looney Tunes? "Ma'am," I said slowly, not wanting to rattle an insane person, "I am terribly sorry about your loss, but my sister and I don't—"

"—do murders, I know, I know," the woman interrupted me, following it up with a few dry coughs.

Good Lord. She did sound terrible. Could this really be the woman who had alarmed Nan enough that she'd ended up asking *me* to keep her company? The woman really didn't sound well enough to be terribly threatening.

In fact, for a minute there, I was sure the lady was going off into one of those long hacking spasms again. But then she took a long ragged breath and went right on. "Your fool sister said the same thing, but I know you're both lying. You are. I read the papers, I know what you two can do."

"Ma'am, you need to talk to the police."

"The police!" she croaked. The very idea started her coughing again, until my own lungs seemed to ache just listening to her. "I tried the police," she finally managed, after the coughing subsided a little. "Them policemen think they've already found the killer." She was creepy-sounding now, her voice hoarser and more rasping then ever, as she talked. "As far as them police are concerned," the woman wheezed, "the case is closed."

Sounded good enough to me. I was thinking about saying this, when the woman began to cough one more time.

Lord, Lord, she was sounding worse by the minute. What if she died right there, holding the phone, like Marilyn Monroe? And I hadn't even tried to get her medical help? Not to mention, her phone line would still be connected to mine, and I'd once again be talking to the police about a dead body.

OK, OK, I know that sounds a bit selfish, but listen, after what Nan and I had been through, I'd pretty much had it with dealing with the police.

When the woman finally calmed down this time, I said, "Ma'am, where are you? I'll be happy to call 911 to—"

My answer was another cough. And then, "Hell, no, I ain't telling you where I am! Not until you agree to help me find the person who took my sweet baby from me. I got to know, and I don't have a lot of time—"

Speaking of which, it was almost quarter after three. I was going to have to step on it to meet Nan. "Ma'am, I don't know how to get this across to you, but my sister Nan and I *don't* investigate murders. We do *not*, OK? You need to call the police or a private investigator or somebody like that, OK?" There was a short pause while I waited for her to say something. When she didn't, I hurried on, encouraged, "Ma'am, I do wish you the very best of luck, and I do sincerely hope—"

"Fuck you, shithead," the woman said.

I jerked the receiver away from my ear as if it had just bit me. Almost immediately, the dial tone sounded.

Goodness. That little conversation had certainly taken an ugly turn.

If this lady—and I use the term loosely—really had been Looney Tunes, no wonder Nan had been rattled. The woman did not sound as if she were any too tightly wrapped. Not to mention, she had a trigger temper—and a potty mouth.

Who exactly was this woman anyway?

I knew I was in a hurry—that Nan, indeed, would be waiting on me, but if I wanted to find out exactly who this nasty woman was, I had to do it now. I happen to have one of those caller options on my phone that redials the last number that phoned you. Nan has always said that Caller Return was a useless expense, but here was where I could finally prove her wrong. I hit the call return code on my phone, and I waited. I could hear the tones of a number being dialed, then a telephone beginning to ring on the other end. Less than a minute later, someone picked up.

"Jewish Hospital," said a prim, nasal voice.

Jewish Hospital is a major part of a large medical complex located in downtown Louisville. I was still digesting that little nugget of information—*Potty Mouth had been calling from a hospital?*—when the nasal voice hurried on, "How may I direct your call?"

That one stumped me. Who was I supposed to ask for? The sick woman with the bad cough? In a *hospital?* Oh, sure, she'd be a snap to find.

"I'm sorry," I said, "I dialed the wrong number."

OK, so proving Nan wrong about Caller Return was going to have to wait. It also looked as if Nan herself might have to wait a little. If I didn't get a major move on.

I hurried out the front door. Hurried to my car. Hurried toward Shelbyville Road.

I guess I would've been late, regardless. But I would not have been a half hour late, if it hadn't been for the dumb traffic. Which was not, I repeat, *not* my fault.

When traffic started moving again, I all but careened into

the mall parking lot. I parked in the first spot I saw empty, and then I hit the ground running as soon as I got my driver's side door open. High heels were never meant to be worn by runners, which is probably why you never see high-heeled sneakers. Still I made pretty good time, for somebody in extreme pain by the time I'd gotten no more than twenty feet away from my car. I ran toward the closest door, raced through it, and headed for the Food Court. My footsteps sounded like little explosions on the gleaming hardwood floor.

I could barely hear them, of course, over the sound of my own labored breathing—and the sound of whoever that man was at the mike in the middle of the Food Court. As soon as I saw that the person at the mike was most definitely not Nan, I came to a screeching halt, my heart in my mouth. Where was Nan? Was she already finished? More important, was she all ready to strangle me?

Then I saw her. She was standing across the room, off to the side of the man at the mike, talking with a man in faded jeans and a woman in pink, neither of whom I recognized.

Oh dear. And Nan had been depending on me to keep anybody from buttonholing her. She really was going to strangle me.

I started to hurry toward the three of them, and then I noticed something else.

The man in the jeans was holding Nan's hand in his.

I quickened my step. Good Lord, what was he doing? Was he trying to grab her?

And yet, Nan didn't seem to be making any effort to take her hand out of his. The two of them were just standing there, staring into each other's eyes.

And smiling.

Dreamily.

I peered at the guy a little closer.

As Nan herself used to say in my ear every time we saw a cute guy on campus: *No more phone calls, ladies. We have a winner!*

This guy was a winner, all right. In fact, he had to be one of the best-looking men I'd ever seen. Even if you count all those prominently featured in *People* magazine.

I looked back over at Nan. I couldn't be absolutely positive—she was turned so that I could only see about three-quarters of her face—but I was pretty sure that her tongue was hanging out.

Chapter 3

●

NAN

My tongue was *not* hanging out.

I admit that I may have been guilty of staring—just a little—but that was only because I thought I might've seen the man now standing in front of me somewhere before.

Like, oh, say, in my *dreams*, for instance.

All right, so I admit it, I did happen to notice that the guy was gorgeous. Several inches over six feet tall, with deep blue eyes, dark hair, and the longest eyelashes I'd ever seen on a man, he was what Rob Lowe might've looked like had Rob lifted weights.

He was wearing faded Levis, scuffed boots, and a blue chambray shirt with the sleeves turned up at the cuffs—an outfit worn by so many men in the country music business, it practically amounts to a uniform. And yet, on the Incredible Hunk, this particular uniform looked terrific. I'd often wondered why women were supposed to be crazy about men in uniforms, because uniforms had never done a thing for me. Until now. In an instant I'd become a believer.

Under the circumstances, I don't think I could be faulted for staring a little. And it wasn't like I was the only one. The minute Hunk had walked in, he'd started turning the heads of nearly every woman in the Food Court. He hadn't seemed to notice, though, mainly because Hunk had been doing some staring of his own. His eyes had never left my face as the woman who'd walked up with him said, "Oh, my dear, I certainly didn't mean to alarm you. But, Nan, I was so glad to see you again, I just had to rush right over!"

She had called me by name, and she'd said *again*. With some effort I pulled my eyes away from Hunk, and focused on the woman. She looked to be about ten years older than me, and to be cruelly honest, about thirty pounds overweight. Her auburn hair had been pulled back from her plump face into a tight chignon at the back of her neck. This hairstyle looked sophisticated and professional, I'll give it that, but unfortunately, it also accentuated how round the woman's face was.

She had the every-strand-in-place look that comes from either a terribly expensive hair stylist or a terribly cheap hair spray. Judging from the outfit this woman was wearing—a tailored designer suit in shocking pink, with shocking pink designer heels to match, and a shocking pink print designer scarf draped around her shoulders—my guess would definitely be the hair stylist.

My guess was also that I'd never seen this woman before in my life. Of course, this last meant almost nothing. In my line of work you meet an awful lot of people. After a while, their faces all start to blend together.

It doesn't help that most of the people who come up to you usually call you by name and act as if they're your best friend. I suppose it has something to do with the way your voice is so familiar to them. They hear it in their homes, in their cars, even in their *ears* as they're jogging along with their Walkmans. So, somehow, they've mixed you up with all the other people in their lives whose voices are equally familiar. You've been lumped in the same category as relatives, friends, and co-workers.

And you still don't know them from Adam. Or Eve.

I gave Shocking Pink my most cordial smile. "Don't worry about it," I said. "You didn't scare me in the least."

Hey, I always jump a foot in the air about this time of day.

Shocking Pink actually fanned herself, as if maybe she'd been so upset at the prospect of scaring me that she'd been on the verge of passing out.

I continued to smile.

"Oh, thank goodness, *that's* a relief!" Shocking went on. "I did *so* want you to meet a friend of mine, and I certainly didn't want to start things off on the wrong foot." Here Shocking gave a little giggle, which I believe was supposed to indicate that the very idea of her ever getting off on the wrong foot was laughable.

My smile was beginning to hurt.

Stepping back a little, so as to include Hunk in our conversation, Shocking hurried on. "Nan Tatum, may I present Crane Morgan?"

She said this in the same way you might say, *May I present the Prince of Wales*, but frankly, I barely heard her. Crane Morgan was taking a step toward me. "Glad to meet you," he said, extending his hand. It was the first time he'd spoken, and I was surprised to discover that his voice was so deep, he could've sung bass with the Temptations.

"Glad to meet *you*," I said. I put my hand in his, and felt strong fingers tighten around my own. I also felt—because, let's face it, I'm a total idiot when it comes to good-looking men—an almost electric charge the second his hand closed around mine.

Shocking was blathering on, "My dear departed husband bought oodles of commercials for his business on WCKI—of course, I make sure the new owner still does—so I just *had* to meet Nan when she emceed the cancer drive I headed up. At least I think it was the cancer drive, I do so many; anyway, we had the nicest talk . . ."

At this point I gave Shocking a quick glance. I remembered doing the cancer drive a few months ago, but I certainly didn't remember chatting with her there. Her face wasn't the least bit familiar.

"So the minute I met you, Crane, why I just knew I *had* to introduce you to Nan. That's why I asked you to come today, because once I heard that Nan was going to emcee, well, I said to myself, this will be the perfect time to introduce you two!"

I was looking at Crane again. He hadn't released my hand, and yet, he didn't seem to notice. He was smiling at me, his face warm and relaxed, and yet, there seemed to be something behind his eyes. A sadness, a sorrow of some kind. In fact, it was as if—in the back of his mind—there was always some profound grief he never quite lost sight of.

Or was I reading too much into the face of a handsome stranger whose easy smile didn't quite reach his eyes? Of course, on his particular gorgeous face, if you gave me time, I could read an encyclopedia.

"I just knew you two would hit it off!" Shocking was still blathering on. "I just knew it! You two have so much in common!"

"You're on the radio, too?" I said, clearly directing my question at Crane.

The radio industry is a pretty small community, believe it or not. The main way you get a raise in this business is to move to a radio station in a bigger market. So, if you've been in radio for a while, you've seen the same faces again and again, only maybe in different cities, all across the country. I may not be good at faces in general, but I knew if I'd ever seen *Crane's* face before, I would've remembered it.

When I spoke, Crane seemed to notice he still had my hand. He released it, and if I didn't know better, he actually reddened a little. Like a little boy caught doing something he shouldn't.

And my stupid heart actually did this little ba-bump.

Have I mentioned what an idiot I am when it comes to good-looking men?

Shocking was doing her inane giggle again. "Oh, my, no!" she said, giving the end of her scarf a careless little flip. "Nan, dear, Crane's not a radio star! Crane's a photographer! And he does beautiful work, I'll have you know, *beautiful* work. Why, I just had him do my portrait, and believe me, he captured the very *best* side of me!"

I was still smiling, of course, but I couldn't help thinking, *Which side would that be? The inside?*

I was sure my face didn't betray anything of what was going through my mind, but Crane's reaction made me wonder. His dark eyes intense, his smile grew a little wider. "Mrs. Eagleston was a wonderful subject," he told me. "Doing the portrait of such a lovely lady was easy."

I stared at him, wondering if there was a trace of sarcasm in his voice.

If there was, Mrs. Eagleston didn't hear it. "Oh, *Crane,*" she said, giving her scarf yet another flip. "You flatter me! And I *believe* I told you to call me Louise. I haven't been Mrs. Eagleston since my husband died six years ago!"

I gave Louise another quick glance. Was she *flirting* with

Crane? Was she letting him know, in no uncertain terms, that she was currently very available? It wouldn't be the first time an older woman was interested in a younger man. But if Louise was interested in Crane herself, why on earth had she introduced him to me?

Of course, maybe she thought it would make her look more important in Crane's eyes if she acted as if she and a local celebrity were good friends. This last has never ceased to amaze me. Apparently, there are people in the world who truly believe that associating with somebody like me is a feather in their cap. I've always hated to break it to them, but outside of the Kentuckiana listening area, I am no more a celebrity than they are. And to anybody who doesn't listen to WCKI, I'm not even a celebrity here.

"As *Louise* was so kind to mention," Crane said, giving Louise a quick smile as he said her name with a little extra emphasis and then immediately turning back to me, "I have my own studio on—"

"—Main Street, in one of those charming Victorian buildings," Louise finished for him. "You know the ones, Nan, dear, near Third? A lot of them have been renovated inside, but not Crane's. It's still original. Oh, you really should see it, Nan, it's the most darling studio!"

I looked over at Crane to see how he had reacted to having his studio described as *darling*, and his smile had grown wider. "I really would love you to see my studio," he said. "Why don't I show it to you right now?"

It seemed obvious to me that he was leaving Louise out of the expedition, but she didn't seem to realize it. "Oh, what a good idea!" The woman actually clapped her hands together like a delighted child—a delighted child at least fifty years old. "I just knew you two would hit it off! Like I said before, you two have *so* much in common! What with you both being twins and all!"

I blinked at that one. "No kidding. You're a twin?" I said. "Are you . . ."

I'd been about to ask if he and his twin were identical, but something in Crane's face stopped me. He was still smiling, just as before, but now there was a strained look around his eyes.

Even Louise, I think, noticed. "What I meant to say is," she said, glancing at Crane uncertainly, "well, that Crane *was* a twin." She twisted the end of her scarf. "That's what I meant. He was *born* a twin, all right, but he isn't a twin now. He—"

Crane interrupted Louise for once. "My brother Lane passed away two years ago," he said quietly.

I couldn't help it. I did a quick intake of breath.

So that explained the grief I saw in his face. Dear God. How could you ever get over something like that? And this idiot woman said he wasn't a twin *anymore?* Hell, you were a twin forever, regardless of whether your twin was still living.

One of the talk shows—Maury Povich or Sally Jesse or one of the others, I can't remember which—had recently done a segment featuring what was referred to as "twinless twins." I'd started out watching it, but about fifteen minutes into the thing, I'd flipped it off. It had been too sad.

And too awful.

As much as I complained about Bert, I had no doubt that I'd be devastated if anything happened to her.

"I'm so sorry," I told Crane.

Crane nodded, and shrugged a little. "Me, too," he said.

He tried for a light tone, but he didn't quite make it. His dark blue eyes were even more intense than before.

I don't know what made me do it, but on impulse I reached out and touched his hand again. Would you believe, he was already reaching for my hand, too? As if he already knew what my reaction was going to be.

It probably would've been a nice moment, except for one thing.

Behind me a voice as familiar as my own said, "Oh, Nan, I apologize, I really do. I got stuck in traffic, or I would've been here. I hope you haven't been waiting on me long."

Crane immediately released my hand, more's the pity, as I turned around to face Bert. She was standing there, arms folded across her chest, her eyes darting from me to Crane, then over to Louise, and finally back again.

When she got back to me, Bert's look clearly said, *What in the world is going on here?*

I turned toward Bert a little more so that my back was now to Crane, and so that the only person who could get a clear view of my face was Bert.

"Bert!" I said. "How nice to—"

I had every intention of going on, but Louise was apparently going for the record, *Most Interruptions in a Single Conversation.* "Oh, look!" Louise said, her voice an excited squeal. "Look who's here! It's the other one!"

The other one.

Bert and I hadn't heard that little phrase since high school. Even back then, I'd known that there was something unkind about saying this. Now I realized what it was. *The other one* pretty much implied that one of us was the genuine article— and the other one a mere carbon copy. Bert was either *the other Nan,* or I was *the other Bert.*

I might've said something about her choice of words to Louise, but I had more pressing matters to attend to. "Yes," I said, "this is my sister, Bert. And what a surprise!" I stepped closer to Bert. "This is so sweet of you to come by."

As I said this last, I gave Bert the old Twin Whammy.

I realize this last sounds a bit odd, especially if you don't happen to be a twin, but Bert and I have been giving each other Twin Whammies ever since we were small. Whammies go like this: You concentrate very hard on sending your twin a message, and at the same time, you open your eyes very wide and stare without blinking directly into your twin's eyes.

There are those who actually believe that identical twins really can communicate telepathically. I'm not sure whether this is true for Bert and me, but every time I've given her a Twin Whammy, she has always gotten the message. Lest anyone suggest that Bert and I immediately join the Psychic Friends Network, however, I believe I should also mention that Bert might just be picking up on the subtle changes in my facial expression—such as the way my eyes have started to bug out.

Bert's own eyes widened considerably as she stared back at me. "Oh, uh, yes?" she said uncertainly. "Of course? I, uh, just thought I'd surprise you?"

I didn't want to be overly critical, particularly about a person I've just said I'd be devastated to live without, but I was pretty sure that Bert could've delivered her lines with a little more conviction.

Chapter 4

•

BERT

Judging from the look on Nan's face, I guessed I wouldn't be nominated for an Academy Award this year.

And yet, what did Nan expect? Up to a few seconds ago, I'd been under the impression that my mission tonight was to search and destroy. *Search* for Nan, that is, and when I'd found her, *destroy* any ideas that anybody might have about Nan hanging around the mall one second longer than absolutely necessary.

Now, it looked as if that little rescue mission had been scrapped. At least, I thought it probably was. The trouble was, I wasn't sure. What's more, if Nan really believed that zapping me with a few Twin Whammies was going to clue me in, she had to be kidding.

Nan has always put far too much stock in what I call the *hocus-pocus* of being twins. Personally, I think that over the years people have asked us so many times if we can read each other's minds, or send messages telepathically, or feel each other's pain, Nan has actually come to believe that we can do it.

It didn't help any that, back in high school when she and I took part in the University of Louisville Twin Study, Nan had scored unbelievably high on the ESP tests they gave us.

I, on the other hand, had scored so much less than what any normal person could get simply by chance that the people conducting the tests had said that I had ESP, too. Only, unlike Nan, I was "blocking."

I guess I must've been blocking once again, because as Nan directed yet another Twin Whammy my way, I still had no idea what in the world she was trying to tell me. I did, however, feel like telling her: Look, Nan, Twin Whammies were fine when we were ten or eleven, but today I need English. Good old reliable English, actually spoken out loud and everything.

Unfortunately, the only out-loud English I could hear was not coming from Nan, but from the woman in pink. As a matter of fact, she was all but screaming in my ear. "So you're Bertrice! The other one! My, my, how wonderful!"

I begged to differ. For one thing, she was mispronouncing my name. Bert-*rice*, rhyming it with *nice*. Which, strangely enough, did not describe my mood at the moment.

"That's Bertrice," I said, emphasizing the last syllable. Burr-*treese*.

"Oh," the woman screamed, *"Bertreese!* Silly me, of *course!* BERTREESE!"

Have I mentioned how much I hate my name? I looked it up once in one of those baby naming books, and it was listed under the heading: NAMES THAT ARE SO FAR OUT OF FASHION, THEY'LL NEVER COME BACK. And yet, this woman was yelling my out-of-fashion name so loud, people out in the mall parking lot could probably hear her.

"Everybody calls me Bert," I said, stretching my mouth into a smile. "Hardly anyone ever calls me—"

Maybe Nan really does have ESP. She certainly seemed to

know where I was going with this. "Bert," she said, interrupting me, "let me introduce you to Mrs. Louise Eagleston—"

Louise, on the other hand, must have a double-block in the ESP department, because the woman certainly didn't seem to sense that Nan was right in the middle of a sentence. "Your sister and I are old friends," Louise interrupted, fiddling with the end of her scarf. "We met at a charity event; and well, she and I just hit it off."

I glanced over at Nan. Nan was looking straight at Louise, her face totally blank. My guess, Nan couldn't even remember Louise, let alone the mutual hitting it off they'd done.

"Ever since I met your twin sister, I've been hoping I'd get to meet you," Louise continued.

I looked back over at Louise. She was clearly talking to me and mentioning Nan, but she wasn't looking at either one of us. She was staring, instead, at the man who'd been holding Nan's hand when I'd first walked up.

The guy who I believe I mentioned was extremely good-looking and who at that moment was looking unwaveringly at Nan. Who, in turn, was returning his gaze with much the same expression she'd had on her face that day long ago when she'd found all our Christmas presents.

Not that I blamed Nan or Louise, of course. As Mom always said, whenever she saw a handsome man on the street, *Lordy Mercy*. Nan's companion was a *Lordy Mercy*–type guy all right.

With Louise not even looking my way, however, it did make it a little awkward to say, "Glad to meet you, too, Louise," but I did it, anyway.

Nan managed somehow to tear her eyes away from Lordy Mercy, and turned back to me, "And Bert, this is Crane— Crane Morgan."

There wasn't anything markedly different in the way Nan introduced Crane, and yet I could tell just by the way she said his name that Crane had already made Nan's hit parade.

"It's a pleasure to meet you," Crane said, extending his hand.

The moment he spoke, I almost caught my breath.

Oh, Lord, Nan was a goner, for sure.

Nan has always been crazy about deep, masculine voices. She'd actually dated a construction worker by the name of Tab, for God's sake, just so she could hear him say her name. She won't admit it, of course, but I know that's why she stayed with him so long. It took Nan three entire months to notice what I had pretty much surmised the day I met him: Tab could say Nan's name, all right, but when it came to using her name in a complete sentence, he was totally at a loss.

"I'm glad to meet you," I now said to Crane, extending my own hand. Almost immediately, my hand disappeared in his.

Oh, my, a deep voice and a strong, firm handshake, too. Nan might as well throw in the towel.

"You twins are just *too* cute, you really are!" Louise said. "You *are* identical, aren't you?"

I could've explained it to her—how Nan and I aren't exactly identical. We're identical twins, as far as DNA goes and all that, but Nan and I are not duplicates of each other, like most identical twins. We're mirror twins, which is a kind of subset of identical twins—a subset, in fact, that's even rarer.

Mirror twins are, in essence, mirror images of each other. Like, for example, in our case, Nan is left-handed and I'm right-handed; Nan starts off on her left foot, I start off on my right; her hair parts naturally on the left, mine on the right; and so on. Nobody's exactly sure what causes mirroring, but one study I read mentioned that it occurs when the egg takes more time than normal to split. So for a while the cells divide as if it were going to be just one person, with a left and a right. When two people eventually result, one has more left characteristics and the other has more right.

Like I said, I could've explained all this to Louise Eagleston but it seemed like an awful lot to get into. Not to mention, I was pretty sure I didn't want to discuss eggs and fertilization in front of a guy I hardly knew. I know. I know. Call me a prude. Nan certainly has done it, more than once. Calling me a prude, that is—not discussing fertilization in front of guys she hardly knows. Although there's a real good possibility she's done the latter, too.

Prude or not, all I did was nod. "That's absolutely right," I told Louise, "we're identical, all right." Which, of course, was a short version of the truth.

"Oh, how wonderful!" the woman said, clapping her plump hands together as if applauding the two of us.

I glanced over at Nan uncertainly. Did it take very little to thrill this woman, or was I imagining things?

Nan was for once looking straight at me, so I tried to give her a Twin Whammy of my own—one which said, *What do you want me to do now?*

Nan must've gotten something out of my bug-eyed stare, because she actually opened her mouth. In fact, it looked for a moment there as if Nan was on the verge of telling me something in—what a shock—English. Unfortunately, though, Louise piped up with, "Wait a minute! *Bert?* And *Nan?*" She gave her scarf a little flip in the air. "You don't mean to tell me you're named after the Bobbsey Twins?"

Nan and I both nodded in unison. Nan's expression of faint distaste certainly seemed to, no pun intended, mirror mine.

"Oh, this is too cute!" Louise squealed. "It is too, too darling!"

I was getting too, too tired of hearing the words "cute" and "darling." In fact, if Louise said "cute" or "darling" one more time, I was going to have to hurt her.

"Don't you think so?" Louise asked Crane. "Aren't they just too—"

Thank God this time somebody interrupted Louise for a change. "Bert," Crane's deep voice boomed, "I was just suggesting to Nan that I show her my studio."

I turned to look at him; and what do you know, his incredibly long-lashed eyes were resting on my face. "It's downtown on Main," he said, "which isn't too far from here, so—"

I had begun to feel a real rush of gratitude to Crane for shutting Louise up for a moment, but even his deep voice couldn't stop her for long. "Crane has suggested we all come see his studio. He's a photographer, you know—he took my portrait, such a beautiful job—and his studio is the most darling . . ."

As Louise was speaking, I glanced over at Nan. She looked as if she'd just bitten down on a jalapeño pepper, but was determined to act as if she really liked it.

From this, I cleverly surmised that Crane had not included Louise in his invitation.

To confirm this, I glanced over at Crane as Louise was going on about how Crane's too-darling studio and its too-quaint charm had not been renovated out of existence like a lot of the other buildings on Main Street.

Crane had an expression on his face that Nan and I had

come to know well back when we were in high school. He looked just like guys always used to look once they'd made up their mind which twin they were interested in—and they didn't know how in the world to unload the other one. Only in this case, the look on Crane's face was even more desperate. It clearly said, *Oh, great, I've got to be a gentleman and ask the sister and the loudmouth to come, too, but if they accept, I'm going to throw myself under a train.*

"Yes," Crane said, the moment Louise shut up, "I did want to show Nan my studio. And I'd love for you two to come, too."

I had to hand it to him. He was an excellent liar.

His skill was no doubt lost on Nan, however. All her attention was apparently going into the Triple Twin Whammy she was sending my way. Nan had turned so that Crane could only see her back, and if Louise ever took her eyes off Crane, she would only see Nan from the side. I, lucky person that I was, got the full frontal view. Eyes bugging, nostrils wide, and mouth pinched, Nan was sending me a Whammy par excellence.

OK. OK. I got the message, for God's sake.

I took a deep breath. Nan was going to owe me big time for this one.

"Thanks so much, Crane," I said, smiling at him, "but I really couldn't possibly. As a matter of fact, I really don't have much time. Mom is waiting dinner for me this evening." Crane may have been a good liar, but I didn't think he could hold a candle to me. I turned smoothly and faced Louise. "You know, since you've already seen the studio, I did hope that I would have a little more time to talk to you," I went on. "Nan has mentioned you several times, and I've been wanting to meet you, too."

Louise now had another familiar expression on her face. The deer in the headlights expression. "Oh?" she said, clearly surprised. "Nan has mentioned *me?*" She sounded as if she wasn't sure how to react to this development.

"Oh, yes," I said. "Nan has said such nice things about you and . . ." At this point, I was casting around in my mind for something I could say about the woman. And then it came to me. "And all your charity work. I've been wanting to talk to you about it. I do think that people who contribute their time to help the less fortunate are just *too* wonderful . . ."

Oh, God, give me a shovel. As my son Brian puts it so charmingly, I was wading in it hip-deep.

Louise gave her scarf another little flip in the air, smiling widely. "How nice of you to say," she said. "Well, I suppose you and I could get a bite to eat, and talk for a little while. I have always thought that charity work is . . ." She turned back to Crane and Nan, but they were already beginning to move away from us—no doubt, anxious to make their escape. Louise's voice trailed off.

"Well, I'm disappointed that you two aren't coming along, but maybe some other time?" Crane was backing up as he said this, his hand just touching Nan's elbow as she backed away with him. Listening to him, I changed my mind. He could possibly be a more accomplished liar than I was. He actually sounded genuinely sorry.

Louise responded with yet another scarf flip. "Of course, Crane," she said. "Some other time."

Crane and Nan left then, moving—it seemed to me—just as fast as they dared without looking as if they were running.

Louise stared after them, totally silent for a change. In fact, she actually seemed uncertain what to do next, now that most of her audience was doing a fast exit.

I touched Louise's arm. "You were saying something about your charity work?" I allowed myself some satisfaction at having put one over on this unbelievably pushy woman.

Louise glanced over at me, her eyes narrowing just a little, then she looked back at the rapidly disappearing Nan and Crane. Smiling, she called after them. "That's right. You two go on," she bellowed after Nan's and Crane's backs—before they got out of her vocal range—waving them away with her scarf as if she'd been the one who'd arranged their little expedition all along. Her eyes still on Crane and Nan, Louise went on. "Bert and I will just get us a little something to eat and have ourselves a nice, long talk."

My smile froze. Oh God. What had I gotten myself into?

Halfway down the alcove, leading to the exit, Nan stopped. It crossed my mind that Louise's voice had carried to where Nan was now standing—goodness, it had probably carried to Oxmoor Mall down the street—and having heard the woman, Nan was coming back to rescue me.

"What am I thinking of?" Nan said. "I can't go." At this point Nan paused to cast a forlorn look in Crane's direction. "I hitched a ride here so I won't have a way . . ." All the while, Nan looked up at him under her lashes.

What can I say? She was good.

Crane didn't even let her finish. "No problem," he said, his voice booming back to us. "I'll be glad to drive you home," he said. He made it sound like a privilege.

I couldn't help smiling. Crane did seem nice.

Of course, that's what I'd thought about Nan's last boy-friend—a cop, believe it or not, by the name of Hank Goetz-mann. I still wasn't sure exactly why Nan had broken it off with one of Louisville's Finest—Hank had certainly seemed fine enough to me. On the other hand, Hank had clearly not been any Crane Morgan in the looks department.

And it was kind of nice to see Nan's eyes light up when she looked over at Crane.

Nan and Crane were now hurrying once again toward the mall exit doors. In fact, I'd say that the two of them moved faster than rats leaving a sinking ship.

Sinking ship that I was, I stood looking after them. Was I a truly great sister or what?

When they had reached the mall doors, I stopped staring after them and started trying to think of a way to ditch Louise. The woman had already started rattling on about something, while she stared after Nan and Crane and clutched my arm.

"Oh, dear," I said, hitting my forehead, like one of those people in the old *I-could've-had-a-V-8* television commercials, "it just occurred to me that I'm not going to be able to have a bite with you, after all. It's like I said, I'm supposed to go to Mom's for dinner." I glanced at my watch. "Oh dear, she's probably waiting on me right this minute."

I told the lie quite well—Lord knows, I should've, I've had a lot of practice—but I don't think Louise heard a word of it.

She hadn't moved since Nan and Crane had left. She was just standing there, twisting the end of her scarf. "Bert," she said, "I do hope we're doing the right thing."

I just looked at her. *We? The right thing?*

"I guess it'll be OK, though," Louise added.

First, Twin Whammies, and now, riddles. Could this woman be any more annoying? I bit. *"What* will be OK?"

"Oh, you know, letting Nan go off with him," Louise said.

By now Nan and Crane were nowhere in sight. I turned to stare at Louise. "Why wouldn't it be OK?"

Louise shrugged, wrinkling her nose. "Well, you know, after what happened."

The answer to my earlier question was a resounding "Yes." The woman could indeed become more annoying.

"What happened?" I asked.

She was twisting her stupid scarf again. "Oh, I keep forgetting that people here in Louisville don't know a thing about the Morgan twins. And what happened."

"The Morgan *twins?*"

Louise nodded. "Crane Morgan is a twin—that is, he *was* a twin. His brother died a little over two years ago."

"Oh dear." I felt a rush of sympathy for the man. How awful for the poor guy. It was a wonder that he could still be so cheerful after that kind of a loss. Lord, it was a wonder he was still *functioning* after that kind of a loss.

"The story made all the papers in Owensboro," Louise added.

"The story?"

Louise shrugged again. "Let's go get something to eat, and I'll tell you all about it."

I know, I know. The woman was playing me like a harp. She, no doubt, had known very well that I'd been trying to dump her, and now she'd gotten me to follow her without so much as a protest over to the Philly Cheese Steak counter.

I even stood behind her for ten long minutes while she ordered her Philadelphia steak sandwich, with extra cheese and onions, her Coke, her large french fries, and then I finally went and claimed an empty table.

I myself got only a Coke. I would've liked to have gotten more—it was already dark outside, and the sandwich Louise brought to the table did smell awfully good—and yet, how could I? After lying about Mom and dinner, I couldn't very well start chowing down. Oh, yeah, Nan owed me big time.

Louise was slowly unwrapping her sandwich. While I sipped my Coke and tried not to glare at her, she slowly unwrapped her straw, and stuck it through the plastic lid of her Coke. She then slowly unfolded her paper napkin, and laid it carefully on her lap. And then—and only then—did she lift her sandwich to her mouth.

At this rate we could be here all night. "You know, Mom *is* holding dinner for me," I said. "So what were you saying about Owensboro?"

Louise took a bite of her sandwich, chewed it carefully and swallowed it.

I took another quick sip. "You were talking about something that had happened in Owensboro?" I prodded.

Louise nodded, but continued to chew. Finally, she swallowed, and then before she spoke, she slowly patted at her lips with her paper napkin. "It's been over two years now, but people are still talking about it. Crane's twin brother, Lane Morgan, committed suicide."

"Oh my goodness!" I burst out. "How terrible."

Louise nodded. "Lane killed himself because he'd been accused of stabbing his girlfriend, a woman by the name of Marian Fielding—to death."

I felt a sudden chill. Good Lord. Crane's twin brother had committed murder? I glanced at Louise, who was slowly chewing as she kept a beady eye on my reaction. I suddenly did not like this woman. She was having way too much fun telling me this. Could it really be true?

"You said *accused*. Did Lane Morgan really do it?"

Louise had taken another bite, and was chewing with all the speed of a cow chewing its cud. So OK, she couldn't exactly speak. She could, however, have nodded her head. Or shook it to indicate "No." She did neither. She chewed, she swallowed, and she dabbed at her lips with her napkin, all before she spoke again.

By that time I was seriously considering wringing her neck.

"Well, there were two witnesses who put Lane at the scene of the crime," Louise finally said. "Plus tissue and fiber samples. And Lane's DNA conclusively matched that of blood drops found near the body of the victim."

I took another sip of my Coke, and stared at Louise. She sounded as if she'd been one of the investigators on the case.

I guess I must've been looking at her a little oddly, because she cleared her throat and said, "I read all about it in the *Owensboro Herald*. The paper more or less interpreted Lane's suicide as a confession."

Louise took another bite of her sandwich and chewed it even slower than before. I wasn't sure if she was an incredibly slow eater, or if she was just trying to drive me nuts. Finally, she said, "You cannot imagine how sorry the whole town felt for Crane. He and his brother had been inseparable."

Well, not exactly, I thought. Lane had had a girlfriend, after all, so he'd had to have gotten away from Crane occasionally.

"Oh, yes, Crane was absolutely leveled," Louise said. "I just know he moved to Louisville simply to get away from all those too-horrible memories. And yet, he can't really get away. Just look what happened when I hired him to do my portrait—a simply beautiful job, he did, too. But right away there were those who just had to call me up and remind me about the whole mess."

I looked at her, puzzled. "You got phone calls about *Crane?* When Lane was the one who—"

Louise dabbed at her mouth. "Well, that's just it, my dear. No one knows if it really was Lane. Identical twins do have the same DNA, don't they?" She leaned forward and lowered her voice for the first time since I'd met her. "There was a rumor going around that *both* Crane *and* Lane had been going out with Marian Fielding at the same time."

I couldn't be sure, but Louise actually seemed to *enjoy* repeating this little tidbit of news. I stared at her. "Oh, come on. You don't really think Crane had anything to do with Marian Fielding's death? You can't possibly."

I didn't spell it out, but I thought it: Surely, Louise wouldn't have had her portrait taken by somebody who she actually thought might be a murderer?

Louise was watching me closely as she took another bite. If she hadn't been chewing, I was almost sure that the woman would've been smiling.

I shifted position in my chair, and took a long, long sip of Coke.

Maybe old Louise here had ulterior motives for passing on these sordid little stories. Maybe she'd made a play for Crane herself, and he'd rejected her. Maybe that was why she was spreading such awful tales. It had been obvious that Crane was interested in Nan. So maybe Louise's plan was to turn Nan against Crane. Louise had to know that I'd repeat everything she told me to my twin sister.

Actually, when you thought about it, the whole thing was preposterous. I felt myself relaxing a little, even as I asked, "Look, if Crane were the real killer, why on earth would his brother commit suicide? Why kill yourself over something you didn't even do?"

Louise's eyes actually sparkled as she leaned across the table again. "Lane is *supposed* to have drowned himself," Louise whispered. "The official version is that Lane jumped from the Second Street Bridge in Owensboro and drowned in the Ohio River. His brother Crane identified the body when it was finally recovered days later." Louise glanced around, as if checking to see if anybody in the Food Court could hear her. The maneuver made me more annoyed at the woman than ever.

"I mean," she went on, "it stands to reason that if Lane wasn't the killer, then his death wasn't a suicide, was it?" She slowly patted her lips again with that infuriating napkin. "It can't be that hard to push somebody off a bridge, you know. Especially if that somebody wasn't expecting it."

I reached for my Coke again, and as I did, I couldn't help but notice that my hands were now shaking.

"Ready to go?" A voice sounded in my ear.

I jumped so much, I spilled a little of my Coke.

Turning, I saw a balding, middle-aged guy standing behind my chair. He smiled, revealing teeth that had a whole lot in common with a picket fence. A fence with a couple of pickets missing.

It was Bob Grayson, a guy from Nan's radio station who happened to be married and yet, I'd always suspected, also happened to have a huge crush on Nan.

"I'm Bert," I corrected automatically, my mind still digesting what Louise had just told me.

"Oh, of course," Bob said, reddening a little. "Hiya, Bert. I should've known it was you when I saw that you'd changed clothes. Or rather, that you hadn't actually changed clothes, because you never were wearing what Nan was, so what I mean is that . . ." At this point, Bob must've decided that he'd said enough. He abandoned this explanation entirely, and blurted, "So, where's Nan? I've been doing some background interviews, and I thought I was supposed to drive her home." He glanced around the Food Court. "You know where Nan is?"

I just looked at him, my throat tightening up.

Where was Nan? Well, if you believed Louise, Nan was off spending quality time alone with an extremely nice, extremely good-looking guy.

Who'd killed two people.

Chapter 5

•

NAN

I know Bert probably wouldn't believe it, but I did feel a little guilty about leaving her to deal with Louise Eagleston all by herself. Louise seemed only a little less tenacious than Alien at the beginning of the movie by the same name. You know, when Alien first attached itself to that guy's face. Bert could possibly have as difficult a time extricating herself, and I did feel bad about it. I really did.

Of course, my massive guilt didn't slow me down any.

I all but ran toward the parking lot. Crane, amazingly enough, moved even faster. He got to the door at the end of the alcove—the one leading to the parking lot—a moment or so before I did. And wonder of wonders, he actually opened the door, and kept it open, waiting for me to go through first.

It was all I could do to keep my mouth from dropping open. Offhand, I couldn't think of anybody I'd dated who'd ever opened a door for me.

Other than Hank Goetzmann, the cop. Who didn't exactly count. I'd always gotten the feeling that he was just following standard police procedure.

Crane, on the other hand, seemed to have thought this up all on his own. Or rather, he didn't seem to think about it at all. He'd just casually opened the door for me as if it were the most natural thing in the world.

Judging from the behavior of other men that I'd dated, I'd say it wasn't natural. In fact, the one time when I'd ventured to mention to some guy I was dating that it would be nice if he made this little gesture, I'd been accused of being anti–women's lib. No kidding.

Apparently, I had completely misinterpreted the purpose of the women's liberation movement. It had not been to ensure that women had equal opportunity in the workplace, or equal pay, or control of their own bodies. Nope, all those demonstrations and speeches had been to make certain that here in America we women could finally be guaranteed the right to open our own doors.

Crane was now smiling at me, and waving me on through. "Thank you," I said as I passed him. Believe me, I meant it.

Crane led the way to a late-model dark green Toyota Camry. In case you didn't immediately know that this car was expensive, Toyota made sure you got the idea by writing *Camry* on the back in gold. If the gold letters weren't convincing enough, there was also a leather interior and gold-trimmed hubcaps. Evidently, Crane's photography studio was doing quite well.

Without missing a beat, Crane strolled around to the passenger side of the car, and yes, he actually opened the door for me *again*.

I tried not to stare, but let's face it. There was every chance in the world that this man could be genuinely thoughtful.

On the way to his studio, we did the usual thing you do on a first date. We confined our conversation to non-controversial topics. Like our work, the weather, and the topic that is pretty much required discussion for all state residents during the month of April—the month, mind you, that immediately follows the NCAA basketball tournament.

In April, if you live anywhere in Kentucky, you have to talk about whether or not U of L or UK will have a good basketball team next year. Of course, on a first date, you do not, at any time during the discussion, indicate whether or not you prefer one team over the other. Because telling a UK fan that you're a U of L fan, or vice versa, is a lot like telling a Hindu all about the juicy ribeye you ate the night before. Instead of declaring yourself a UK fan or a U of L fan, you say things like, "I really enjoy watching both teams play."

"You know," Crane said after we'd thoroughly discussed who we thought was the best player on each team, "I've always enjoyed watching *both* teams."

I couldn't help but smile. "That must make it really difficult when they play each other."

Crane grinned. "Not at all. That's the only game that I know for sure I'm going to be rooting for the winner."

I grinned back at him. What do you know, it could very well be that this man was absolutely adorable.

Crane was shaking his head. "Can you believe that I've met people who moved to Kentucky from up north, and they have actually expressed amazement at the way Kentuckians are so wrapped up in *college* basketball? Up north, I've been told, people follow *professional* basketball."

I feigned mock horror. "No!" I said.

"Yes!" Crane said, his smile now crinkling the corners of his eyes. "You know what I told them? That here in Kentucky being either a University of Louisville fan or a University of Kentucky fan *is* a profession."

I laughed, nodding my head in agreement, and Crane's grin grew even wider. For a moment, as he glanced over at me, he'd completely lost the air of sadness that seemed to pervade everything he did. In fact, right then Crane looked as if he didn't have a care in the world.

By the time we'd established that both U of L and UK were going to be awesome in the fall, and that the weather was exceptionally warm for April, *and* that both of us really enjoyed our work, we'd arrived in front of 121 West Main. As luck would have it, there was a parking space right in front of the building. Which, on Main Street—one of Louisville's busiest downtown streets—hardly ever happens.

The five-story building clearly belonged to another era. One of several that had been restored on that particular block of Main Street, the Victorian period building had double doors faced in polished copper, a stone facade with ornate scrollwork, and the words G.T. ALCOTT AND SONS MILLINERY EST. 1807 carved into its facade. With stained glass insets in several of the windows, the building made you feel as if you'd stepped back in time.

Crane, amazingly enough, opened three more doors for me after we arrived. First, the passenger door on the Camry. Next, one of the aforementioned copper double doors. And finally, the door just inside and to the left that had the words MORGAN PHOTOGRAPHY painted on the smoked glass.

By the time Crane had held the door for me for the fourth time in only a twenty-minute span, I was convinced. Crane Morgan was indeed the nicest guy I'd ever gone out with.

I moved on into the room, still looking around. On one side of the room a camera on a tripod stood facing a wall draped in a paint-splashed canvas. Large umbrellas and an assortment of lights on stands surrounded this area; this was, no doubt, where Crane did his portrait work.

What interested me most, however, was the large, framed, black and white photographs decorating the walls. Some of these photographs were wonderful—a fire escape casting stark shadows across a brick wall; an overhead shot of a crowd of shoppers rushing along the street, their long shadows seeming to pull them along; and a child's face seen through a goldfish bowl, as fish and child seemed to study each other.

Crane was clearly waiting for my reaction. I gave him another smile. "Your studio is wonderful," I said, walking over to get a better view of the photographs on the wall to my left. "And your photographs, why, they're—"

I didn't mean to break off so abruptly, but my attention had been caught by what looked like several self-portraits. There were at least a dozen of these. Most were routine shots, pictures of the very good-looking man in back of me laughing, smiling, or smirking into the camera. One, however, was very different. It showed Crane, his head turned so that you saw only a three-quarter view. He was looking directly at the camera, his gaze intense and challenging. The dark shadows that played across his jawline made him look almost menacing.

I couldn't help staring at it. Crane certainly didn't look like himself in that one.

Crane followed the direction of my eyes, and moved to stand next to me. In fact, he stood so close, our shoulders touched. "Oh Lord," he said, "I just realized that all these portraits make me look like some kind of ego maniac."

I smiled and said nothing. The thought had crossed my mind, though. What kind of man would hang a dozen portraits of himself on the wall? The words *vain*, *egotistical*, and *narcissistic* did leap to mind.

"The only thing is, none of these are pictures of me," Crane said. "They're all of Lane."

Lane? The twin brother who'd died a couple of years ago? Oh God. I wasn't sure what to say. How could Crane stand to see these pictures every day? On the other hand, what did it matter really? A glance in a mirror would be a constant reminder of his loss.

It suddenly occurred to me that I'd been staring at Lane's portrait in total silence while all this went through my mind. Flustered, I blurted out, "My goodness, you and your brother really do look alike."

Crane's mouth tightened with pain, and I realized too late that I'd used the present tense. There was no way I could correct it now, though. I couldn't exactly say, *Oh, I'm sorry, what I meant to say was that you and your brother really* did *look alike.* That would make things even worse.

To cover my growing confusion, I moved closer to the shadow portrait. "I really like this one," I said, "but there's something about it that's—that's—"

"Disturbing?" Crane finished for me.

I glanced over at him. "Well, I wouldn't say disturbing, exactly. It's just that your brother looks so unhappy." He also looked angry, but I wasn't about to mention it.

Crane was looking at the portrait, too. "Oh, he was unhappy, all right. That one was taken after Lane had gotten involved with a woman named Marian Fielding." Crane looked as if just saying the woman's name left a bad taste in his mouth.

"Lane never was the same after Marian came into his life," Crane went on. "She ruined everything for him."

I blinked at that one. *Ruined everything?* That seemed like an awful lot of power for just one woman. I wanted to ask Crane what she'd done, but I didn't know how to without sounding like an even bigger gossip than Louise Eagleston.

Crane took a step away from the shadow portrait, and took a deep breath. "You know," he said, turning toward me with a rueful smile, "sometimes I feel as if I've had two lives. One, when Lane and I were together; and then the other, after he died."

I tried to return his smile, but the grief in his eyes was so painful to see, I had to look away.

"In my first life," Crane went on, moving to stand in front of a smiling Lane portrait, "Lane and I grew up in Owensboro, graduated from college in Evansville, and majored in art. Our parents both died within a couple months of each other while we were still in college. They'd had us late in life, though, so by that time they were both in their sixties. In my first life, then, my family was mainly just Lane."

Crane paused again, and cleared his throat. When he spoke again, there was an emotion in his voice I hadn't heard before. "In my second life, after Lane was gone, I moved to Louisville, and—I don't know, maybe it was because Lane's death made me realize how fleeting everything is—I did something that he and I had talked about doing for years."

"What was that?" I asked, moving to stand next to him in front of the happier portrait.

He smiled, and now his tone was light again, even casual. "I opened this studio."

Once again, I didn't know what to say. I just looked at him.

The poor man. There was so much grief in his eyes, it broke my heart.

Crane shrugged and added, "Of course, a lot of my work these days is the usual wedding pictures and portraits, but eventually I want to get into advertising work exclusively. And maybe someday see my work in the pages of national magazines."

I blinked again. Now here was a novelty: a guy with actual ambition. I'd dated so many men whose main goal in life seemed to be trying to stay drunk for an entire weekend that hearing a man talk about his work as if it were something he was excited about was a brand-new experience.

"Right now," Crane went on, "I'm sharing studio space with another photographer—Bentley Shepard? Maybe you've heard of him. He does the usual wedding-portrait stuff, too, but also some mail-order work. Sharing the studio with Bentley, though, is really just a matter of economics for me. I don't want to go through the insurance money too quickly in case I need it later on down the road. And since I'm just starting out, I thought sharing rent with somebody else would be the best way to go. Bentley has the other half of this floor. But I do hope to have a studio all my own someday soon. And really build a future."

As Crane said this last, his eyes returned to Lane's portrait. A muscle tightened in his jaw, and I knew what he was thinking. *Lane didn't get to have a future.*

"I am so sorry," I said, going to Crane's side.

I'd meant to just touch his arm, to somehow let him know that I understood and I cared. But before I quite realized what was happening, he'd pulled me into his arms.

And his mouth was on mine.

That first kiss felt like something I'd been waiting for my entire life. It went on and on until I actually felt dizzy. When we finally broke away, I think we were both a little shaken.

I immediately moved away from him, trying to calm my thundering heart. And trying to get hold of myself.

Whoa, girl. What a minute. Things were suddenly moving too fast. *Way* too fast.

I tried to act casual, as if maybe I always kissed men like that on a first date. And while I waited for my heart to stop trying to leap out of my chest, I walked quickly toward the wall farthest from Crane—a wall covered with black and white photographs I hadn't yet looked at. "You know," I said, stopping in front of one, a close-up of the craggy, lined face of an old man, "you are really good."

As soon as the words were out of my mouth, I realized that they could be taken two ways. Once again, though, it was too late.

"You're not so bad yourself," Crane said, sounding amused.

I turned to look at him, smiling in spite of myself. "I *meant*," I said, "that you're a good *photographer*."

Crane grinned and shrugged. "Oh," he said, obviously teasing. "Just a good *photographer*—how disappointing."

His dark blue eyes were so intense, I found that I couldn't look away. In fact, the two of us just stood there like two moonstruck teenagers and just stared at each other. As the minutes ticked by.

God. He was a good-looking man.

God. He was sexy.

God, oh God. I could be in big trouble here.

I finally looked away, turning blindly toward the wall of photographs. And like I pretty much always do when I'm unbelievably rattled, I started babbling like an idiot. "You know, I like this portrait. I really do. I think it might be my favorite. It really is nice."

It took me a moment to actually focus on the pictures, but by the time Crane had crossed the room and asked, "Which one?" I had an answer for him.

"This one," I said, pointing at a portrait of a young woman. In her late teens or early twenties, she was wearing a gauzy dress, a wide-brimmed hat, and she was barefoot. The wind was blowing the woman's long blond hair across her face, and she was laughing as she tried to keep her hat in place.

Crane didn't answer for a minute, and when he spoke, his voice sounded odd somehow. "That portrait won first place in a regional photography exhibit at the J.B. Speed Art Museum three years ago. I think it's one of my best."

I gave Crane a quick glance. He looked perfectly calm; maybe I'd been imagining the strain in his voice. I turned to look at the portrait with renewed interest. "I can certainly see why it won." I took a step closer to the laughing face. The woman really was lovely. I wondered who she was—an old girlfriend, perhaps?

"Wouldn't you know," Crane went on, his voice even more strained, "one of my award-winning portraits would be of Marian Fielding."

I blinked at that one. "This was Marian?" I said, stepping closer to the portrait. What I didn't say, but I thought, was: *This was the woman who you feel ruined your brother's life?* I actually felt a chill, looking at Marian's pretty face. What in the world had she done?

Upon closer inspection, however, I had a hint as to what might've happened. With the sunlight coming from her left, the gauzy dress that Marian wore in the portrait was a blend of shadow and light. In a few places it looked virtually transparent. Anyone could clearly see that beneath this little frock, Marian Fielding was wearing nothing at all.

I blinked again, digesting the implications. This woman was dressed like this in front of her boyfriend's *brother?*

I turned abruptly away, feeling awkward, as if I'd stumbled into some place I shouldn't be. "I like this portrait of the old man, too—" I began.

Crane interrupted me. "No, Nan, we're going to talk about it," he said. "I want to tell you about Marian. And about Lane."

I turned to look at him. He may have wanted to tell me, but I wasn't sure now if it was something I wanted to hear.

"If you and I are well, if we're going to see each other, I want you to understand. And—and . . ." Crane was talking hesitantly now, picking his words carefully. "If you don't want to see me after what I'm about to tell you, then it's good that I told you now. Before—before things got out of hand."

I just looked at him. I hated to break it to him, but things were already out of hand. And what on earth did he think he could tell me that would make me not want to see him?

Crane looked back at the laughing portrait, took a deep breath, and then clearing his throat, he said, "Why don't I get us a drink? What would you like? I've got a little bar behind that door over there." He pointed toward a closed door on our right.

I nodded. If he was about to tell me something awful, a drink might be a very good idea.

Crane made me a Bloody Mary and himself a gin and tonic, and then he and I sat down on a large black leather sectional sofa backing up to a window looking out onto Main Street. Miniblinds protected our privacy, but you could see the street clearly from where I was sitting. Sipping my Bloody Mary—which seemed a bit heavy on the vodka—I eased off my shoes, tucking one foot under me.

Crane gave me a sad smile. "You know," he said, "I've never wanted to tell anybody this before."

After he said *that*, I would've been willing to listen to anything he had to tell me. I even leaned forward a little.

Crane took a deep breath. "Marian Fielding was one of those women who enjoy getting her hooks into a man, and then flirting with other men right in front of him. She even flirted with me, if you can believe that."

She's wearing a see-through dress with no underwear right in front of you? It wasn't exactly a stretch to imagine her doing a little flirting, too.

Crane took a long drink of his gin and tonic. "It was torture for Lane," he said. "Marian would dance too close with somebody at a party, or she'd kiss some guy she'd just met, right in front of Lane—and he would just go wild. Once she had Lane all worked up, Marian would stand to one side, watching and smiling that sick little smile of hers. I remember once she actually laughed when Lane totally lost it, and ended up getting into a fist fight with a bartender that Marian had been coming onto all night long."

"She sounds cruel," I said, taking a sip.

"She *was* cruel." Crane closed his eyes. "It all came to a head one night after they'd gotten back from a party. Lane and Marian apparently had a violent argument, fueled probably by how much liquor they'd drunk. At her apartment Lane finally lost complete control, and he—he hit her."

I had been about to take another drink, but I froze. Lane had hit the woman?

"Lane didn't mean to hit her that hard, I know he didn't," Crane went on. "He would never have intentionally hurt Marian. Never. But she—she died."

I almost dropped my glass.

Oh my God.

Crane's voice was ragged. "When Lane came home that night—we shared an apartment—he acted crazy. Pacing. And crying. And screaming Marian's name." Crane took a deep breath. "I don't think he could stand knowing what he'd done."

My hand had begun to shake a little. I put my glass down on the end table next to me.

"The rest of that evening is still a blur, even today," Crane said. "I tried and tried to get Lane to go to the police. I told him that he could claim temporary insanity. He could tell the police he didn't know what he was doing. Unfortunately, as it turned out, nobody had to tell the police anything. There was enough evidence at Marian's apartment for them to figure out who'd done it—they all knew it was Lane. He'd cut himself—drops of his blood were on the floor. I think he and I both knew it was only a matter of time until he was arrested. I started talking to attorneys for him, to doctors, trying to get him some help. But then, when I came back home, he wasn't there." Crane's voice was getting more and more ragged. I reached for his hand. "And then—then the police came to tell me that Lane had . . ." Crane couldn't seem to bring himself to finish what he was saying. His fingers tightened around my own. "That he'd killed himself."

"Oh, Crane."

I was so shocked, I could hardly breathe for a moment.

Poor Crane. How could you ever get over something like that? I don't believe I'd ever felt so sorry for anybody in my entire life.

We sat there for a minute or so, holding hands. Finally, Crane broke the silence.

"Don't hate me," was all he said.

I blinked. "Hate *you?* Why should I hate you?"

Crane looked miserable. "Some people seem to think I have to be just like my brother. Since we were identical twins. And that if Lane could hurt somebody, then so could I."

"Nonsense," I said.

I guess I said that awfully quick, because Crane sort of blinked. "Nan, you just may be one of the few people in the entire world who understands how different Lane and I really were."

I smiled at him. One thing a twin definitely knows, identical twins aren't identical in every way. Bert and I share the same genes, sure, but, good Lord, we're not the same person.

"You may also be one of the few people," Crane said, his eyes darkening as he looked into mine, "who understands how much I miss my brother. No matter what he did." He gave my hand a little squeeze, and shrugged. "You know, when you're accustomed all your life to having a certain person with you, suddenly not having him is like, well, it's like having a limb amputated."

I knew, of course, exactly what Crane meant. If anything ever happened to Bert, I knew I'd feel as if I'd lost something of myself.

With the worst out of the way, it seemed as if Crane and I were suddenly free to discuss everything else. For the next several hours, we sat side by side, and talked. I told him about how I'd gotten my first job on the radio (I'd begged and pleaded), and Crane told me about his first portrait session (he'd paid the subject rather than vice versa). We talked about parents, high school, college, and anything else that came to mind.

It was almost three in the morning by the time I realized how late it was. "I've got to get some sleep, or I'm going to be incoherent on the radio tomorrow," I said. "Or rather, *today*."

Having talked so much, Crane and I were very quiet driving back to my house. When he turned onto Napoleon Boulevard, Crane reached over and took my hand. Holding it against the side of his thigh.

I would never have believed how sexy a little gesture like that could be. I could feel my heart speed up, my breath quicken.

When Crane got out and opened my car door, then took my elbow as we walked up the sidewalk to my door, his touch seemed almost electric.

My porch light was off, but the moon was full. Everything around us was bathed in a cool blue light.

When we got to my door, I moved into his arms as if I'd always belonged there. His kiss this time was as passionate as before, but now there was an urgency to it that had not been there earlier. I could feel myself sinking into that kiss, sinking down, down, to a place where I no longer cared about anything except the intoxicating feel of his lips on mine.

His hands moved to my hips, pressing me against him.

And then, for some idiotic reason, I suddenly realized I was standing there, in front of my entire neighborhood, making out, for God's sake, on my own front porch, like some high school kid.

Hell, *Bert* was probably watching us right this minute.

That little thought was a splash of cold water. I took a deep breath, and then I stepped away. When Crane immediately closed the gap between us, pulling me back into his arms, I put my hands on his chest and gently pushed.

"Crane," I said, my voice not much more than a whisper, "I don't on a first date."

I didn't spell out what it was that I didn't, but I thought he could probably fill that one in for himself.

Apparently, he could. Smiling a little, he said, "Do you on a second date?"

I returned his smile. "I'm not sure."

"Well, then, let's have a second date this evening, so we can both find out."

I grinned at him, wishing suddenly that I could tell him that I had never in my life ever gone to bed with anybody on a first date. It wasn't true, though. Back when I'd first started working at the radio station, I suppose I'd been trying on personalities, trying to decide who I really was. One of the personalities I'd tried on was Slut. I'd quickly found out that Slut wasn't me.

I'd also found out that the sexual revolution that was supposed to have occurred in the sixties really hadn't changed anything much at all. If you went to bed with a near stranger, you pretty much woke up with a near stranger. In fact, there was every chance he wouldn't even remember your name.

I also found out that, with a lot of men, once you start going to bed, you never got more than two sentences out of them again. What's more, one of those sentences was most likely to be, "Let's go to bed."

"A second date sounds great," I told Crane. We decided that Crane would pick me up here at six-thirty. Then I got my key out of my purse, turning toward my door, but Crane immediately took it out of my hand. For a second, I was afraid I was going to have to resist the temptation a second time, but Crane only unlocked my door, opened it for me, then handed me the key. He leaned closer to give me another kiss, and that's when the porch light next door went on. And off. And on. Off. On. Off. In rapid succession.

Crane's head sort of jerked in that direction, then looked questioningly back at me.

I, of course, knew exactly what was causing the porch light to malfunction.

Or rather, *who*.

When Bert and I were still in high school, this was how Mom used to signal us that we'd been standing far too long out on the porch, in front of all the neighbors, kissing our dates. Or that we'd been parked in the driveway too long. As subtle as a train wreck, this little light maneuver meant that whatever we were doing, we were to stop it and get inside.

Back in high school I'd dreamed of having my own place one day, and never ever seeing a flashing porch light again.

Well, I did have my own place, but apparently, I'd been mistaken about the rest of it.

The porch light flashed again. I took a deep breath, and tried not to grit my teeth. "Damn. There's a short in that light," I told Crane. "I keep forgetting to call an electrician."

I wasn't sure if Crane believed me, but he nodded his head as if he did.

Then, as the porch light across the way continued to blink on and off, Crane reached over and softly touched my cheek, his eyes on mine. For a moment, he didn't say a word; he just looked at me, his dark blue eyes intense.

"See you tonight," he said softly. He turned and headed down the sidewalk toward his car.

Me, I just stood there. Smiling.

Until Crane was out of sight.

Then I headed over to Bert's. Frowning.

I was going to fix her porch light once and for all.

Chapter 6

•

BERT

Oh dear.

The second I opened the door and saw the look on Nan's face, I knew she hadn't come barging over to my apartment in the wee hours of the morning to thank me for my help.

"Bert, what the hell did you think you were doing?" Nan said, pushing past me and heading into my living room.

"Why, what do you mean?" I said, closing the door and turning to face Nan. In all modesty, I am very good at sounding innocently surprised. I even managed to sound a little hurt that Nan would use that nasty tone with me.

"Cut the crap, Bert," Nan said.

OK, so maybe I wasn't quite as good as I'd thought.

"You know damn well what I'm talking about," Nan went on. "The porch light bit. What was *that* all about?"

I have always thought that a good defense was a strong offense. I crossed my arms, shifted my weight to the other foot, and assumed an expression that I hoped looked long-suffering. This was pretty difficult to pull off since I was wearing my Warner Brothers sleep shirt with Daffy Duck on the front, and I had pink sponge rollers all over my head. Still, I gave it my best shot. "Well, Nan," I said evenly, "I think it's obvious that I was trying to help. As you can see,

I'm all ready to go to bed, and yet, I've stayed up way past my bedtime just to let you know something very important that I found out tonight."

Nan rolled her eyes. "Something so important you couldn't have waited until tomorrow?"

"Well, I *could* have," I said, "but when it started looking as if you were going to invite Crane to stay the night, I thought I'd—"

Nan cut me off, her eyes blazing. "I most certainly was *not!* Really, Bert, I only just met him, for God's sake. Do you actually think that I'd spend the night with some guy I just *met?*"

I, of course, just looked at her. Unwaveringly. I really hoped that I would not have to remind her of that unfortunate time back when she'd first started working at WCKI. According to what Nan had told me back then—which, believe me, I remembered word for word—she'd been trying out personalities in order to discover, as she'd so dramatically put it, "the real Nan."

Wouldn't you know, of all the personalities that Nan could have tried out—like, for example, *Mother Teresa*, or *Joan of Arc*, or maybe even *The Singing Nun*—Nan had decided to give *The Happy Hooker* a whirl. Only without the monetary rewards, more's the pity.

Thank God the tryout hadn't lasted more than a week. Nan had discovered almost immediately, as I recall, that if *The Happy Hooker* was the real Nan, then the real Nan had some real problems with self-esteem.

The entire episode was far behind Nan these days, and I could understand if Nan wanted to forget this little chapter in her life. But let's face it, had she really forgotten it?

"Oh, yeah, throw *that* in my face!" Nan said.

No, I'd say she hadn't forgotten it.

Nan was pacing now, walking back and forth in front of my coffee table, waving her arms. "I can't believe you'd bring up something that I told you a long, long, long time ago in strictest confidence! That is really low!"

Nan does outraged indignation almost as well as I do surprised innocence. I didn't blink an eye. "Nan," I said, "I wasn't throwing anything in anybody's face. I was just trying to explain where in the world I might have gotten the wild idea that you might be on the verge of inviting Crane Morgan to stay over. That's all I—"

Nan cut me off. "Besides, even if I did intend to ask him to stay—which I *didn't*"—here she stopped pacing for a moment in order to devote all her attention to glaring at me—"what business is it of yours? Are you my mother?"

"*Our* mother," I corrected her.

Nan looked as if brushfires had just been lit behind each eye. Perhaps I should've just let the *my mother* stand. "Bert, do you really think that you have any right whatsoever to be telling me what to do? Huh? Do you?"

I decided that was one of those rhetorical questions that really didn't need an answer. "Nan, I wasn't telling you what to do. I just wanted to stop you before you—"

I guess I should've used a different choice of words. Nan suddenly looked as if an invisible someone had painted a bright red circle in the middle of each of her cheeks. "Stop me? *Stop me?*" Her voice went shrill with anger. "Bert, if I wanted to go to bed with a—with a *Saint Bernard*, it wouldn't be any of your business!"

I hate it when Nan starts saying ridiculous stuff like this. For one thing, it's pretty hard to maintain a straight face when you're listening to this kind of thing. "OK, Nan, I'm sorry, OK? I had no idea. Feel free to sleep with all the enormous, brandy-carrying canines you want. But before you move on to Crane Morgan, there are a few things you should know . . ."

Nan drew a long, beleaguered breath, much like the long-suffering one I'd drawn earlier. "Like what, Bert? Like what am I supposed to know that's so damned important that you'd start doing Mom with the porch light?"

I shrugged, trying to act almost casual. "Like what happened to Crane's brother, for instance. Louise Eagleston told me that Lane Morgan had—"

"—killed his girlfriend?" Nan finished.

I blinked. Oh. Well. Apparently, Nan had heard about that. I nodded. "That's right, and did you know that right after that, Lane committed—"

"—suicide?" Nan finished again.

I blinked again. "Well. Yes. Uh-huh. He did—"

Nan cut me off again. "So what's this got to do with Crane?" she asked, putting a hand on each hip and glaring at me.

That was a good question. The answer, of course, might be, "Nothing." On the other hand, Lane had been Crane's *identical* twin. Identical, like Nan and me. Before this, I'd never really thought about it, mainly because the subject had never come up. But now I wondered. If Nan turned out to be capable of committing murder, did that mean *I* was also capable of killing someone?

Or were there really such things as an evil twin and a good twin, like so often portrayed in books and movies? One twin who could do terrible things, and another totally incapable of it?

If there was indeed such a thing, then I'd say that, as the

evil twin, Nan certainly had my vote. Particularly at this very moment as she hurried on, still glaring at me. "I mean, really, Bert, of all people, *you* should know that Lane and Crane were two very different people. Just because Lane did something, there's no reason to—"

"*If* it really was Lane," I put in.

Nan took that little comment well. Her voice shut off so quickly, you might've thought she had an on-off switch. For a long moment she just looked at me, her eyes narrowing. "Now what exactly did you mean by that crack?" she asked finally.

I'd been meaning to break everything to her gently, but since it was obvious that Nan was not going to listen quietly, I decided to just blurt it all out. Looking at the creases growing deeper and deeper between Nan's brows, however, I had a pretty good idea how this little news flash was going to be received. "Well, Nan, now that you mention it, according to Louise Eagleston—"

"—the gossiping, old biddy—" Nan put in.

I ignored Nan's interruption. "—there has been a lot of talk around Owensboro since Lane Morgan's death. They're saying that Marian Fielding—that's the girl who was killed— was dating *both* brothers, and that maybe it wasn't really Lane who killed her."

Oh, yeah, that one went over extremely well. Nan just stood there for another long, long moment, glaring at me. Actually, to be totally factual, she wasn't glaring at me so much as her dark brown eyes were more or less bugging out in my direction. Not a pretty picture, I might add. In fact, looking at the expression on Nan's face, I made a mental note never to glare at anyone. *Ever.*

"Well, that's the sickest, cruelest, most insensitive thing

I've ever heard," Nan said. "I can't believe how awful some people can be."

I wondered if she was including me in "some people." "Nan," I said, "I didn't say it was true. I was merely repeating what—"

Nan interrupted me yet again. "No wonder the poor guy left Owensboro and moved here to Louisville. If people were saying that kind of thing behind his back, why, he certainly couldn't stay there. But how could they even think that about him?"

I didn't say a word. But the phrase "where there's smoke, there's fire" did leap to mind.

Nan must've picked up on some of what I was thinking, because she rolled her eyes. "Oh, Bert, if you knew Crane, you wouldn't believe any of it," Nan went on, crossing over to my sofa and plopping herself down in the middle of it. "You'd know just how awful this gossip really is. Hell, Crane could no more hurt another human being than he could fly."

I didn't say a word. I did, however, resist the impulse to go to the window and check out the night sky for UFOs.

"Crane is funny, and charming, and witty, and . . ."

I took a seat in the Queen Anne chair next to the sofa, and tried to overlook the sinking feeling I had in the pit of my stomach as Nan went on.

And on.

And on.

Oh dear. The whole time Nan talked, she had a dreamy, faraway look in her eyes. "And he's polite, and gentlemanly, and—and—"

How about *homicidal?* I thought, but I didn't say a word. Not a word.

"—and, well, wonderful." As Nan said this, she swept

aside the orderly pile of magazines I had stacked on top of the coffee table and put her feet on top of the polished surface. I watched as several magazines headed for the floor.

It has been patently obvious ever since we were little that, before we were born when Nan and I had been splitting things up between us, I had gotten far more than my share of the neatness genes. Nevertheless, I'd kept hoping that Nan had gotten a few. Evidence, however, continued to mount that I had probably hogged them all.

It was at this point that I believe I demonstrated admirable restraint by letting the fallen magazines stay where they'd landed. And by not even mentioning that coffee tables should not in any way be confused with ottomans.

Nan probably wouldn't have heard me anyway. She was still extolling Crane Morgan's virtues. "He's smart and ambitious and artistic."

I shifted position in the Queen Anne chair. Goodness, Nan wasn't just on cloud nine with this guy. She was on cloud thirteen or fourteen, at least.

I tried to remain calm. After all, it wasn't as if I knew for sure that Crane was a two-time murderer. Although, let's face it, just the possibility that he *could* be a multiple murderer would probably be enough to get him crossed off my list of date possibilities.

Nan, obviously, did not agree. In fact, it continues to amaze me that we women will check *Consumer Reports* whenever we buy a car or a major appliance; we'll require boatloads of references from people we hire to paint our house or repair our roof; and yet, we always seem to be more than willing to accept a boyfriend at face value. In Crane's case, in particular, *heavy* emphasis on the *face*.

Nan hadn't stopped extolling. "Oh, Bert, Crane seems to

be everything I've ever dreamed of. He's sweet and kind and sensitive. I know I haven't known him very long—"

Nine measly hours or so, but who's counting?

"—but I really think he might be the one." She paused and added, "And I know for sure that he's the best kisser I've ever gone out with."

Nan actually giggled as she said this. Really. Up to that very moment I would've bet actual money that I'd see Hillary Clinton giggle before I ever saw Nan do such a thing. Obviously, it was a good thing I wasn't a gambling woman.

I shifted position in the Queen Anne chair again, and hoped I didn't look as uneasy as I felt. After all, I told myself, there was really nothing to be alarmed about. Just because Nan seemed far more concerned with how a person kissed than if he'd murdered anybody lately, well, that was no reason to worry. No reason to wonder if perhaps Nan had lost her mind. Of course not. Not at all. Silly me.

Having finished giggling, Nan was hurrying on. "So is that it?" she asked. "Is that everything you had to tell me? Is *that* what was so urgent that you felt it necessary to flash the porch light in my eyes?"

I sat up a little straighter, and before I spoke, I cleared my throat a little. "Well, yes, Nan," I said, "I really thought that you should know—"

Nan interrupted me again. "Look, Bert, I'm going to make this very clear, OK? I don't ever want to see that stupid porch light going on and off again. I mean it, I saw all the flashing porch lights I ever wanted to see back when I still lived at home. I for sure don't want to see any now."

OK, that did it. Nan was now talking to me as if she were my—that is, *our*—mother. And correct me if I'm wrong, but I believe she herself had already made it abundantly clear just how much she enjoyed being talked to like this. If *she* didn't like it, I don't know how she could've thought that I would.

I held up my hand, signaling her to stop. "Wait a minute," I said, and yes, my tone was a little clipped. "I wasn't flashing my stupid porch light for fun, you know. I was trying to tell you something I thought you ought to know. I lost sleep, for God's sake, to stay up and tell you this. And now, it's only a few short hours until I'm supposed to be getting up, and I'm exhausted. Too exhausted to have you jump all over me for doing you a favor."

"A favor? A *favor?*" Nan said, her voice getting shrill again. "Are you *joking?*"

I went right on as if she hadn't said anything. "Of course, now I realize that just because a guy could be a murderer, that's no reason to assume that he might not be a great date. I mean, what was I thinking? From now on, if I find out that you're going out with Ted Bundy, I'm not saying a word!"

Nan just looked at me, her eyes narrowing again. "Crane is not Ted Bundy," she said quietly.

"How would you know?" I asked. It was a pertinent question, I do believe.

Nan seemed to think my question was *im*pertinent. "Well, for one thing," she said, "Ted was executed a while back, so I don't think he and I will be going out anytime soon."

I could have done without the sarcasm.

"And before you start thinking otherwise, you ought to know that Lane wasn't Ted Bundy, either," Nan added. "In fact, what happened to Lane was a tragedy."

I just looked at her. "What happened to Marian Fielding didn't sound like any walk in the park either," I said.

Nan shrugged. "What goes around comes around," she said.

I leaned forward. "What does *that* mean?"

"Well," Nan said, "all I can say is that you should've seen the picture of Marian that Crane has at his studio." Nan went on then, describing the photograph in detail, right down to the total lack of undergarments. I listened, and when Nan was done, I did have to agree with her on one point. I really couldn't think of any good reason a person would forget to put on underwear. Particularly if that person knew that she was going to have her picture taken.

Unless, of course, you were Sharon Stone.

It sounded to me, then, as if Marian might not have been the world's best fiancée. The world's best flirt, maybe, but *fiancée?* No. And yet, what difference did that make? She certainly didn't deserve to die just because she would not make a particularly good role model for young wives-to-be.

Nan started going on then about how Marian Fielding had taunted poor Lane for years, how she'd enjoyed flirting with other men right under Lane's nose, and how she'd pretty much driven Lane crazy until the day he'd finally snapped.

Listening to Nan, I could hardly believe my own ears. Nan was actually summing up what she and I call "the SDI Defense." The SDI Defense is a term that, in fact, Nan and I made up. Having heard this defense so many times on television and on the radio—and having read it so often in newspaper coverage of highly publicized criminal trials— Nan and I had finally given it a name.

The SDI Defense was simply this: At some point or another, the defense attorney always begins to detail—as a final explanation for whatever horror the defendant had done to the defendant's girlfriend or his wife or whoever—all the myriad reasons why *She Deserved It*.

There was, no doubt, a corresponding HDI defense for male victims, but to tell you the truth, Nan and I have noticed the SDI defense a lot more often.

Nan and I have always agreed that invoking the SDI Defense was pretty underhanded, and now, Nan was spouting an SDI Defense of her own? Good Lord. They say love is blind, but if this kept up, Nan was going to need a Seeing Eye dog by tomorrow.

"According to Crane," Nan said, "Lane just exploded one night. He regretted what he'd done immediately, and that's why, of course, Lane ended it the way he did. He just couldn't live, knowing what he'd done." Nan ran her hand through her hair. "Why, poor Lane was as much a victim as Marian."

I just stared at Nan. Yeah. Right. Except there was one gigantic difference. Marian didn't choose to be a victim. *Lane* had chosen to make her one.

Nan was on her feet again, obviously getting ready to leave. "So see, Bert? You don't have to worry. Crane has already told me everything I need to know. You can go on to bed, and relax."

Hearing that stubborn tone in Nan's voice, I knew that whatever I might say from this point forward would make no difference. It was obvious that Nan was in New Man's Land right now. And in New Man's Land, the new man could do no wrong.

And as much as I hated to think it, I had to admit that if this relationship went like all of Nan's other great loves, Crane Morgan wouldn't stay in New Man's Land for long. And Nan's blind goo-goo eyes would suddenly pop open and she'd be seeing twenty-twenty again. I only wondered how long it would take.

I guess I was still looking more than a little concerned as I followed Nan to the door. "Come on, Bert," Nan said. "Don't judge Crane before you even know him, OK?"

I recognized the cajoling tone immediately. It was the same tone Nan had used when she was convincing me that our joining the glee club in high school was a dandy idea. She hadn't, of course, told me in advance that any actual singing would be involved. Or that the reason she'd suddenly decided to become gleeful was that a boy she liked was a member of the club, too.

"Come on," Nan repeated, "I can't be all *that* bad a judge of men, can I?"

I thought of the last two guys Nan had dated for any period of time—Tab the construction worker, who mainly spoke in monosyllables and grunts, and Hank the policeman, the one guy I still didn't quite understand why Nan had dumped. The parting had been mutual, Nan had said; and she'd mumbled something about "needing space," by way of explanation, but that had been so vague, I still had no real idea why the two of them had split up.

So was Nan a good judge of men? The answer had to be: sometimes.

Standing just inside my front door, Nan had finally picked up on the fact that I had not immediately responded to her question. "Really, Bert," Nan said, "I don't think I'm *that* easily fooled."

Oh, please. She certainly could be fooled. Under the right circumstances, anybody could be fooled. But I decided not to point this out. Besides, I wasn't exactly a role model or anything myself when it came to choosing a partner. In fact, it had taken me nineteen years and two kids to decide that Jake had been a mistake.

I gave Nan an uncertain smile.

"And you know, it wasn't like Lane Morgan killed Marian Fielding on purpose," Nan added, reaching for the doorknob. "It *was* an accident."

That one got my attention. "An accident?"

Nan nodded, turning back toward me. "Lane just lost his temper," she said, "and he hit Marian too hard."

"He hit her too hard? Is that what Crane said?"

Nan nodded again. "He hit her, and when she fell, I guess she hit her head or something."

I was already shaking my head. "Nan," I said, "he hit her all right. He hit her with a knife!"

Nan blinked. "What?"

I made it as clear as I could. "Marian Fielding was stabbed to death."

Nan tried to hide her surprise, but I could tell right away that this last was news.

Bad news.

Chapter 7

•

NAN

The bad thing about being shocked in front of Bert is that there's no way she's not going to know. She knows my face as well as her own—no surprise there—so she's pretty much tuned into the slightest change of expression. I tried to bluff my way through, of course, but I knew I probably wasn't fooling her a bit.

"Oh, yes, that's right," I said. "That's what I meant to say. Marian Fielding was *stabbed* to death, that's exactly right."

Bert leaned back against the door jamb, crossed her arms, and just stared at me. "Then you already knew?" There was skepticism in every word.

I crossed my arms, too. "Sure," I said, nodding. "I knew that Lane had lost his temper, and killed Marian—by stabbing her," I added quickly. "Crane told me all about it. Really, Bert, don't you think it's kind of awful for us to be standing here, gossiping about it?" I reached for the doorknob again.

I had hoped this little criticism would change the subject, but I should've known better.

Bert's chin went up, as she stood upright. "I am not gossiping. I certainly wouldn't gossip about something like this. Goodness gracious, this isn't something that anyone should gossip about, like maybe it's some kind of lurid movie plot or something . . ."

Oh, God. She could go on like this for hours.

"My goodness, Nan, I can't believe that you'd even *think* that I was just gossiping, because what I—"

Before I went stone deaf, I interrupted. "I agree. It *is* too awful to gossip about. I mean, two people ended up dead. So we really shouldn't even be talking about—"

"But only one of those dead people got to decide how it would end," Bert put in. She'd crossed her arms again, and her mouth had that stubborn set to it that I've seen quite a few times over the years. She was not going to let this one go. "Only Lane got to *decide* to die. Marian didn't decide anything. She—"

Oh, for God's sake. It was getting later and later, and I had to go to work tomorrow. I was certainly not going to stand here, holding on to the doorknob, waiting for her to have the last word. "OK, Bert," I said flatly, "Lane stabbed Marian until she was dead. *Very* dead. OK?"

Bert looked at me uncertainly. "Well, yes, that *is* what—"

I cut her off. "So what's your point? I mean, really, Bert, how important is it how the woman died? The outcome is still the same. And Crane's brother certainly paid for his action with his own life. So what does it really matter now?"

Bert frowned, fiddling a little with her sponge curlers. "Well, it matters a lot, that's what. It seems to me that your new friend was distorting the truth a little. He was obviously trying to make it seem as if what his brother had done wasn't quite so bad, so that you would think—"

I interrupted. "Bert, Crane's version still has a woman and his brother ending up dead. Now, I don't know about you, but death still sounds kind of bad to me. Hell, Crane

even admitted that Lane had done it. What else do you want
him to say?"

Bert's eyes were all but snapping sparks now. "I'm *just*
saying that if the woman was stabbed, then Crane should've
said she was stabbed. Why pretend that all that happened
was that she just got smacked a little too hard? Really, Nan,
don't you think that Crane should've—"

I'd had it.

I grabbed the doorknob, wrenching the door open. "For
God's sake, Bert, the poor man is still dealing with the death
of his twin brother. He's still working through his grief. You
could at least make an effort to keep an open mind about
the guy."

Bert was not going to let me have the advantage of leaving
her with a word unspoken. She reached over my shoulder
and pushed the door shut with a bang. Oh, for God's sake.
I turned around. We were now pretty much nose to nose, but
her pink sponge rollers gave her a bit of a height advantage.

"I've got an open mind, believe me, it's *wide* open," Bert
practically yelled right in my face, "I mean, *air* is blowing
through my mind, it's so open. If it wasn't, I certainly would
be—"

"Crane warned me about this very thing," I said, raising
my voice a little louder than Bert's, "but I didn't believe it.
I just couldn't believe people would treat him this way when
he hasn't done a damn thing!"

Bert took a step back, and eyed me warily. "What do you
mean—Crane warned you? What did he warn you about?"

This time I did roll my eyes. First, Bert attacks Crane.
And then she starts acting all suspicious because he thinks
he's being attacked. Oh, yeah, that made sense. "Bert," I said,
"Crane merely told me that people have treated him like

shi—" Bert's eyebrows shot up the second I started that last word. Oh boy. It has always been hard for me to believe that a twin of mine would actually act offended, of all things, if you use curse words in her presence.

Cursing, of course, is an occupational hazard for disc jockeys. After spending hours on the air, being careful not to say any of the truly expressive words the FCC won't allow you to say, you've got a shitload of unspeakables saved up.

Still, since I was trying to make a point, I didn't need any digressions from Bert on how Southern ladies should not talk like sailors. I quickly altered what I'd been about to say. "Crane has been treated like *cow manure*. Evidently, there are *some people* who just assume that Crane and Lane are one and the same. I can kind of understand it, actually. They just have the idea that a twin is an exact duplicate. But, Bert, I would think that *you*, of all people, would know better."

I lifted my chin and grabbed the doorknob again, fully intending to make my dramatic exit again; and oh, maybe slam the door for good measure. Wouldn't you know Bert would spoil the whole thing?

"Nan, wait a minute," Bert said, grabbing my arm, "you know that I don't mean to be badmouthing your new beau."

I stopped and turned to face her, shrugging off her hand. "Bert, let's not call anybody my beau anymore. OK? Bows are something *your* boyfriends wear as ties."

That little news flash went over big. Bert was back to glaring at me. "Oh, that's right, I'd forgotten, you're the one who's been out in the world and knows everything. I'm the dumb one who's been at home too long, and is out of touch. How dare I try to tell you anything—"

Oh, now we were getting ugly. "Look, Bert—" I began.

Bert was now wagging her index finger at me—something

she knows I hate. "Well, let me tell you, Nan," she said, her sponge rollers bobbing up and down as if they had a life of their own, "when it comes to men, you can sometimes be a—an *idiot.*"

Hey, I know I've said the same thing myself, but it's an entirely different thing to hear it out of the mouth of your sister. "This, from the woman who married Jake Powell," I said, wagging my finger in *her* face this time.

Bert crossed her arms, and her sponge rollers calmed down. "We're not talking about me."

"We're not talking about me either," I said, turning on my heel again and grabbing the damn doorknob one more time. "Not anymore." It would've been still another great exit line, but Bert grabbed my arm again.

When I turned around this time, all ready to pull away, Bert wasn't frowning. Oh hell, she was looking upset. "Look, Nan, I'm just worried, that's all. I don't want anything to happen to you."

She looked so genuinely upset that for an awful moment I thought she might start to cry. Which I don't believe I've seen Bert do since the day that Jake left her.

All of a sudden I wasn't mad anymore. My big sister— with the vast life experience of ten whole additional minutes—clearly was just trying to protect me. On an impulse, I gave her a quick hug. "Don't worry, hon," I said. "Nothing's going to happen to me."

Bert still looked every bit as worried as before.

"Hey, I'll hide all the sharp instruments every time Crane comes into the house."

I meant it as a joke, but Bert still didn't smile.

"Nan, I'm serious," she said. "If you intend to keep on going out with him, be careful. And if you need me for any-

thing—to come pick you up somewhere, to bring you anything—cab fare—"

"A tourniquet—"

She ignored me. "Or, well, anything—just call me."

Lord. She sounded as if I were being hunted by the mob.
Or rather, dated by it.

"Bert, sweetie, you're making too much of all this. There
was just a death in Crane's family. That's all."

"And a death *outside* of his family," Bert added. "That's
the one that really bothers me."

In fact, Bert was still looking plenty bothered when I
finally decided I'd said all there was to say, and I headed
back to my apartment to grab what few hours of sleep there
were left.

Believe me, there weren't many. When I woke the next
morning, I felt as if an anvil were sitting on my head. My
legs felt as if I'd been dancing the Texas two-step all night
long. I pulled on my country music uniform—faded jeans, a
turtleneck, and a denim jacket with WCKI RADIO embroidered
on the back, and I was out the door.

Driving into downtown Louisville, I did what I knew irritated every single male driver around me. Every time I had
to stop and sit for a minute at a stoplight, I put my makeup
on, using the rearview mirror. In actuality, I didn't use the
mirror all that much. Getting that close a look at my face
after as little sleep as I'd gotten wasn't something I wanted
to do.

In fact, what I really wanted to do was turn around and
crawl back into bed. I couldn't remember the last time I'd
felt so beat.

Fortunately, I had a little pick-me-up waiting for me when
I got to the radio station to begin my five-hour shift. There

was a slim white cardboard box with a big red bow around it on the receptionist's desk, waiting for me. It's terribly shallow of me, I know; but let's face it, one of the nice things about getting flowers at work is having everyone know about it.

While our receptionist, Bambi, looked on, green with envy, I opened the box, spreading the green tissue paper. Inside were not just one, but two-dozen long-stemmed, deep red roses.

Wow.

I touched a velvety petal. The pristine white card nestled in the rich green leaves read, "Thank you for the happiest evening I've had in a long time. Yours, Crane."

Double wow.

Oh, yeah, I was pretty much grinning my head off during my first few sets—that's radio-ese for what a disc jockey says between songs. I felt like crap, my eyes felt as if I had sand beneath the lids, and I was suddenly in a wonderful mood, just thinking about the roses.

And about last night.

And about Crane.

Unfortunately, the mood didn't last.

One phone call was all it took to deflate it. Although Bambi answers most of the station phone calls, it still falls to the deejay on duty to pick up some of them. Especially those calls that come in on the contest line—that's the phone line WCKI uses whenever we run one of those "the twentieth caller wins two free trips to Lithuania" or some equally sought-after prize. Contest line calls, of course, do not always come from contest players.

I get calls from listeners making obscure song requests, or from kids staying home from school just goofing around, or from clients complaining about their spots (more radio-ese for commercials) not being played during prime times. Prime time, of course, being when the clients or their spouses *think* the most people are listening, regardless of whether their estimation is correct or not.

Some days these phone calls bug the hell out of me—particularly the ones from clients yelling about why I didn't play their spot at the right time. I'm not, you see, the one who programs the playing times—that's done by the traffic director, who hides out behind the anonymity of that title and the computer she uses to program the spots.

The computer made me do it, in fact, is the excuse I generally tell clients. In fact, I'd just told a client that very thing and was even smiling when I picked up the next call on the request line. Unfortunately, my smile pretty much vanished the second I recognized the voice.

"Nan? This is Mrs. Gerard Eagleston. I mean . . ." There was a momentary pause, and her voice dropped about an octave. *"Louise."*

I felt an immediate flash of annoyance. Oh, great, you mean, I could still call her Louise? Gosh. What a thrill to be on a first-name basis with the woman filling Bert's head with tales of murder and mayhem about Crane Morgan! So what on earth could the bitch want now?

I was opening my mouth to ask that exact question when it occurred to me that Louise did happen to be influential with a client of the radio station—hadn't she said the new owners of her husband's business bought time on CKI? And, God knows, Charlie Sims would kill me if I did anything to piss off an advertiser regardless of how much the advertiser may piss *me* off.

"How nice to talk to you again, Louise," I lied. "And so

soon. What can I do for you?" I made my voice sound as pleasant as I could, even though I was speaking through clenched teeth. I glanced at the clock on the wall in front of me. Fortunately or unfortunately, I'd just switched to the network feed, and Paul Harvey was launching into his noon *News and Commentary*. It'd be several minutes before I'd have to return to the air. Of course, Louise probably knew that. That's why she'd called now.

"Well, you can come to my house for dinner tonight, Nan," Louise said, her tone light, "and mind you, dear, I won't take 'no' for an answer."

Well, *dear*, you're just going to have to, I thought. "Oh, Louise, I am so sorry, but I really can't make it—"

"I *sa-i-i-id*," Louise said, her voice bordering on musical, "I won't take no for an answer. You have to come, Nan. I make a divine shrimp scampi. I just know you'll enjoy it."

Obviously, the woman didn't realize she was speaking to someone who'd just as soon eat a Quarter Pounder from Mickey D's than a fresh lobster from Maine. I repeated myself. "I really am sorry, Louise, but I have other pl—"

"But you have to. You do! I have something very important to discuss with you!" Louise's light tone had evaporated. "It's of . . . well, it's of a criminal nature."

Oh, really. What now? She'd found out where Hoffa was buried? This woman struck me as just wanting to hobnob with somebody she thinks is a celebrity. No doubt, she'd do or say anything to get a hobnobbing opportunity. Well, telling my sister horrible stories about the guy she'd introduced me to last night wasn't exactly the way. Now, no doubt, she wanted to pass on her vicious gossip to me.

Well, believe me, I had better things to do. In fact, just

thinking about going out with Crane tonight made me feel warm all over.

I cleared my throat. "Like I said, Louise, it's not possible," I told her. "Another night, perhaps?" Please, God, let her say no.

"No!" she snapped. She'd said no, all right, but it didn't mean what I'd hoped. "It can't be another night—it has to be tonight! Before things—that is, before everything gets— Look, I've got something to tell you that you really should know."

The hysterical note that had crept into her voice made me think old Louise here was not at all accustomed to people turning her down. It also occurred to me that, at Louise's, the word "unhinged" might not necessarily refer to a door.

What's more—it's a failing of mine, I know—but I have never much liked to be pushed. When we were growing up, Bert used to say the surefire way to get me *not* to do something was to insist that I do it.

"Why not tell me your little story now?" I asked, still keeping my voice friendly. With a supreme effort, I might add.

Louise sighed, obviously exasperated. "Nan, I'd much rather tell you in person." She was no longer bothering to sound friendly. "Besides, Nan, I have something rather disgusting to show you, too."

Oh, goody, Hoffa's underwear, too. "Look, Louise, what's this all about?"

There was a long pause, while Louise apparently weighed the pros and cons of owning up to what she really wanted. Meanwhile, I noticed that Paul Harvey was on page three. In another minute or so, I had to be back on the air.

She sighed again. "It's about Crane and Lane Morgan."

No kidding. Why was I not surprised?

"I know you must find Crane Morgan charming," Louise went on. "Everybody does at first, but there are things you should know."

"Oh, really?" I asked. I was beginning to do a slow burn. Who the hell did this woman think she was? And what kind of stupid game was she playing? "Then maybe you can tell me why you introduced us in the first place? And why you told my sister all those awful stories about Lane Morgan and his fiancée?"

"*Stories?* They weren't stories," Louise said huffily. "I'll have you know everything I told your sister was absolutely true. I'm really trying to help you out, you know. Now, are you coming to dinner or not?"

I opened my mouth to tell her that the answer was *not*, and then I remembered all the things Bert had heard from Louise about Lane Morgan. I was certain Louise was, at the very least, now preparing to embellish her story. Or at the very most, to lie outright. I wondered if Louise would be able to keep her fabrications going, or if she might trip herself up. Hell, the more Louise blabbered, the sooner she was going to show herself up for the vicious gossip that she was.

Not only that, but I had to admit—at least to myself, if not to Bert—I *was* a tiny bit curious as to what Louise had to say this time. She did sound a little rattled. And let us not forget, Louise was a semiclient. Charlie Sims would not react well if I gave this woman the cold shoulder.

I clenched my teeth. "All right, Louise, I'll be there," I said. "What time?"

Louise's tone changed immediately as soon as I accepted. "Oh, wonderful, Nan," she said. "I'll expect you at seven." She gave me her address, once again told me that I was going to love what we were going to have for dinner, and then I was out of time.

Paul Harvey was just wishing everybody a good day when I hung up the phone. As I intro'd the next tune, I planned how I was going to handle everything.

Of course, I had no intention of missing my date with Crane. After all, it was Bert who'd listened to Louise's gossip about the Morgans in the first place. So it stood to reason that Bert would be the one who would notice any changes in fact from what she'd been told earlier.

Not to mention, hadn't Bert just told me to call her if I needed her?

I couldn't help smiling a little as I picked up the phone and started to dial.

Bert, of course, was true to her word, as always.

"Absolutely not! You are out of your mind," she said.

"Come on, Bert," I said, "think of it as a free dinner."

There was a noise on the line that I thought at first was static, and then I realized that it was Bert. Snorting. "If I want a free dinner, I can go down to the Wayside Mission, and stand in line."

I suppressed a sigh. "Then think of it as doing your beloved sister a really big favor."

"How about thinking of it as lying to Louise Eagleston? Lying to that poor, unsuspecting woman so that you can go out with—"

I cut her off. "First, Louise Eagleston is hardly a poor woman. She's got to be rolling in it. And second, I never said you had to lie. In fact, you don't have to *say* that you're me. If the subject doesn't come up, then so be it. The way I see it—there's no real reason to even mention my name."

"Don't you think Louise might guess?" Bert said. "Come

on, Nan, I talked to her for quite a while—she'll be able to tell, for sure."

"You mean, like Mrs. Montgomery?"

Mrs. Montgomery had been our teacher in second grade. She'd gone to the trouble of seating us on opposite sides of the room, just so she could tell which was which. Bert and I had switched places all year long, and Mrs. Montgomery had never known the difference.

I could almost hear Bert turning the whole thing over in her mind. Mrs. Montgomery had known us for an entire year, and Louise had only talked to her for an hour or so.

"Come on, Bert, please," I coaxed. "You're the only one who'd notice any discrepancies in her story. Besides, don't you think you owe it to yourself to find out the truth?"

There was total silence on the phone.

Garth Brooks's latest megahit was almost over, too. I didn't have much time. "Bert?"

Still, there was silence.

Damn. I'd probably lost her now. Bert would never buy that last argument in a million years. She'd see through it for sure. Hell, it was just another version of the "it's for your own good" argument that our mother had used when she was trying to get us to do something we didn't want to do.

"Well," Bert said finally, "I guess I do owe it to myself. Not to mention, to you. So, OK, what time am I—that is, *you*—supposed to be there?"

I couldn't help grinning.

Was I good, or was I good?

Chapter 8

●

BERT

Driving to Louise Eagleston's house, I kept calling myself names. *Wimp* and *Idiot* topped the list. I couldn't believe that I'd let Nan talk me into this crazy switch. Have I mentioned that I've never been good at being Nan? I wasn't even sure that I was any too great at being me.

Even if I'd had no doubts about this little charade to start out with, I would've come up with some as soon as I started picking out clothes to wear. I knew Nan would be perfectly content to show up at Louise's home on Alton Road in St. Matthews—one of the nicer areas in the east end of Louisville—looking like a bag lady. If I were playing Nan accurately, I should follow suit.

I only wished *suit* were an option.

I just couldn't bring myself to wear Nan's customary getup: faded jeans with the knees worn thin, a seedy denim jacket, and a T-shirt. I compromised by putting on a pair of very nice Ellen Tracy taupe linen slacks, a cream-colored linen blazer, and a gray silk pullover.

I admit it, I was ruining Nan's image. So what was the worst that she could do? Tell me she never wanted me to switch with her again?

Oh my, yes, *break* my heart.

Louise's home turned out to be a lovely white frame Cape Cod surrounded by an antique wrought iron fence. It had a wide front porch and a huge magnolia tree in the front yard. The magnolia's white blossoms were just beginning to open.

As I got out of my Festiva, I couldn't help but think wistfully of the gorgeous magnolia at my house—or rather, my ex-house—on Ashwood Drive. The one that I used to own with my ex-husband, Jake.

Divorce sure changes things. At least, it certainly does for the woman involved.

It had not, oddly enough, changed all that much for Jake. He still lived to this day in the same house he'd lived in since our children were born. I'd had to sell him my half. My half of the house, and my half of the magnolia. I really didn't have a choice. I couldn't possibly afford either one on what I brought home as an office temp.

Oh well. I took a deep breath, straightened my shoulders, and started up the sidewalk. I was being Nan, after all, and Nan would not be lamenting over magnolias. As I headed toward the front door, I noticed that the door to the garage was open. I could see a shiny black, late-model Mercedes parked in there. I also noticed a professional lawn care sign in the yard, a digital satellite dish perched on top of the roof, and what looked to me to be brand-new storm windows. My, my. Widows certainly seemed to fare a whole lot better than divorcées. That little fact probably went a long way toward explaining the murder rate in this country.

I rang the doorbell, still looking around. I wasn't really all that interested in Louise Eagleston's manicured lawn or new storm windows, but I wanted to keep my mind off the performance I was about to give. God, I hated doing this. Still, I had agreed, and as they say, the show must go on.

I tried a confident little toss of my head, like I've seen Nan do more than once. It didn't feel natural. I probably looked like I had a spasm in my neck.

Louise seemed to be taking an awful long time to answer her door. Of course, it could be that her doorbell wasn't working. I hadn't heard it ring inside. Then again, I hadn't exactly been listening for it either.

I hit the doorbell a couple more times without results, and then I went for the large brass door knocker positioned at eye level in the center of the front door. The noise the thing made was unbelievably loud.

And yet, there was still no answer.

By this time, I admit it, I was actually beginning to hope. Maybe I wouldn't have to do an impersonation of Nan tonight after all. Maybe something had come up, and Louise couldn't make it after all.

Let me see, if I were Nan, I'd probably be getting unbelievably irritated by now, at being stood up and all. I believe, in fact, that I'd be just about ready to call it quits. So, strictly in the interest of accuracy, I should be doing the same. I made use of the door knocker a couple more times, again got no response, and then, trying very hard not to smile, I turned to go.

Wouldn't you know, it was just then that I heard someone call out from inside the house. "Nan."

At least, that's what I thought I heard. The sound had been so faint, I couldn't be sure.

Well, I *was* being Nan. So I said exactly what she would've said under the same circumstances. "Shit."

If Louise was inside calling me, she knew I was out here. I couldn't very well leave now. I tried the front doorknob. Damn. It turned easily.

I opened the door, stuck my head in, and called, "Louise?"

I didn't hear a sound. Closing the door behind me, I stepped into the cool shadows of the spacious entry hall. "Louise? It's Ber—" Wouldn't you know, I almost blew it in the first minute. Fortunately, I caught myself just in time. "It's Nan Tatum," I called. "From, uh, WCKI?"

As soon as I said this last part, I felt like an idiot. The woman had invited me—that is, Nan—to dinner. Did I really think Louise might not remember who I was?

I peeked into the living room to the right of the foyer, beginning to feel more than a little awkward. Where in the world was my hostess?

I was now doing something I knew that Nan would never do. I was tiptoeing, trying to make as little sound as I could on the beige wall-to-wall plush carpeting. I moved hesitantly into Louise's living room, glancing this way and that. "Louise?" I called.

The house seemed unnaturally quiet. I was beginning to identify with one of those people in all the horror movies who keep right on walking farther and farther into the house of doom even though everybody who'd gone in earlier had never been seen again. My heart was beginning to pound. "Louise?" I called again. "Mrs. Eagleston? Yoo-hoo?"

Once again, no answer.

Louise's living room was done in the faux country look that's so popular these days. Faux country, I've noticed, is considerably more expensive than genuine country. I'd seen Louise's blue plaid sofa and coordinating print chairs in a recent Ethan Allen catalog. Fake wood beams crisscrossed her living room ceiling, and a little heart-shaped wooden sign above the doorway read WELCOME.

Uh-huh.

Well, I certainly didn't feel welcome. In fact, as I stood in the middle of the living room and waited, what I felt more than anything else was ignored. Louise Eagleston may have thought she was well bred, but I had news for her. It was bad manners not to come and greet a guest promptly.

Of course, Louise *was* entertaining Nan, who never stood much on formalities. Maybe Louise knew that. Maybe what Louise had called out—but that I'd barely heard—was for me to join her back in the kitchen. I could smell something cooking back there. Surely, then, that's what she'd said. I headed down the hall, more or less following my nose. Through a swinging door and into what turned out to be a brightly lit kitchen about the size of my living room and dining room put together.

The first thing I noticed when I went through the door was that Louise was nowhere in sight. The second thing I noticed was that her kitchen was gorgeous. With shiny ivory tile floors and glass-door cabinets painted a warm beige, this was the kind of kitchen I'd always dreamed of. Louise's appliances were pale almond, and she had not one but two stainless steel wall ovens. A large center butcher block island with a built-in stovetop dominated the room.

Unfortunately, a burning smell dominated the room even more. What I'd smelled was not something cooking, but something burning. Something dark and gooey was bubbling its last gasp in the bottom of a large sauce pan on the stovetop. Little wisps of smoke rose from the goop.

To my left, I could see through the spattered glass window of the upper wall oven, a terra cotta pot in which something was baking. Or rather, *blackening*. I moved toward the oven for a closer look. Oh, my. Unless Louise was making Cajun, I'd say dinner was a disaster.

My God, and Jake used to tell me that *I* was a bad cook? Louise could give me lessons on bad cooking.

I hurried around the center island, turning off the wall oven and the stove top as I went. I was looking everywhere— at the island, the kitchen counters, the stove—trying to find a pot holder or an oven mitt so that I could move the saucepan off the hot burner. Evidently, things like oven mitts and pot holders were too mundane for a kitchen as high class as this one. I spotted two neatly folded plaid dishtowels lying on top of the counter next to the sink, and I hurried toward them, intending to use the dishtowels as makeshift pot holders.

That was when I tripped over something large, soft, and unyielding, lying on the floor.

Since I was being Nan, once again I said precisely what she would've said. "Shit! Shit! Shit!"

I looked down to find out what it was that had almost caused me to fall flat on my face.

And that was when I screamed.

Lying at my feet was Louise Eagleston.

She didn't look well.

The woman was sprawled on her stomach, her face turned to one side, her eyes open, as if she were staring at the shiny no-wax, ivory tile floor of her perfect kitchen. Her left arm was half-hidden under her body, and her right was flung out as if she'd tried to break her fall. A black-red, wet-looking stain was spreading down the back zipper of her pink ging-ham dress, and the handle of perhaps the biggest butcher knife I'd ever seen protruded from the middle of the stain. Splotches of dark red dotted the large fluffy white bow tying Louise's apron in the back.

I took one long look at all of this, and I think I might've screamed the entire time. Somebody was screaming, and since I was pretty sure it was not Louise, I guess it had to be me.

After I managed to stop screaming, I did a terrible thing.

I turned and ran out of the room.

Staring at Louise, it had suddenly hit me that the person who'd done this terrible thing might still be in the house. Moreover, I'd just notified them exactly where I was by screaming my head off.

I was out of the kitchen and running wildly toward the front door when something else hit me. *Louise could still be alive.* Just because you've got a knife in your back didn't necessarily guarantee that you're dead. True, the prognosis didn't look good, but I was pretty sure I'd seen somebody recover from just such an injury on a recent episode of *ER.* Or maybe it was *Unsolved Mysteries.* Whatever. If Louise wasn't dead, she needed help.

A quick look around the living room told me that there was no telephone in sight. Surely, though, Louise had one in the kitchen. I didn't remember seeing one in there; but then, Louise herself had been taking up pretty much all of my attention.

I took a deep breath, closed my eyes for a moment to steel myself, and then I turned around, heading back the way I'd come. On the way, just in case Louise's attacker had not gone, I shouted into the silent house, "I've got a GUN! In my purse! So you better not mess with me!" On the off chance that somebody was watching me, I patted my purse confidently. "I'll shoot you! I will! And I'll *enjoy* it! It'll make my day!"

The house remained silent as ever. I was hugely relieved, of course. Not just because Louise's attacker was obviously no longer around, but also because it looked like nobody had heard me trying to sound like Dirty Harriet.

Louise, unfortunately, looked exactly like I'd left her. I stepped closer to her, looking for some signs of life, and, yes, fighting nausea. Oh God. Louise looked bad. If the poor woman was breathing, she could've fooled me. Still, I wasn't a doctor. Fooling me wouldn't be hard.

I forced myself to kneel down and pick up Louise's hand in order to feel for a pulse. Just like they do on *E.R.* Louise didn't feel terribly cold, but then, the kitchen was pretty warm, what with the food burning and all. "Oh God, oh God, oh God," I heard myself whispering as I pressed my fingers against the spot on Louise's wrist where I thought I should feel a pulse. There wasn't any. I moved to different pressure points on Louise's wrist, but I still didn't feel anything. Either I was doing it all wrong, or Louise really was dead.

Which meant I was holding hands with a corpse.

The minute this thought went through my mind, I'm ashamed to say I screamed again.

I also dropped Louise's wrist as if it were a roach, letting her hand fall to the floor with a soft, wet-sounding, little plop.

That sound was so awful, I screamed again.

With all that screaming, I guess I expected someone to come rushing in the back door, just like in the movies, but nothing happened. Outside the kitchen window opposite me, I could see a red brick house next door, the neighbor's empty driveway, and their open garage. Nobody seemed to be home. I could also see a little of the road out front. There were no cars or people in sight.

In fact, the only thing that seemed to be moving inside or out was the dark stain on Louise's back. As I watched, transfixed, a black-red puddle began to form very slowly on the shiny, white tile floor. Heading directly for my nearly new taupe suede Papagallo shoes. I know it sounds shallow, but I think it was my shoes being at risk that got me moving again.

I spotted a phone cord snaking down the wall, and disappearing into the cabinet on my left. Apparently, Louise didn't think a phone was the sort of decorator accessory you left out in the open. It had been hidden in a drawer. It was only a couple of steps away, though, so I got to my feet and hurried toward it. I dialed 911, and when the operator answered, I gave her my name, Louise's address, and said, "Send an ambulance. Quick!"

That was probably all I needed to say. Unfortunately, I was a little rattled, and as soon as the words were out of my mouth, I realized that an ambulance was going to be a waste of time if Louise was dead. So I added, "No, make that the coroner." After I said *that*, it occurred to me that what had happened to poor Louise didn't exactly look like an accident. So I corrected myself again. "No, no, wait a minute, make that the police."

Too late, I realized I sounded as if I were at a drive-in window, ordering a Big Mac. Oddly enough, the operator started acting strange right after that. She made me repeat everything twice, and describe Louise's current condition in detail. Finally, I'd had it. "Look, she's got a knife sticking out of her back. OK? She looks really dead to me."

As I said this, something outside the kitchen window caught my eye. I leaned toward the window, pulling the phone cord along with me, trying to see what it had been. I was thinking that maybe somebody was out there who could help. Maybe they'd know CPR, or at the very least, be able to tell for sure if Louise was no longer with us.

Somebody was out there, all right. But it didn't look as if he were going to be any help.

A man was running, arms pumping, legs straining for distance, turning left out of the neighbor's driveway, past Louise's house, heading down Alton Road. It looked to me as if he might've come out of the open garage next door. Was this one of Louise's neighbors, out for a jog?

Out for a jog in a gray three-piece suit, pink dress shirt, bow tie, and black and white loafers with white socks? Somehow, that didn't seem likely.

I leaned even closer to the window, stretching to get a better look. Even as far away as I was, I could see that the guy was balding, and that he seemed to have a kind of egg-shaped head on top of an extremely long neck. With long legs and arms, he looked like a gazelle with a turtle head. A sweaty turtlehead at that.

I could only see him from the back, so I couldn't exactly tell how old he was. He must've been unaccustomed to exercise, though. Turtlehead was wheezing and sweating buckets by the time he rounded the corner.

"Hello? Ma'am? *Ma'am?*" When I'd leaned toward the window, I'd taken the phone away from my ear, but I could hear the 911 operator's voice. I would've answered her, too, right then except that I suddenly felt something touch my foot. Something damp and clammy.

I glanced down.

There was a bloody hand on my ankle, its fingers red and sticky, smearing crimson stains on my hose.

I screamed all over again.

I wasn't sure what Louise had been trying to do, holding on to my ankle, and I didn't have the chance to find out before she sank back to the floor. Her eyes closed again, but her hand still clutched my ankle.

"Ma'am! Are you all right? Ma'am! Are you all right?"

It was the operator again. When I'd screamed, she'd apparently feared the worst. "I'm OK," I said, my voice trembling a little. "But make that a doctor now. Quick."

The operator's voice was all business. "A doctor? Where are you hurt?"

I blinked, confused. "Not me. The dead woman. I mean, the woman who isn't dead after all," I babbled. "That is, Louise Eagleston, you know, the woman with the knife in—"

I must've sounded a little incoherent, because the operator interrupted me. "Ma'am," she said coldly, "do you know it's against the law to make fraudulent 911 calls?"

I gripped the phone. Did this mean she hadn't sent the ambulance *yet?* "Look, lady," I said, "get the police here, and an ambulance! Do it right now! There's a woman dying, and she needs help! Hurry up!"

I'm not sure whether it really took them forever, or it just seemed that way. When you've got a bleeding woman hanging on to your ankle, time doesn't exactly fly by. I guess I could've shaken Louise off, but it seemed like a pretty rude thing to do to a person who seemed to have enough problems to contend with already. Besides, the 911 operator made me stay on the line until the paramedics arrived, so it wasn't like I had anyplace to go.

I probably would've remained in that exact same position, too, as motionless as a mannequin, except that Louise suddenly let out a groan. When I jumped at the sound, she let go of my ankle. She groaned again, only this time the sound was so weak, she sounded like a kitten. Suffering. My throat tightened. Poor Louise. I bent down and took her cold hand in mine, squeezing it, trying to will warmth back into it. "Hold on, Louise," I said. "You're going to be all right. You're going to be just fine."

I didn't expect any reaction, but Louise shocked me by opening her eyes. This time, though, I didn't scream, I leaned closer to her. "I've called an ambulance, and you're going to—"

Louise clutched at my hand. "Too . . ." Louise gasped. "Too . . ."

I thought she was just repeating the last word I'd said. Or maybe she knew she was dying, and she was saying it was too late. "No, really," I said. "You're going *to* be OK."

Louise shifted a little, moving with an obvious effort, and then slowly pulled the hand she'd been lying on into view. In her hand was an envelope, a crumpled, red-stained envelope. She pressed it into my hand, her breathing coming in short gasps.

The envelope, I immediately noticed, felt a little damp. I suppressed a grimace.

"Too . . ." Louise said again, her voice even weaker. Louise's eyes were on mine, willing me to open the envelope. I tugged at the flap, and looked inside.

It was about thirty color snapshots of various sizes. I pulled them all out, flipping rapidly through the photos. Mostly, they were of a pretty, blond woman in her early twenties and—I blinked when I recognized him—Crane Morgan. The photos had been taken on a beach somewhere. You could see the bright blue stripe of ocean in the background of several of the shots.

You could also see that Crane had a terrific tan that he must've enjoyed showing off. In almost all the photos, he was wearing a swimsuit that was little more than a thong, revealing long muscular legs, broad shoulders, and a flat washboard stomach. In some of the pictures, you could see a tattoo on Crane's left arm, just above the wrist—a small purple flower.

I raised my eyebrows as I came to the last few photos in the packet. Maybe what Louise had been trying to say was "too revealing." Because these last photos were not snapshots. These, in fact, looked as if they'd all been taken in a studio, professionally lit and posed. It was kind of a good thing they'd been taken indoors, or else the subjects of these pictures might've gotten pretty cold. Every one of them were nude. Brunettes, redheads, blondes, in various poses, all smiling seductively at the camera.

None of these women was the girl in the other photos with Crane. I turned one of the nude photographs over. On its back was a square block stamp with the letter S in the middle. I flipped the rest of the nude photos over. All of them bore the same stamp.

"What are these? Why did you give me these pictures?" I asked Louise, but her eyes were slowly closing even as I spoke. "Louise? Louise?" There was no response. Once again, she did not look alive.

My throat started to tighten up, but then I reminded myself that I'd been wrong before. Moments later, I heard the squeal of a siren, and then—thank you, Lord—a knock on the front door. I ran to answer it.

Yanking open the front door, I barely acknowledged the men in white uniforms as I pointed toward the kitchen. "She's in there! *Hurry!*"

The paramedics rushed by me, and I was about to close the door when a white Camaro pulled up out front and parked at the curb. These days the unmarked car of choice for the

Louisville police department seems to be the white Camaro. I stood there and watched, hardly daring to hope. Please, God, please, oh, please, let this be Louisville's Finest. I would be so relieved if this were the cops. Then somebody else could take over this nightmare.

As it happened, it was the police.

But I wasn't the least bit relieved.

The cop who got out of the Camaro on the side facing me was fiftyish, muscular, and totally bald. He bore a remarkable resemblance to G. Gordon Liddy, but I barely gave him a glance. I was looking instead at the cop who'd been driving— the one with the square jaw, the marine haircut, and the build like a prize fighter who'd been out of training for a few years. The one who I'd always thought looked a lot like Brian Dennehy, the actor who'd starred in *Cocoon*.

That's right. I'd seen this cop before.

It was Detective Hank Goetzmann—the cop Nan had dated for three months and then dumped.

Goetzmann didn't look any happier to see me than I was to see him. I could understand how he felt, of course. After some woman has dumped you, the last thing you want to do is run into her sister.

At least, I thought he knew I was Nan's sister.

Oh God.

What if he thought I was Nan?

I stared at him as he and the policeman with him hurried toward me. Goetzmann was no longer looking in my direction. Instead, he was muttering something to the other guy. The other guy nodded, his face grim, looking first at Goetzmann and then at me.

So what was that all about? Was Goetzmann telling G. Gordon that he knew me—or that he'd dated me? And yet, surely after going out with Nan three entire months, Goetz-mann could tell us apart. On the other hand, he really hadn't seen Nan and me together all that much once he and Nan had started going out. Nan and I have discovered over the years that people get us most confused if they haven't seen us together all that often. So, let me see, I'd seen Goetzmann maybe four times in the time they were dating, but none of those times had been for very long. I'd run into him usually just as he was leaving. So he never really got a good look at me for more than a few minutes.

It was my understanding, however, that he'd gotten an extremely good look at Nan.

Goetzmann and G. Gordon were now on the front porch. "Miss Tatum," he said, "this is my partner, Allen Charles." Goetzmann's tone was all business.

I extended my hand toward the bald cop almost automatically.

And then all three of us stared in horror at my hand. It was sticky with dried blood. Louise's blood.

I actually felt a little dizzy, looking at it.

Goetzmann immediately took my hand, turning it over, evidently looking for cuts. "Are you hurt?" he said.

I shook my head, pulling my hand away. "Oh, no, I'm fine. It's Louise Eagleston who's hurt. I guess I got this on me when she grabbed my hand."

Goetzmann and Charles didn't move. They just stood there, staring at me. They seemed to both expect me to go on, so I did. Talking a little faster like I always do when I'm nervous.

"She was lying on the floor, and she grabbed my ankle first. Then when I bent down, you know, to see what she wanted, she grabbed my hand."

They were still just staring.

I talked even faster. "The two paramedics are with her now. They just got here, I was just letting them in when you pulled up, so I guess that's why I didn't notice my hand." Oh God. I was babbling. "Of course, I *was* a little rattled. But then, if seeing a woman with a knife in her back doesn't rattle you—"

I was going to say, "—*something's wrong*," but Detective Charles cut me off. "Where's the victim, Ma'am?"

"In the kitchen," I said, stepping aside and waving vaguely toward the back of the house. "She's lying in front of the island. Of course, you'll see the paramedics back there, so I guess I didn't have to tell you exactly where she was, because once you see the paramedics, you'll—"

I didn't know why I was still talking. Both men had already gone by me, heading down the hall in the direction I'd indicated. Goetzmann, however, paused long enough to interrupt me. "Look, stay right here, OK? We'll want to talk to you as soon as we've had a look around."

Goetzmann was hurrying away from me, and I still didn't know if he knew who I was.

"I'm Bert, Detective Goetzmann!" I called after him. Like a moron, I might add.

He stopped and stood there, motionless for a moment. Then he turned to look back at me, scowling. "Yes, I know," he said and then lumbered on into the kitchen.

Oh dear. I wondered if I'd insulted him, suggesting that he couldn't tell me and Nan apart. I also wondered if he really expected me to just stand there with blood on my hand and my pantyhose, waiting for him to return. If I hadn't noticed the blood, it wouldn't have been so bad. But now, knowing it was there made me feel a little nauseous. Surely, if given the choice between (A) my washing my hands and ankle, or (B) my staying right where I was and throwing up all over the foyer, Goetzmann would choose option A.

I headed into the house and down the hall in search of the bathroom. I didn't see Goetzmann or the others, but I was moving in the opposite direction from the kitchen. I could hear them, though, moving around on the other side of the kitchen door and talking.

The bathroom turned out to be the second door on my right. I made a beeline for the sink, turned on the tap, and then just let warm water run over my hands for a while. I was horrified to see the water actually turn a little pink.

It made my stomach churn all over again.

Which made me start looking around for a washcloth. I read somewhere if you put cold water on a cloth, and place it on the back of your neck, it's supposed to keep you from vomiting. I didn't get to test this out, though, because by the time I had the washcloth wet, I wasn't feeling sick anymore. Since I had the cloth, though, I sudsed it up with soap and began scrubbing first at my hands, and then at my ankle and shoe.

This time when I rinsed the cloth, the water turned red.

My stomach lurched.

I was testing out the cold-cloth theory, leaning over the sink with my eyes shut, when somebody big and rude pushed past me and shut off the water.

"What the hell do you think you're doing?"

It was, of course, Goetzmann. In the small bathroom, he looked enormous. And a little irritated.

"Well, I was washing my hands." My tone indicated that I was explaining the obvious. "And I was trying to get the blood off my ankle. Then I started feeling a little sick so—"

Apparently, Goetzmann wasn't all that interested in my answer. He cut me off.

"I told you to stay where you were for a reason," Goetzmann said. "I didn't want you trampling all over the crime scene, destroying evidence."

I just looked at him. "This isn't the crime scene. This is the bathroom. The crime scene's in the kitch . . ."

My voice trailed off when Goetzmann's eyes started bugging out. He reminded me a little of Nan when he did that. "Bert," he said, in the tone of someone who's dredging up his last ounce of patience, "if the killer used—"

I broke in. "Killer? What do you mean, *killer?*" I stared at Goetzmann, not really wanting to hear his answer.

Goetzmann looked as if he didn't want to tell me either. "Bert, I'm sorry, but Louise Eagleston is dead."

My throat went dry. "Are you sure?" I said weakly. "Because a little earlier I thought she was dead, and—"

"Bert," Goetzmann said, "we're sure."

I didn't know what to say. I couldn't say that I'd really liked Louise, but nobody deserved to die like that.

"And, Bert," Goetzmann said, his gruff voice a lot gentler, "I don't want to make you feel bad, but I really wish you hadn't washed your hands in this sink."

I was still thinking about poor Louise. I looked at him, genuinely puzzled, trying to figure out why he was talking about sinks, of all things, at a time like this.

"Because," Goetzmann went on, "if the killer happened to have washed his hands after attacking Mrs. Eagleston, then you've just washed all the evidence down the drain."

Oh dear. That pretty much explained why we were discussing sinks. I was clearly in the wrong. I'd been so anxious to get clean that none of this had occurred to me.

In an effort to make amends, I said, "Well, it might not be much to go on, but I do still have the pictures Louise gave me."

Goetzmann suddenly looked significantly more alert. "Pictures?" he said.

After that, he more or less led me out of the bathroom and back into the living room, sat me down on the couch, and insisted that I tell him every single thing that poor Louise had done and said from the time I'd first discovered her lying on the floor.

The only thing I didn't tell Goetzmann was the switch that Nan and I were doing. The way I saw it, Louise was not going to be telling anybody, so there was really no need to mention it. It would just complicate things.

And things were complicated enough.

So complicated, in fact, that it took a while to tell it all to Goetzmann. It also took a while to go through the pictures. It was a little awkward when Goetzmann got to the studio shots. I tried to act nonchalant, as if in the past I'd sat on quite a few couches with quite a few of Nan's old boyfriends, looking through tons of nude pictures, but I guess I must've looked pretty uncomfortable. Right after Goetzmann saw the first picture, he flipped through them very fast and then put them out of sight on the bottom of the stack of photos.

"I was thinking that maybe Louise meant 'too revealing,'" I told him. "When she said 'too.' I didn't know her very well, of course—I'd only met her the other night—but I got the feeling that Louise was sort of prudish about things like that."

Goetzmann just looked at me. "And you're a woman of the world," he said.

I stared back at him, not sure what to say. What exactly had Nan told him about me? Nan was always painting me as some gullible babe in the woods. To hear her tell it, Louisville's panhandler population cut cards for the right to approach me first thing every morning as I walked to work.

"Well, I think—"

Goetzmann must not have wanted to explore that little topic further, because he interrupted me. "About these other pictures," he said, tapping the pictures of Crane and the pretty blond girl. "Do you recognize any of these people?"

I identified Crane Morgan for him, and then something else occurred to me. "Actually, now that I think of it, this might not be Crane. It could be his twin brother, Lane."

Goetzmann's eyebrows went up "*Another* set of twins?" he asked.

I couldn't tell if that was just a comment or a complaint, and I was pretty sure I didn't want to know. "Well, there's only one Morgan twin now." I hurried on, repeating to Goetzmann everything I could remember that Louise had told me about Lane and the murder of Marian Fielding and Lane's subsequent suicide. When I got to the part about Louise suspecting that Crane Morgan might be the killer, rather than his brother Lane, Goetzmann pulled a notebook out of his suit pocket, flipped it open like a *Star Trek* communicator, and started furiously scribbling in it.

"Oh dear," I said, trying to see what he was writing. "You don't think all this has anything to do with Louise's death, do you?"

Goetzmann leaned back so that I could no longer see what he was putting on the page. "It might have something to do with it," he said. "Then again, it might just be a robbery gone bad. We haven't been able to find the victim's purse yet."

That reminded me. "You know, I did see a man running

down the street," I said. "But I think I would've noticed if he were carrying a purse."

Hank's eyes bugged out again. "What else haven't you told me?"

The way Nan and I had switched did, of course, leap to mind, but I held my face perfectly still, so Goetzmann wouldn't see that his question had hit home. Instead, I described Turtlehead for him in as much detail as I could.

Goetzmann kept writing and nodding. "I may have you look at a few mug shot books later." He finished writing, and then looked up at me. "There's one thing you haven't told me," he said.

I know my eyes widened. I couldn't help it.

"How do you know Louise Eagleston?"

Oh dear.

I looked at the beige carpeting at my feet. And then over at the WELCOME sign next to the door. There didn't seem to be any way to get out of it, so I just told him the truth. "Louise is a client of WCKI. Nan and I met her at the mall last night when she introduced Nan to Crane Morgan."

There was a beat—just a beat—during which Goetzmann didn't say a word. Then he went smoothly on. "Oh, well. I guess I'll need to talk to Nan, too," he said, getting to his feet. "I'll give her a call right now."

I looked at him. Was he secretly pleased to have an excuse to phone Nan? I kind of hated to rain on his parade. "Nan's not home right now."

Goetzmann turned to stare at me. "How do you know?"

I cleared my throat. "She's out on a date with Crane."

There was a longer beat this time, while Goetzmann apparently digested what I'd just told him. That, yes, Nan is, at this very moment, out on a date with the great-looking hunk whose likeness can be seen wearing the thong bathing suit in the photographs you're now holding. Or put another way, *Yes, Goetzmann, Nan would rather date a possible murderer than you.*

Goetzmann cleared his throat, and then looked over at me. "Well, that's good. Because now I'll be able to interview them both at the same time."

I hoped I was mistaken. It sounded to me as if he was planning on following me home and then waiting around until Nan showed up with Crane.

"I'll just follow you home and wait around until Nan shows up with Crane," Goetzmann went on.

Oh dear. Nan was not going to be happy with me. In fact, there was every possibility when Nan got home, there was going to be another murder.

Chapter 9

●

NAN

The evening started out awful.

Once again I'd tried to sneak out of WCKI right after my shift, but just like the day before, Charlie had caught me in the hall on the way out. This time he marched me into his office, and indicated with a nod in that direction that I should take a seat in the fake leather chair in front of his desk. As soon as I sat down, Charlie started going on and on about what a great job I was doing.

I tried to keep right on smiling, as if I were buying every bit of what he had to say, but I couldn't help being suspicious. Charlie has never been overly generous with his compliments. If I ever needed to prove it, I'd offer as Exhibit A what Charlie had said when somebody asked him if he thought Cindy Crawford was beautiful. He'd replied, "She's OK."

The way I saw it, if Cindy Crawford couldn't get a decent compliment out of the man, my chances had to be zero to none. And yet, here was old Charlie, smiling wide enough to show his back teeth and saying what a "consummate professional" I was.

To paraphrase Shakespeare, something was rotten in Louisville.

I might've given the whole thing more thought, but frankly, my mind was elsewhere. In fact, while Charlie was going on and on about how wonderful I was, I was trying to decide what I should wear on my upcoming date with Crane. Last night Crane had not exactly spelled out what we were going to do, and stupid me, I hadn't thought to ask.

So now, here I was, trying to make up my mind. Should I dress up in order to subtly encourage Crane to take me someplace expensive? Or should I dress down in order to avoid looking as if I were subtly encouraging him to take me someplace expensive? I didn't want to look like one of those gold-digging females who equate how much a guy spends on you with how much he cares. Of course, one reason I didn't want to do this is that if I ever truly believed such a thing, I'd have to admit that just about every guy I'd ever dated didn't care two cents about me. Literally.

I'd just about made up my mind to dress somewhere in the middle—not black satin, but not blue jeans either— when Charlie's voice cut into my thoughts. "So, tell me, Nan, how do you feel about flagpoles?"

I blinked. Flagpoles? Uh-oh. This conversation had a certain déjà vu quality to it. Had I missed something while I'd been mentally going through my wardrobe? "Well, as a support for flags, I guess I'm all for poles," I said uncertainly. "I mean, without flagpoles, you'd have an awful lot of flags lying on the ground, wouldn't you?" I finished up with a big smile.

Charlie has no sense of humor. He just stared at me for a long moment before he hurried on. "What I mean is, Nan, how would you feel about sitting on top of a flagpole?"

I stared. "What, *again?* You're kidding me." About a year ago, the station had actually had me climb up a flagpole and sit up there until the ratings climbed, too. What was shocking

was that I'd actually agreed to do it. Charlie had been delirious over the publicity it generated; I'd just been delirious.

"We'd build you a better platform, of course," Charlie
said, "so it's not as if it'll be uncomfortable staying up there
or anything. Not like last time."

Oh, yeah, now *that* was a load off my mind. When Charlie
had made me do this before, the gentlest of breezes had sent
the whole thing rocking like a canoe. With a seasick passenger.
Oddly enough, the day I barfed on the air had been the exact
same day Charlie had decided our ratings had risen enough.

Charlie apparently interpreted my appalled silence as
interest. "It'll be a follow-up campaign that'll really grab listeners. We'll put you on top of the flagpole again, and we'll
say you won't come down until WCKI is number one this
time." Charlie gave me another wide, teeth-revealing grin.
"We've even got a slogan already—WE'RE GOING TO NEW HEIGHTS
FOR OUR LISTENERS."

He was nodding his head, still grinning. "So what do you
say? You'll do it, won't you?"

"No," I said.

That seemed pretty clear to me, but Charlie acted as if
he hadn't heard me. "It'll be a real attention-getter. We'll have
you do your show from up there, of course. Hell, we got
coverage by all the TV stations before; this time, maybe even
the networks will—"

I shook my head again. "You could get coverage. *I* could
get pneumonia. The answer's still no."

Can you believe, it took me almost an hour to convince
Charlie that I meant it? In the end, the only thing that got
him to shut up about it was to tell him a tiny white lie. I told
him that in the last year I'd become deathly afraid of heights.
I had vertigo so bad, in fact, that the only sound they'd be

broadcasting from the top of the damn flagpole would be one continuous scream.

After Charlie finally agreed that hysterical screaming would probably not attract all that large a radio audience, I got up and all but ran out of his office. Before Charlie thought up something else. Like, oh, say, tying me to the front end of a moving automobile in order to illustrate the slogan WE'RE GOING THE EXTRA MILE.

It didn't take me two minutes to get out of the building. I just grabbed my purse and took off for the front door. WCKI is located on the first floor of one of the quaint Victorian-era office buildings on Muhammad Ali Boulevard in downtown Louisville. Which means, of course, no nearby parking. It seemed to take forever to travel the three blocks to the parking lot where I'd left my car, but maybe that was just because I was in a hurry.

The quickest way to get home is usually Broadway to Bardstown Road to Napoleon Boulevard, a fifteen-minute drive if it isn't rush hour. During rush hour it can take as much as an hour. During *pre*-rush hour—the period from three to five during which anybody who can possibly leave work early does, in order to beat the real rush hour—it takes about thirty-five minutes.

Thanks to Charlie and his dumb flagpole scheme, it was pre-rush hour. There was already enough traffic on Broadway and Bardstown Road to slow me down considerably. By the time I got home, it was only a scant hour and a half before Crane appeared at my front door. Under other circumstances, of course, that would've been plenty of time to get ready. Believe me, if I couldn't shower, dry my hair, put makeup on, and find something semi-nice to wear in an hour and a half, I needed help.

Unfortunately, I didn't exactly have an hour and a half. If I didn't want Crane to walk in, take one quick look around, and immediately discover which twin was the pig, I had to clean my apartment.

Or at the very least, I had to hide a lot of stuff. Which to me, come to think of it, is pretty much the same thing as cleaning. In my living room alone there were four empty glasses I'd forgotten to put in the dishwasher. There was also what looked like a hundred magazines stacked here and there, and enough newspapers to start a recycling yard. Not to mention, a pair of jeans on the couch, a dish towel on the coffee table, and one sock lying out in the hall.

I briefly considered putting a quarantine sign on the door, and letting it go at that. Unfortunately, it occurred to me that this particular strategy might discourage Crane from going out with me at all.

There seemed to be no way to avoid it. For the next forty-five minutes, I did my own personal imitation of the Tasmanian Devil, whirling around the apartment faster and faster, and no doubt, slobbering and muttering, too. What I was muttering, of course, was curses. Man, how I hate to clean. It's one of the reasons I don't like people just dropping in. It's not that I don't like company; I just don't like witnesses.

After I'd filled up all my garbage cans out back, I still had a few magazines and newspapers left. Enough, in fact, that if I just left them, the place would still bear a distinct resemblance to a pig sty. I got rid of as many magazines as I could by putting them in any drawer that had space—this turned out to be the drawers of my buffet and china cabinet. When that still didn't quite do the trick, I put what was left in my dishwasher, on top of the empty glasses I'd just gathered from all over my apartment.

That problem solved nicely, I vacuumed the floor, the sofa, the drapes, and my overstuffed chairs, still whirling around the room Taz-style. After that, I dusted every horizontal surface in the living room—except, naturally, the baseboards. If Crane was the type to get down on his hands and knees to inspect my baseboards, the woman he was looking for was Cinderella, not me.

I gave my living room one final look, making sure there was nothing incriminating sticking out anywhere, and then I ran upstairs, shedding clothes as I went. I stepped into the shower, turned on the taps full blast, lathered my hair only once, and rinsed it as fast as I could. Then, still drying off, I hurried into my bedroom to make the final decision as to what the hell I should wear.

I decided on a black knit dress that came to just above my knees and was clingy enough to make me look a lot curvier than I am. I'd like to say I chose it because I had the fashion sense to realize that it would not look out of place in either an expensive restaurant or in a pizza parlor. Frankly, though, its most compelling argument was that it didn't need ironing. I put on black underwear, pulled on black pantyhose—no easy task over damp skin—and I eased my feet into black high heels. I had the dress on and was hurrying back into the bathroom to finish drying my hair at exactly twenty-four minutes to seven.

Wouldn't you know, once dry, my bangs were straight as a poker and hanging in my eyes. I plugged in my instant hot rollers, wrapped my bangs around a single large roller, rolled them away from my eyes, and sprayed them with hairspray so that the curl would take. It was probably not a good idea to spray hairspray on something as hot as that curler—my luck, I'd follow up my Taz impression with one of Michael

Jackson and set my hair on fire—but at this point, I was desperate. I hurried on to my next project: my face.

Oh my yes. I intended to slather on as much makeup as I could without looking as if I had done any slathering. This, believe me, takes skill. One that, if it were men who had to master it, would probably be listed on résumés. Moving as fast as I could, I put on undereye concealer, ivory foundation, smoky eyeliner—and then something terrible happened.

The doorbell rang.

I jumped at the sound, nearly putting my eye out with the eyeliner pencil. My heart began immediately trying to leap out of my chest. Could this be Crane? I checked my watch. It was only five minutes after six. I breathed a sigh of relief, and my heart slowed down. There was no way that this was Crane.

In my experience, men were punctual in direct proportion to the number of strikes they already had against them. For example, those who had less than a full set of teeth, who were unemployed, and who at some time during the evening intended to ask me to pay for the date—these guys always showed up right on the dot.

They were never early, though. Hell, a guy could be appearing on a regular basis on *America's Most Wanted;* he could be picking you up in a stolen car; hell, he could still be wearing the ski mask he'd worn in all the videos they'd taken of him at automatic teller machines; and he would *not* be early. In fact, I'd always thought that this was one of the male Rules. Like the female Rules outlined in that bestseller published a year or so ago? Male Rule #1 had to be: Never let her think you're eager to see her.

It was even more unbelievable that Crane would arrive early on this, our second date. Usually at this stage of the dating game, the last thing a guy wants to do is to look as if he's anxious to see you. In fact, he's generally going to a lot of trouble to make it clear that you want this relationship a lot more than he does. So far be it from him to drop by any earlier than ten minutes or so *after* he says he'll be there.

I was sure that my doorbell ringer could not possibly be Crane, but just to be on the safe side, as I hurried downstairs, I pulled the roller out of my hair and stuck it in the side pocket of my dress. My bangs felt a little stiff, so I ran my fingers through them, loosing them up. The hairspray had been even more effective than I'd thought, so I was still running my fingers through my bangs, trying to finger-comb them, as I opened my front door. I intended to get rid of whoever it was as fast as I could so that I could finish putting on my makeup.

The only problem was, it really did turn out to be Crane standing there on my porch, smiling at me.

I'm not sure, but I might not have returned his smile. Instead, I did such a quick intake of breath, I sounded like somebody was standing on my air hose.

"Nan," Crane said. His voice was even deeper than I remembered. Dressed in a dark gray designer suit and one of those shirts that didn't have a collar, like Tom Cruise wore in *Rain Man*, Crane Morgan was easily the best-looking man I'd ever seen in person. My silly heart started beating faster.

In distinct contrast to what he was wearing, Crane was holding a dozen colorful helium balloons. He extended them toward me, his smile getting wider. Every balloon had my name written on it, except for one. It had a big red heart. "I was going to get you flowers," Crane said, "and try to impress you. You know, make you think that I'm really suave and debonair . . ."

Hey, I was impressed that he knew how to pronounce *suave* and *debonair*.

"But I knew you'd know better." He shrugged and added, "Besides, flowers are so ordinary . . ."

His dark blue eyes were intense.

I met his eyes, and of course, I immediately wondered if I had on any lipstick whatsoever.

"And you most definitely are no ordinary woman."

He was smiling the entire time he was talking, but I couldn't help noticing that his eyes seemed to keep darting to a spot just above my forehead.

"Thank you so much," I said, taking the balloons. I really did love them, and I might even have shown it except that as I stepped aside, indicating to Crane to come in, I caught sight of myself in the mirror of the antique oak medicine chest that I have hanging by my front door.

I took one look, and I stifled a scream.

Evidently, finger-combing my bangs had not worked. They were still in a fairly tight roll.

Oh God. All I needed was a chicken bone to stick in that big knot on the front of my head, and I could find work as a witch doctor.

Crane was now standing just inside my door, obviously waiting for me to say something.

I cleared my throat. "Well," I said, not meeting his eyes, "as you can see, I'm not quite ready to go."

Crane shrugged again. "That's my fault. I'm really early."

I just looked at him. He knew he was early? He even *admitted* it?

He took a step toward me, and I caught the scent of Aramis—a cologne I like so much, I once let some guy kiss me just because he was wearing it. I, of course, immediately discovered that you need something more than cologne to be a good kisser.

"To be honest," Crane was saying, "I was so anxious to see you again, I couldn't wait until seven."

I blinked and, for a moment, forgot that I had a Tootsie Roll on top of my head. Crane was *volunteering* this? Without my even twisting his arm?

My God, I could possibly be nuts about this man.

I must've looked a little surprised because Crane shrugged again. "Yeah, I know, I'm supposed to act as if I think you're lucky I'm here, but to tell you the truth, I've never liked all those stupid games we're supposed to play."

I was smiling sincerely now. "I've never liked them either," I said.

Crane grinned. "Well, good, then you'll understand that I don't mean to be rushing things, but I really want to do this . . ."

And then, all of a sudden, it seemed, I was in his arms, and he was kissing me, as the balloons softly bounced all around us.

I have to say this little turn of events certainly took my mind off my *hair*. It even made not wearing lipstick seem like pretty good planning.

When I finally pulled away, I actually felt dizzy. "I—I guess I'd better finish getting ready." I sounded breathless.

Crane sounded a little out of breath himself. "So, I guess, you don't on a second date either?"

I met his eyes. "My goodness, you really *don't* play games, do you?"

Crane smiled, his dark eyes still on mine. "Games just waste time," he said quietly. "And we could be spending our time doing something that we both know is going to be wonderful."

OK, so I'd be lying if I said I wasn't severely tempted to just take his hand and lead him upstairs to my bedroom right that very minute. My heart was going like a trip-hammer, and as I admitted earlier, I have certainly been this stupid before.

I took a ragged breath. The fact that Crane would even make such a suggestion when I was wearing only half my makeup and had a bad case of Tootsie Roll hair was terribly flattering. Or maybe he was just hard up. The last two words made me flush at the thought.

"I don't know," I said honestly, "I think I might *not* on a second date." I gave an extra emphasis to the word *not*, but that wasn't the word Crane seemed to hear.

Crane grinned and moved closer. "Might? Did I hear you say *might?* Does that mean you haven't quite made up your mind?"

I stepped away from him, moving toward the stairs. "It means I'm still considering my options."

Crane grinned. Which was a lot better reaction than some I'd gotten in this same situation in the past. One guy I'd turned down on our second date had actually called me names—really ugly names, rhyming with bunt and what.

"So, let me see," Crane said, grinning even wider and crossing his arms, "what you're saying is that I've got all evening to help you continue considering your options. Am I right?"

I didn't answer, but I couldn't help smiling. I looped the ribbons to the balloons around the banister and, without looking back, headed on upstairs to finish my makeup—and, oh, yes, to comb my stupid bangs out.

As it turned out, Crane was right. Whether or not we were going to end the evening in bed was an unspoken question between us from that point forward.

We went to a movie at the Showcase Cinemas that had

been advertised heavily on TV all week, and it turned out to be one of the most awful movies I'd ever seen. Even worse than *Johnny Mnemonic*, which was going some. The movie being awful, though, turned out to be wonderful for Crane and me, because he and I laughed through the whole thing. Sitting side by side in the darkness, our shoulders and legs touching, it seemed oddly intimate as we whispered comments into each other's ear, and of course, stuffed each other with popcorn. Crane even echoed my own sentiments: "You can't watch a movie without popcorn. It would be un-American."

After the movie, we went to a wonderful restaurant called L'Apéritif, which had been open only a few months, but had already become one of Louisville's finest and busiest. I was sure we wouldn't be able to get in, it was getting so late, but Crane told me he'd made reservations early that morning.

A man who actually planned ahead, and took care of reservations all by himself? Oh, yes, I could be crazy about him, all right.

We ate the house specialty, something with beef and scallops and a delicious cream sauce, but to tell you the truth, I wasn't sure what I was eating. All I remember is that I drank entirely too much wine, and that Crane was funny, and intelligent, and sweet. He even talked about his brother again, only this time he didn't mention any of the sadness. Instead, he talked about all the happy times the two of them had had, growing up—how they'd switched places in school, fooling teachers and students alike; how one Halloween the two of them had actually egged the police station; and how Lane had talked Crane into going out for basketball in high school.

Crane had looked sad for the first time when he told me about this last. "When Lane made the team, but I didn't, Lane refused to play without me. Can you believe that? He wouldn't even go to the games." Smiling, Crane shook his head. "I think I would've played without *him.*"

I nodded, returning his smile, but I didn't believe him.

The rest of the meal was pretty much a blur. I do remember that after we'd eaten whatever the specialty was, and we were waiting on our desserts, Crane reached over and took my hand. Without saying a word, he raised my hand to his lips and kissed it.

Maybe it was the wine, or maybe it was just that I felt so close to him, as if maybe he and I had always known each other. Whatever the reason, I made up my mind right then that the answer to our unspoken question was yes.

I know, I know. I could just hear Bert. *Are you out of your mind? You barely know this guy.*

I mentally tuned Bert out—after all, what did she know? She'd been married, for God's sake, so she'd had sex on a regular basis for years. *Years.* I couldn't even imagine what that would be like. I could, however, imagine what it would be like to go to bed with Crane. In fact, I'd say my imagination was working overtime on the way home. The closer we got, the faster my silly heart beat.

At the turn off Bardstown Road onto Douglass Boulevard, only a minute or so from my driveway, Crane glanced over at me. "Still considering your options?" he said.

I shook my head. "I've made up my mind." I moved closer to him, and he reached over and put his right arm around my shoulders.

Leaning against him, I could feel his heart beating fast, just like my own.

And then, when Crane pulled into my driveway, my heart almost stopped.

I sat up, staring at my house. And in particular, at Bert's front door. What on earth was going on?

For an awful moment I thought I had to be asleep and having one of those ghastly date-nightmares. You know the ones—where everything you ever imagined that could go wrong on a date actually does. Like you show up at your boyfriend's house to meet his mother and you're stark naked.

Or how about this one? You come home from a really wonderful second date with a fantastic new guy that you think you could be falling in love with, and your old boyfriend is there waiting for you with a shitty look on his face?

Usually, though, the dream ends when you wake up, soaked in sweat and relieved as hell it was only a dream. This time, though, I knew that wasn't going to happen.

Coming out of Bert's apartment next door—and oh, yes, looking about as disagreeable as he did when I was dating him —was Detective Hank Goetzmann. Goetzmann had that bull-dog look on his face I'd seen about, oh, a thousand too many times—and he was lumbering straight toward Crane and me.

In Goetzmann's wake came Bert, trotting after him like a nervous terrier trying to keep up. Behind Goetzmann's back, she was making wild little gestures in my direction. If I were interpreting them right, those gestures meant she was *not* to blame for this fiasco. Again and again, she mouthed what looked to me to be the word *Please*. I thought I knew what she was trying to say. *Please don't be mad. Please don't blame me.*

I glanced over at Crane. His eyes met mine, and seemed to mirror my own feelings.

Well, shit.

It didn't look as if I had all that many options, after all.

Chapter 10

●

BERT

Nan couldn't say that I didn't try to warn her. I believe I did everything except turn somersaults to let her know that Hank Goetzmann was not paying a social visit, but was here in an official capacity.

The entire time Goetzmann was walking from my front door over to Nan and Crane, I was following him, gesturing, making faces, and mouthing the word *Police*. Behind Goetzmann's back, of course. I wasn't sure if warning a person that she was about to be interrogated by a police officer was something that you could get arrested for, but I didn't want to take any chances. It would be just my luck that *spoiling the surprise* would turn out to be a misdemeanor.

Of course, it would've been easier to get the message across to Nan if G. Gordon Liddy, or whatever his name was, had come along. If Nan had seen Goetzmann's partner—in addition to Goetzmann—coming toward her, she might've realized right off the bat that he had not dropped by just to talk about old times. Unfortunately, though, G. Gordon had stayed behind at Louise's house to supervise the collection of evidence from the crime scene.

His staying behind had been unfortunate in another way, too. It would've been a lot less tense for me if Goetzmann and I had had some company while we waited. Mainly because there was no way he would've started quizzing me about Nan if his partner were within hearing distance.

As it was, I spent the hour before Nan showed up, getting more and more nervous, as I kept waiting for Goetzmann to get around to asking me the questions that Nan's exes always ask. Over the years I've found that these questions generally fall into three categories: *What Went Wrong? How Can I Get Her Back?* and *Is She Seeing Somebody Else?* I've also found that if you act totally befuddled—something that, in all modesty, I have a real talent for—Nan's dumpees soon get the idea that you're just as much in the dark as they are.

And they go away.

This had worked beautifully when I'd acted bewildered with Tab, the construction worker who proudly announced one day that he hadn't read a book since 1983. It had also worked when I'd acted totally shocked with Will, the guy who I'd always secretly called Won't, because to my knowledge he didn't work a day in the entire four months Nan went out with him. And it had worked like a charm when I'd acted absolutely amazed that Nan had finally broken it off with Chuck—the guy I'd secretly called Upchuck because listening to his inane jokes and accompanying horse laughs always made me nauseous.

Even though with Goetzmann, I knew I wouldn't even have to act—as I mentioned earlier, I really *didn't* understand why Nan no longer wanted to go out with him—I also knew that no matter how I acted, he wasn't going to go away.

Not tonight anyway.

He was going to continue to sit in the Queen Anne chair to the right of my sofa, sipping one cup of coffee after another, until Nan eventually showed up.

I think Goetzmann had been a little ill at ease, too. He hadn't said much. He'd just made me go over again what Louise had told me, taken a few notes, and then sat there, looking around my living room. At the books in my bookcase, at the neatly stacked magazines on my coffee table, at the patchwork wall hanging I'd quilted and hung in the hall. I'd followed his gaze, of course, as he'd looked around the room, wondering uneasily if there could be some obscure ordinance regarding dust on baseboards that I could get a ticket for.

The second we heard the car pulling up next door, Goetzmann jumped out of his chair, only a little faster than if he'd been spring-loaded, put his coffee cup down on the nearest end table, and headed for the front door.

I followed right behind him, and when I saw in the light from the street lamp across the way that it really was Nan and Crane pulling up next door in a dark green Camry, I felt a wave of relief wash over me. Relief that Nan was OK, in spite of the awful things that Louise had suggested about Crane. And relief also that Goetzmann apparently had no intention of quizzing me about what I knew about his and Nan's relationship.

Following Goetzmann across the lawn, I did everything I could think of to signal Nan about why Goetzmann was here. By the time he had reached Crane and Nan—Crane having gone around to the passenger side of the Camry to hold the door while Nan got out—I felt as if I'd had my exercise for the week. Judging from the look on Nan's face, though, I might as well have saved my energy. I wasn't sure what Nan thought I'd been trying to tell her, but it must not have been anything even close to what I'd been attempting to convey.

I even tried sending her a Twin Whammy, bug eyes and

all, but the second Nan opened her mouth, I knew it hadn't worked. Glaring at Goetzmann, Nan said, "What in the world are *you* doing here at this hour of the night?" Nan's tone was not friendly.

Goetzmann didn't exactly look warm and fuzzy himself. He barely gave Nan a glance, totally ignored her question, and focused all his attention on Crane. "Are you Crane Morgan?"

Having been only a few steps behind Goetzmann, I joined the group at this point, moving to stand right in back of Goetzmann. Following Goetzmann's lead, I turned toward Crane, too.

And barely stopped myself in time before I did an audible intake of breath.

Crane was wearing a *suit*.

Up to now I'd only seen Crane in jeans, and I guess he'd looked so great in those, I'd been under the impression that he couldn't possibly look any better.

I'd been wrong.

Crane Morgan—wearing a dark gray suit and a collarless pale blue shirt—was truly a sight to behold. In the cool light of the street lamp, the dark gray made Crane's tan look almost golden, and the light blue of the shirt made his eyes look even bluer.

There was really only one word to describe him.

Wow.

I couldn't help staring at Crane a little. Could a man this good-looking really be capable of killing another human being? With Crane standing right in front of me, the idea seemed preposterous.

I gave Goetzmann a quick glance. *Wow*, I guess, was not a word you'd ever use to describe Goetzmann.

Although to be honest, I believe I personally preferred

the square-jawed ruggedness of Hank Goetzmann's face over the finely chiseled features of Crane Morgan's. If I were ever on a date with Crane, I think I might find myself spending an inordinate amount of time staring at his perfect face, looking for flaws. Or worse, thinking about my own.

Not only had Crane beat out Goetzmann in the looks department, but he seemed to be winning the Mr. Congeniality Award, too. In fact, Crane was the only one so far who even sounded civil. "Yes, I'm Crane Morgan," he said, his deep voice rumbling amiably around us. "What's this all about?"

For an answer, Goetzmann reached into his suit pocket and pulled out a wallet. Opening it and holding it out so that the streetlight fell across it and the police badge inside, he said, "I'm Detective Goetzmann. Louisville Police, Homicide Division."

Nan rolled her eyes.

I rather hoped Goetzmann didn't see her do that.

If he did, he ignored her again. "We're conducting a routine investigation, Mr. Morgan," Goetzmann said, "and I need to ask you a few questions."

Crane glanced over at Nan, looking puzzled, and then he turned back to Hank. "Routine investigation? In the middle of the night?" Crane didn't sound annoyed, merely curious. And maybe even a little amused.

Nan, on the other hand, sounded annoyed enough for the two of them. "Routine, my foot!" she burst out.

I stared at Nan. Usually, the part of her body that she mentions in this particular context is not her foot. She must have been cleaning up her language a little in front of Crane.

Nan stood there, hands on hips, glaring at Goetzmann, wearing the DKNY black knit dress she'd gotten at T.J. Maxx's on sale. She'd tried it on for me the day she'd bought it, but on that particular day she'd also been wearing white crew socks and an ancient pair of Converse high tops. The tennis shoes had pretty much spoiled the effect. Now she was wearing black opaque hose and unfashionably narrow high heels. Unfashionable or not, Nan looked gorgeous.

I know. I know. Given that I'm supposed to be Nan's carbon copy, saying such a thing sounds as if I'm conceited beyond belief. I'd agree with that assessment if I'd ever truly believed that I look like Nan. The truth is, though, that neither Nan nor I have ever thought that we look all that much alike. I guess if you've never really seen your two faces together in real life, and you've always thought of yourselves as two very distinct people, you just don't see all that many similarities. As a matter of fact, it has always been something of a surprise to me when somebody gets Nan and me confused. Because we really are very different.

Like, for instance, there was no way I'd ever say to a cop what Nan was now saying to Goetzmann. "This is no routine investigation. This is police harassment, *that's* what it is!"

Oh dear.

Have I mentioned that Nan has a bad habit of leaping to conclusions when she's upset? I tried to interrupt her. "Nan?" I said, lifting a finger in the air. "Uh, Nan? Can I speak to you for just a minute?"

She didn't even glance in my direction. Instead she looked over at Crane. "I used to date this guy," she told Crane, jerking her thumb toward Goetzmann. "We only went out three months, but—"

"Uh, Nan?" I tried to interrupt again. *"Nan?"*

Once again Nan didn't even look at me. She went right on, her eyes still on Crane. "Ever since we broke up, he's been calling me and calling me, trying to talk me into going out with him again."

Nan also has a bad habit of exaggerating when she's upset. She'd mentioned to me that Goetzmann had phoned her a couple of times after they broke up, trying to see if they could somehow work things out. She was making it sound, however, as if he'd been calling her even more often than MCI does after you switch to AT&T.

Goetzmann evidently noticed Nan's slight exaggeration, too. "Now just a minute . . ." he said. He'd been frowning a little right from the start, but now his frown had deepened so much that his heavy eyebrows looked as if they were almost touching.

"Nan . . ." I said again, a little louder.

Nan, however, was on a roll. She ignored both Goetzmann and me one more time. "Well, I won't put up with this kind of harassment," Nan said, shaking her head emphatically. "I mean it, Goetzmann. I'll complain to your boss—I'll tell the Chief of—"

"Nan!" I all but shouted.

That got her attention. She finally stopped midsentence, and turned to look at me. *"What?"* she asked.

Unfortunately, I not only had Nan's attention, but also Crane's and Goetzmann's. With everybody looking at me, I hated to just blurt out what I had to say, but I couldn't think of a more delicate way to put it. "Louise was murdered tonight," I said, looking at Nan.

My eyes were not on Crane, but I could hear him do a quick intake of breath.

Nan, however, didn't look anywhere near as shocked as I expected her to look. She just stared back at me for a moment, her face blank. She looked over at Crane, then at

Goetzmann, and finally back at me. "Louise? Louise *who?*" she asked.

I couldn't believe it. I knew Nan ran into a lot of people in her line of work, so it was easy to forget a few. And yet, she'd just met Louise, for God's sake. How could she have forgotten her this quickly? Of course, maybe it was just that— once Nan had passed the problem of Louise on to me—she hadn't given the woman another thought. Then, too, the sight of Crane in a suit might have wiped her mind clean.

I gave Nan a pointed look. "Louise Eagleston. You know, the woman you and I met at the mall yesterday? The woman who invited *me* to dinner with her tonight?" As I said the word *me* in that last sentence, I gave it a little extra punch.

I could see the light dawning in Nan's eyes. Oh, *that* Louise. The Louise you were pretending to be me with.

"She was murdered?" Nan's hand went to her throat. "Is that true?"

"Bert found her," Goetzmann said, his face still tight with anger. "Bert called 911 . . ."

Here, Nan's eyes widened and quickly flicked to me, the question in her expression readily apparent to me: *Are you OK?*

I shrugged, giving her a tiny smile. *I'm fine* was my unspoken answer. Satisfied, Nan went immediately back to glowering at Goetzmann.

"But Mrs. Eagleston was already deceased," Goetzmann continued. "Mrs. Eagleston's murder is why I'm here." He gave Nan an unwavering look as he added, "No other reason."

Nan glared at Goetzmann all over again. "Is that so?" she said. "Well, I barely knew Louise, so I don't exactly understand why you'd come here. I should think you'd be talking to people who were close—"

Goetzmann cut her off. "Your new friend here knew Louise pretty well."

Nan blinked, and then she and I and Goetzmann all turned to look at Crane.

Crane didn't look at all amused now. In fact, more than anything else, he looked surprised. "I don't know where you got that idea," he said, looking straight at Goetzmann. "I hardly knew Louise Eagleston. She walked into my studio one day, wanting to have her portrait taken, and I did it for her. End of story."

Goetzmann was now leveling a look at Crane. "That's not what she told Bert."

"Bert?" Crane repeated, turning to look at me. "I—I don't understand." He seemed totally baffled.

I stared back at him. If Crane was acting, he'd missed his calling.

"I don't understand either," Nan put in, turning to Goetzmann. "If you wanted to ask Crane some questions, why didn't you go to Crane's place? Or his studio? Why did you come here?"

Goetzmann gave Nan a look that questioned her intelligence. "Bert told me that you and Mr. Morgan had gone out for the evening. So I knew that he'd be bringing you home."

Now, not only Crane, but Nan, too, was staring at me. Nan was wearing an expression that I've learned to recognize over the years. It was the same expression that, no doubt, Julius Caesar had on his face when he ran into Brutus on the Ides of March. Oh my yes, Nan was giving me her *Et tu, Bert* look.

I've always felt that the best defense is a strong offense.

I lifted my chin, and met Nan's look head on. OK, so I blabbed to Goetzmann. Did she really expect me to keep my mouth shut when a woman had been stabbed to death? Did Nan actually think that I'd sit idly by if there was a chance— any chance at all—that she might be spending the evening with a murderer? Was she kidding?

It also seemed to me that Nan was overlooking a little something. Excuse me, but as she herself had pointed out earlier, I'd been doing her a *favor*. As a matter of fact, it was all because of Nan that I'd even been in a position in the first place to hear what Louise had to say. It certainly had not been *my* idea to while away a few hours with Louise.

I took a deep breath. "When Detective Goetzmann asked me if you were home," I said evenly, "I simply told him that you weren't, but that I expected you later."

Nan did not look the least bit placated.

Neither did Crane. "What did Louise say about me?" Crane had moved closer to me, and was now leaning a little in my direction so that, apparently, he wouldn't miss a word of what I had to say.

Oh dear.

I glanced over at Goetzmann, expecting him to jump into the conversation right about now, saying some pat speech about how this topic was privileged information, or some such.

He didn't.

Instead, he just stood there, his eyes riveted on Crane. The detective was obviously waiting for me to spill everything I'd heard, so that he could see Crane's reaction when I accused him to his face of murdering his brother and his brother's girlfriend.

Oh dear.

I cleared my throat.

I ran my hand through my hair.

I looked over at Nan.

She, of course, was now glaring at me. And yet, what could I do? Lie and say I didn't remember?

Somehow, I knew that one wouldn't fly.

On the other hand, I really didn't want to get into what all Louise had said out here in the middle of Nan's driveway, in front of all our neighbors. Even if they were all probably asleep.

Finally, I took a deep breath and said, "You know, it's getting awfully cool out here, don't you think?" I, of course, was sweating in the cool night air, but I saw no reason to mention it. "Why don't we all go inside, have something to drink, and talk all this over?"

I didn't give anybody a chance to answer. I just turned on my heel and headed back across the lawn to my apartment.

I knew without looking that they were all following me.

More's the pity.

Chapter 11

●

NAN

OK. So I admit I'm a callous slug. A woman was dead, and yet, what was on my mind as I followed Bert across the lawn toward Bert's half of our duplex? It wasn't outrage that such a horrible thing had happened. It wasn't even determination to bring the poor woman's killer to justice.

Nope, as I picked my way across the damp evening grass in my uncomfortably high heels, what I was thinking about was that I'd had an entirely different idea in mind as to how Crane and I were going to spend the rest of this evening. It did not include sitting in Bert's living room, talking about Louise Eagleston's murder, let me tell you.

It also did not include watching Bert bustle around, acting as if she'd suddenly become possessed by the spirit of Martha Stewart. Can you believe, after Goetzmann, Crane, and I all trooped through her front door, Bert actually made this sweeping gesture toward her living room, saying, "You all just go right in and make yourself comfortable. Who would like coffee? Detective Goetzmann? I know you've been drinking coffee all night long but would you like another cup? And Crane, what about you?"

You'd have thought that she was hosting a bridge party.

I couldn't help but stare as Bert took coffee orders from

the men. Black with sugar for Goetzmann. Cream and sugar for Crane. Bert actually sounded delighted that she was getting this wonderful opportunity to discover how they liked their coffee. Turning to me, she said a tad too brightly, "Now, Nan, I know you're not crazy about coffee, but could I get you a Coke? Or how about some nice hot chocolate? How does that sound?"

How it sounded, believe me, Bert didn't want to know. Her twin vibes must've given her a little hint as to what was going through my mind because she didn't give me a chance to answer. She just gave me a quick glance, blinked once, then disappeared into the kitchen. Where she started rattling what sounded like a few thousand cups and saucers and spoons.

I suppose, if I were a warm, forgiving sort of sister, I would've followed Bert into the kitchen, and helped her rattle whatever she was rattling. I was clearly not that kind of sister, however, because I just stomped across the living room and plopped myself down on Bert's sofa.

Crane sat down right next to me. Goetzmann, still frowning like he did throughout most of our dating life, immediately moved toward the antique rocker. This rocker happens to be Bert's favorite piece of furniture in the entire world. It holds a special place in her heart because it is her all time greatest thrift shop find—a genuine antique oak rocker with a handwoven cane seat for the grand sum of fifteen dollars. The rocker cracked and squeaked a little when Goetzmann sat down, and in a moment of pure spite, I hoped that under Goetzmann's 200-plus pounds, that stupid rocker broke into so much kindling.

I was—to put it delicately—*pissed.*

I didn't want to believe it, but it seemed pretty obvious:

Bert had spilled her guts to Goetzmann. My very own sister had blabbed to a *policeman* every single slanderous thing that Louise Eagleston had told her about Crane. The man I was dating. The man I could very well be falling in love with.

Oh my God. The moment the thought crossed my mind, my mouth went a little dry. And yet, as soon as I considered it, I realized it was true. I actually could be falling in love with this remarkable man. And the way I saw it, at this point in our relationship, hurting Crane was pretty much the same as hurting me. If spreading tales about Crane didn't amount to blatant betrayal on Bert's part, I didn't know what did.

What's more, Bert had told Goetzmann even *after* we'd talked about Louise being a gossip.

Even now, let's face it—as much as I didn't want to be speaking ill of the dead—the truth was: Louise Eagleston had been a gossip. When you considered what she'd had to say about poor Crane, who was obviously still in major pain over the loss of his twin, you had to admit that she'd been a vicious gossip.

That did not, of course, mean that what had happened was any less awful. On the other hand, the fact that she'd been murdered didn't exactly guarantee that everything she'd ever said was now Gospel truth. I believe even women who were no longer alive have been known to lie a time or two in their lifetimes—or to put the best spin on it that I could— to *exaggerate.*

I had thought I'd made it pretty clear to Bert that Louise was a gossip. But had Bert made it clear to Goetzmann that Louise was not exactly a reliable witness? Apparently not, or else Goetzmann wouldn't have sat there, looking at poor Crane as if he were Ted Bundy, Jack the Ripper, and Jeffrey

Dahmer all rolled into one, the entire time that Bert was out in the kitchen, playing Ms. Southern Hospitality.

Goetzmann would also not have asked the questions he asked. "So, Mr. Morgan, you were saying that you and the victim were friends?"

Crane immediately shook his dark head. "No, I didn't say that," he said. His tone was puzzled. "What I said was that I hardly knew Mrs. Eagleston at all. Ours was a work relationship. Nothing more."

"You don't say," Goetzmann said. He still had the pencil in his hand he'd been scribbling with outside, and he tapped the thing against his massive jaw.

Crane leaned back against the back of Bert's sofa, crossing his arms over his chest. If I hadn't been sitting right next to him, I might've thought he was perfectly relaxed. I could see, however, a muscle jumping in his jaw. Crane must've been seething inside at the way Goetzmann was treating him, and yet, he remained outwardly calm.

I was impressed. When I get angry, I usually can't stop myself from showing it. As, unfortunately, I believe I'd amply demonstrated in my driveway only a few minutes ago.

"You never *ever* went out with Mrs. Eagleston?" Goetzmann asked. He made it sound as if the idea of the two of them never having dated was preposterous.

Crane just looked at Goetzmann for a long moment. "Detective Goetzmann," Crane said, his tone now one of infinite patience, "I just told you that Mrs. Eagleston and I only had a working relationship."

Goetzmann nodded, tapping that idiotic pencil against his chin again. "Right," he said. "Then you didn't take her out?"

Crane's eyes still rested on Goetzmann's face. "Detective,

if Mrs. Eagleston and I only had a business relationship, that means we never went out socially."

Crane just said the words, that's all, but there was an undercurrent of sarcasm in the way he said them.

I couldn't say I blamed him. He'd answered Geotzmann's question, for God's sake, more than once.

Goetzmann's frown, however, deepened. "You don't say," he said again, his tone deliberately casual. He tapped his chin with the pencil again, and then said, as if it were just an offhand remark, "Then I take it you don't count that little excursion to the mall a couple of days ago as social?"

Crane blinked and looked puzzled again. "You mean, when Mrs. Eagleston and I went to see Nan emcee the library event?"

Goetzmann was already nodding. "That's the one. Some people might've called that a date."

"A date to introduce me to another woman?" Crane was now actually looking amused. "Detective Goetzmann, Louise Eagleston invited me to accompany her to the mall for the sole purpose of introducing me to Nan. Mrs. Eagleston had already met both of us, and evidently, she fancied herself an amateur matchmaker." Crane uncrossed his arms, and looked sideways at me. "I, for one, think she really did have a talent in that department, and I'm sorry that I'm now never going to have the opportunity to thank her."

With Crane looking into my eyes, my silly heart started going triple-time. He reached over and squeezed my hand. "I think I'll always be grateful to Mrs. Eagleston," Crane said quietly.

It would've been a nice moment except that just as Crane finished what he was saying, Goetzmann seemed to get something caught in his throat. He started coughing and hacking like somebody badly in need of the Heimlich maneuver.

Or badly in need of having his face slapped.

One or the other.

His handsome face impassive, Crane waited for Goetzmann to stop coughing without saying a word. When Goetzmann seemed to be done, Crane said, "Are you OK, Detective?"

Goetzmann nodded, frowning. "I'm fine," he said, patting at his throat as if there really had been something caught here—a fact which I severely doubted. "It's just that occasionally I have trouble *swallowing.*"

Crane's glance didn't waver. "You don't say." He mimicked Goetzmann's earlier comment almost exactly, right down to the casual, offhand tone.

I wasn't quite sure if Crane did it consciously—he certainly didn't act as if he realized what he was doing—but Goetzmann seemed convinced of Crane's intent. His eyes flashed. "Look, Morgan, if you—"

It sounded like the beginning of a pretty interesting sentence, but we didn't get to hear all of it. Martha Stewart, cleverly disguised as Bert, came bustling back in, carrying a tray, of all things, with four steaming coffee cups and accompanying saucers artfully arranged around a sugar bowl and creamer. I recognized the dishes. It was Bert's wedding china, an embossed ivory Lenox pattern edged in 18-karat gold.

Bert had carefully folded four floral cloth napkins in neat triangles and placed them on the saucers, tucking the napkins under sterling silver spoons. The spoons were from silverware place settings she'd also received as wedding gifts—

Gorham silver in a floral pattern. I stared at the tray for a moment, and then I stared at Bert.

Was it possible that she and I were ever the same thing? I know identical twins are supposed to start life as a single egg, but when I see Bert do things like this, the concept of us ever being one pretty much boggles the mind.

Evidently, Bert was under the impression that being interrogated by the police about the murder of an acquaintance was an event that demanded her finest china and silverware.

As Bert bustled around, handing each of us a coffee cup, I actually had to bite my tongue to keep from saying, "So I guess you couldn't get a caterer on such short notice?"

Bert must've been picking up twin vibes again because she didn't even glance at me the entire time she was handing out coffee cups. She also didn't look at me when she finally took a seat in the rose chintz–covered side chair to the left of the sofa. After smoothing her napkin in her lap, she sat very straight, looking around the room, her cup raised to her lips. Before she took even one sip, though, she said, "Would anybody like anything else? If your coffee is too cold, just let me know, and I'll be glad to microwave it for you. Or if you'd like a little pastry to go with your coffee, I could get you some."

I tried to stop staring at her, but I couldn't help it. This was getting serious. If Bert didn't stop this soon, I might have to call in an exorcist.

After we'd all assured Bert that she didn't have to get us anything else, Goetzmann took a sip of his coffee, and said, "Now, Bert, I believe you were about to tell us something?" He continued to frown, but his voice was gentle. Far gentler, in fact, than I believe I myself had ever heard the man speak.

I turned to look at Bert again. What did Goetzmann think?

That if he didn't handle her with kid gloves, she just might bolt from the room?

Come to think of it, that could be a distinct possibility. Bert's cheeks looked as if she'd just applied two smears of bright red rouge, and when she spoke, her voice sounded dry even though she'd just taken a sip of coffee. "Yes, well," she said, "before I go on, I do want to make it clear that I'm just repeating what Louise told me. That I'm not, you know, making any accusations or anything myself. I'm just acting like a sort of tape recorder really, just repeating what I was told."

Goetzmann was nodding like a jack-in-the-box. "Right, right. Now what did Louise tell you about Mr. Morgan and his twin brother, Lane?"

I could feel Crane suddenly tense beside me, but he didn't say a word. He just turned to look at Bert, his gorgeous face revealing nothing.

Bert looked even more uncomfortable. Unfortunately, though, that didn't keep her from repeating everything she'd told me last night. To give her credit, she did try to just cover the details of her finding Louise Eagleston's body; but apparently Goetzmann had already heard all he needed to about that.

Under his coaxing, Bert finally launched into Louise's gossip. All about how Louise Eagleston had suggested that Crane had killed Marian Fielding and his own twin brother when he'd lived back in Owensboro. After which Crane had moved to Louisville to hide out.

Crane took it all pretty well. When Bert finished, he just stared at her for a long moment. "So," he said quietly, "how many people am I supposed to have murdered?"

Bert's eyes widened. "What?" she asked weakly.

She looked so startled, I would've smiled except that it seemed pretty inappropriate to be grinning at a time like this. Crane was being maliciously accused, and he couldn't even confront his accuser anymore.

Crane didn't smile either. Still looking at Bert, he asked, "Did Mrs. Eagleston happen to mention how she knew so much about my brother and me? I never saw her before she came into my studio to have her portrait taken, so I don't understand." He glanced over at Goetzmann. "I share a studio downtown with another photographer, Bentley Shepard, and it's true that I knew Bentley from Owensboro—Lane and I went to Owensboro High School with him—but I can't believe that Bentley would repeat all of this to a virtual stranger." Crane shook his head again, his eyes puzzled. And filled with pain.

Bert looked pained herself. "You mean," she said, *"none* of what Louise told me is true?"

Crane swallowed once, but he still met Bert's eyes straight on. "The circumstances of my twin's and his fiancée's deaths were very much like what Mrs. Eagleston described. But the only thing I ever told Mrs. Eagleston was that I was a twin. And that was only after she'd remarked on a portrait I had sitting on my desk." He cleared his throat and glanced over at me. "The portrait was of Lane and me. In, uh, happier days."

His voice cracked a little, and my heart went out to him. I don't believe I'd ever felt so sorry for anybody in my life.

Goetzmann—Mr. Sensitivity himself—did not exactly have the same reaction. "So, let me see if I get this straight," Goetzmann said, his voice no longer the least bit gentle. "What you're suggesting is that the dead woman went around telling wild tales about people she didn't even know."

Crane just looked at him. "I'm not suggesting anything."

I'd been quiet long enough. "Well, maybe she did do that," I said. "Maybe Louise Eagleston learned a few things about her acquaintances, embellished the details, and then went around telling half-truths and innuendoes as if they were fact. Maybe that's why she's dead—she made up vicious lies about people, and someone didn't appreciate it."

For a reply, Goetzmann made a derisive noise in the back of his throat. It sounded pretty disgusting.

"Not to speak unkindly of the dead," Bert said, staring into her coffee cup, "but Louise did seem to enjoy telling me all this."

Goetzmann shot her a quick, disappointed glance. I guess he'd been expecting Bert to back him up, and leap to Louise's defense.

"Looks to me as if Louise Eagleston could've been attacked by any number of people she might've been spreading ugly rumors about," I said, looking directly at Goetzmann. "Or it could be that what happened was just a random event. She could've been in the wrong place at the right time, and surprised a burglar."

Bert looked up briefly from her coffee. "There *was* that guy I saw running away," she said.

We all turned to stare at her after that little comment. Bert continued to stare at her coffee cup the whole time, but she did describe in detail a guy she'd seen running down the street away from the Eagleston home. Bert made it sound as if this guy were the identical twin of one of the Ninja Turtles, but it seemed to me pretty significant that she'd seen anybody running away from the house, period. Regardless of how turtle-like he happened to be.

Goetzmann apparently saw it differently. The more Bert

talked about Turtle Man, the more he frowned. When she'd finished, he immediately jumped in. "Look, I realize there are a lot of ways this could've gone down. Nobody has to point them out to me." He took a long, long sip of coffee and added, "Let's just say, I'm keeping my options open."

I sort of wished he hadn't used that particular phrase. At the word "option," Crane and I exchanged a glance. I wondered if Crane was thinking what I was thinking.

There were a lot better ways to have spent this evening. Damn.

Crane was still looking at me when Goetzmann pulled something out of his pocket, and tossed it on the coffee table in front of us. "Maybe you could explain one more thing," Goetzmann said, turning again to Crane. "Since you say you don't know this woman, how do you explain what she's doing with all these photographs of you? And maybe you could also hazard a guess as to why, as Louise Eagleston was dying, she gave these photographs to Bert."

Crane and I both turned to look at what Goetzmann had dropped on the table. It was a packet of snapshots. The front of the packet was crumpled and marred by rust-colored stains. I didn't even want to think about what those stains could be.

A few of the snapshots had spilled out onto the gleaming maple surface, and I leaned forward to get a better look. They seemed to be just photographs. One after another of Crane and the woman whose portrait I'd seen back in his gallery.

Marian Fielding.

Crane reached out and picked up one of the snapshots. And then another. And then another.

He swallowed once, and then said, "Detective, these aren't

pictures of me. These are snapshots of my brother Lane. With his fiancée." He rapidly leafed through the rest of the packet, his mouth tightening. "Wait a minute. Here's one of me. And this one here."

I looked at the photographs he was indicating. Each was a photograph of him alone.

"All the rest, though, are Lane," Crane went on. "And his fiancée, Marian Fielding." His voice was completely void of emotion.

I looked at the photos again. Good Lord. Crane and his brother certainly had looked alike. I mean, *exactly* alike. I leaned closer, squinting a little. I wasn't at all sure if I could tell which was Crane and which was Lane if he hadn't told us.

For the first time, as I stared at those pictures, it hit me. Dating somebody who happened to look exactly like somebody else could be a real nuisance. I'd never really thought about what it might be like to date Bert or me, with a duplicate running around to embarrass you if you made a mistake identifying your date. What a pain in the neck.

Goetzmann leaned forward, tapping the snapshots. "And you have no idea why Mrs. Eagleston would have these pictures?"

Crane looked completely bewildered. "No, I don't."

For his part, Goetzmann looked like he was playing poker and he'd just thrown down three aces and was about to play a fourth. He reached into his suit pocket one more time and drew out even more snapshots. These he fanned in front of Crane, too.

I blinked as I saw what was in them. Nudes. Women lounging on fur rugs, leaning against pillows, clutching stuffed animals, all smiling coyly at the camera. Blonds, brunettes, redheads. The kind of shots on which *Playboy* magazine had made its reputation.

"Ever seen these before?" Goetzmann asked, tapping one photo with a forefinger. His finger landed square on the bare breasts of one of the playmates.

Crane looked through every one of the photographs, one by one.

It made me a little uneasy, sitting next to the guy I was currently dating while he perused a few dozen naked ladies.

Not to mention, some of these women had figures that I sincerely hoped had been surgically enhanced.

Crane cleared his throat. "Detective Goetzmann, not only have I *not* seen these pictures before, I have also not met any of these ladies. Ever." There was a trace of testiness creeping into his voice now; and hell, I couldn't blame him.

Crane turned over one of the photographs, and I saw a stamp on the back—a green S in a rectangular block. He cleared his throat. "I do recognize the stamp on the back, however," Crane said. "It's the mark of my associate, Bentley Shepard. He stamps all his work this way."

"I take it you and old Bentley take nudie pictures, then?" Goetzmann asked, tapping away now at another playmate's derriere.

Crane shook his head. "*I* don't take such pictures, no," he said. "But I have no control over what Bentley does. However, I'd like to point out that there is a difference between what you call 'nudie pictures' and art. The figure you keep goosing I would term *art.*"

"Oh, art? Is that what they're calling it now?" Goetzmann asked, removing his finger from the nude's rear. "You're telling me you didn't know your partner was snapping nude models for fun and profit?"

Crane stood up. A muscle in his jaw was jumping now. "As I said, Detective, I have no idea what Bentley is doing in his half of the office. He is not my partner, as you say, either. We operate separate businesses—we just split the cost of the office, phone and electric service, that kind of thing. That's all. We have separate studios; and if you care to inspect it, there *is* a wall between my office and Bentley's."

Goetzmann made another one of those disgusting noises, his Neanderthal way of letting everybody within hearing distance know that he believed nothing of what Crane had just said—beginning with the part about how the nude pictures were art. Goetzmann stood up now, too, facing Crane.

"You know what I hate?" Goetzmann asked.

Bert and I glanced at each other. We'd heard this little tune before, back when we were involved in that other murder. Oh, sure, maybe the words would be a little different; but hell, it was going to be the same old song.

Goetzmann leaned toward Crane. "I hate coincidences. Mainly because I don't believe in 'em. So you can see that I would just hate it when a woman turns up dead who, just by coincidence, has just told somebody about this murder she knows about. Where a certain twin brother murdered his fiancée. And then, just by coincidence, she mentions how she suspects a certain photographer of maybe killing the brother and the fiancée both."

Crane's hands tightened into a fist. "Now just a minute—"

"And just by coincidence," Goetzmann went on, as if Crane hadn't even spoken, "this murder victim has on her person photographs of these same twin brothers *and* the murdered fiancée."

Goetzmann bent down and rummaged quickly through

the photos on the coffee table. He snagged one between his thumb and forefinger and held it up in front of Crane's nose.

It was one of the photographs of Marian—a picture showing both brothers with Marian in the middle, her arms around both their shoulders.

Crane barely glanced at the picture, and then turned back to Goetzmann.

"Isn't it odd," Goetzmann asked, "that all the pictures Louise Eagleston gave Bert seem to have some connection to *you?*"

Still sitting on the sofa, looking up at the men, I was beginning to feel like a child left out of the adult conversation. I got to my feet, too. "Aren't you forgetting something, Goetzmann?" I asked. "I was with Crane this evening. It seems to me, just judging from when Bert was supposed to get there and the condition of the stuff on the stove, that Louise had probably been attacked only a few minutes before Bert arrived."

Goetzmann gave a curt nod. "We figure she was attacked sometime between six and seven."

I shrugged. "Well, Crane picked me up at five after six, and I was with him from that point on. We went to a movie at the Showcase Cinemas, and after that we went to dinner at L'Aperitif. A lot of people saw him, not just me."

Goetzmann just stared back at me, looking sad.

He actually looked as if he thought I could be lying. Lying to protect Crane.

"Look, I'm telling you the truth!" I said. "Crane was never out of my sight for more than a minute or so. I admit I did go to the ladies' room before the movie, but believe me—I wasn't gone long enough for him to dash out, attack Louise, and hurry on back." Now I leaned toward Goetzmann, poking him in the chest this time. "Now, you know what I hate? I hate a former boyfriend who harasses a current boyfriend, just because he got dumped. I hate a guy who makes a murder investigation a personal attack, just because he got dumped. And I hate a guy who uses his position as a police officer to badger some other guy for personal reasons. Just because he got dumped."

Goetzmann's face turned redder than I'd ever thought it possible for a face to turn. "Now just a cotton-picking minute!" He says this a lot when he's upset. "I did not get dumped. As I remember it, we dumped each other. It was a mutual decision! And I resent your suggesting that I would interrogate anybody just to harass him!"

As Goetzmann spoke, he took a step toward me. Crane must've thought Goetzmann might actually strike me and he quickly stepped between us, putting me behind him protectively.

Lord. If I'd thought Goetzmann's face was an odd color before, I'd had no idea how odd it could get. It went from red to a deep purple.

Then, glancing over at Bert, who was still seated, watching all of us with eyes the size of saucers, Goetzmann took a deep breath. "Nan," he said, looking past Crane directly at me, "watch yourself around this guy. People seem to die around him."

I couldn't believe it. What Goetzmann was trying to do was so transparent, it was almost funny. He was trying to drive a wedge between me and Crane. Well, it wasn't going to work. "Thanks for the safety tip, Goetzmann," I said. "I'll make a note."

Goetzmann's reaction to what I said seemed extreme. He actually looked as if I'd slapped him. He seemed about to say something else, but thought better of it. He reached down and gathered up the photographs, stuffing them into his inside pocket. "Thank you for the coffee," he told Bert stiffly, and then without looking at me again, he headed for the front door.

Bert got up and started after him, probably planning on seeing the jerk out, like a good hostess. But Goetzmann was already out the door, giving it a little slam behind him.

Bert came to an abrupt halt, or else the door would've hit her in the face. "Well," she said. "Well." She stood there a minute staring at that stupid door, then turned slowly back to me and Crane. "More coffee?" she asked weakly.

Chapter 12

●

BERT

The second Goetzmann left, Crane started apologizing. "I am so sorry about all this," he said, looking first at Nan and then over at me.

Nan didn't give me a chance to reply. She immediately leaped in with, "Oh, Crane, you don't have anything to be sorry about. None of this is your fault."

I turned to stare at Nan. *None* of it? How did she know that? True, Crane could probably be eliminated as a suspect in Louise's murder, since it certainly looked as if he had indeed been with Nan at the time. As for the rest of it, though, I hadn't heard anything that totally exonerated Crane in the deaths of his brother and Marian Fielding. And when you thought about it, it would not have been impossible for him to have hired somebody to kill Louise. So, let me see now, did Nan know something I didn't know? Or was she still tripping through the tulips in New Man's Land?

"Well," Crane was now saying, "I feel bad about it anyway. After all, you two have to get up and go to work tomorrow. The last thing you need is some cop badgering you all night long with questions."

I stopped staring at Nan, and turned to stare at Crane. Goetzmann had hardly been asking questions *all night long.*

It looked to me as if I'd just discovered something that Crane and Nan had in common: Both exaggerated under stress.

How cute.

"It's OK," Nan was now saying. "Really. We don't mind . . ."

I'm not quite sure what she said next. My guess it was something along the lines of *Hey, we LIKE to talk to the police. We look forward to it. Talking to the police is what we do for fun.*

To tell you the truth, I wasn't paying much attention. I was too busy studying Crane, and trying to figure out what it was about the man that made me feel so uneasy. Other than, of course, that he could be a murderer—a thing which apparently should not bother me since it certainly didn't bother Nan.

Other than that one tiny little detail, though, I couldn't think of anything. Crane appeared to be warm, and considerate, and kind. And, let us not forget, one of the best-looking men I'd ever seen. So why didn't I like him?

Maybe it was just that I didn't quite trust anybody who was that smooth. Crane didn't seem to make any mistakes. Even now as he said, "Well, Bert, I guess I'd better be on my way, so you can get some sleep," he moved toward me as effortlessly as if he were skating on ice. There was a hardrock maple end table between him and me, but did Crane bump into the edge like I do at least once a week? Nope, he sort of glided around it, and arrived directly in front of me without missing a beat. "Thanks so much for the hospitality," he said, extending his hand. "You make a great cup of coffee."

I felt like I was in a television commercial, but what could I do? His hand was right there, and he was smiling at me, his eyes crinkling a little at the corners. I took his hand, and was immediately rewarded by a quick squeeze. "You're welcome," I said, returning his smile, and for a moment, staring into Crane's perfect blue eyes, I almost meant it.

Glancing over at Nan, I caught her all-but-dazed "isn't he wonderful" look full force. This was not, of course, the first time I'd seen this look on Nan's face. It was, however, the first time I'd ever seen it when Mr. Wonderful was a possible murderer. Call me picky, but I really did prefer Nan to go out with men who had no chance whatsoever of appearing on *America's Most Wanted* in the near future.

On the other hand, in the grand scheme of Nan's life, who was I to tell her whom to date? My own vast experience with men—translated as, *my ex-husband Jake*, because I'd hardly dated anybody else—did not exactly establish me as an expert in the art of picking out the right man.

Maybe the awful truth was: I was a little jealous. Nan had this gorgeous hunk, and I had nobody. Maybe subconsciously, I was bound and determined to find something wrong with Nan's hunk. It could very well be—on some level I wasn't even aware of—that I really didn't *want* to like him.

Crane had slipped his arm casually around Nan's shoulders, and he was now more or less guiding her toward my front door. "I'll walk you home, OK?" he told her. "I'd worry if I thought you were walking around outside all by yourself at this time of night."

He made it sound as if there were several blocks between my door and Nan's, and that these several blocks were the disputed turf of rival street gangs. The distance between my door and Nan's was less than the width of a pretty narrow building, for Pete's sake, and it was lit all the way by two porch lights and a street lamp across the way. Not to mention, the last time I checked, this was the Highlands area in Louisville, Kentucky. Not L.A. The only gangs you'd ever see in this neighborhood were hordes of little old ladies descending on the local K-Mart every time they had a half-price sale.

Wisely, however, I mentioned none of this.

Nan said, "Thanks, Bert," as she headed out the door, still looking at Crane as if he were some kind of wonderful mirage. What Nan was thanking me for, I wasn't at all sure. What's more, if I read the expression in her eyes correctly, she didn't really feel the least bit grateful to me.

Still I waved almost cheerily at the two of them as Crane—with Nan more or less glued to his side—glided smoothly out my door, down the porch steps, and across the lawn toward Nan's duplex. On the way Crane deftly avoided not one but two bayberry bushes, and neatly sidestepped a clump of irises. Nan, on the other hand, caught the hem of her dress on one of the bayberries, and had to stop and disentangle it from the shrub's thorny clutches.

After that momentary lapse, Crane moved smoothly on, looking back at me with a quiet smile and lifting his hand in one final wave.

I waved back one more time, but as I closed the door behind me, I couldn't help thinking, *Was it possible to get any more polished than Crane?* As my son Brian would've said, Crane was majorly cool.

So why on earth wasn't I impressed? What's more, why didn't I feel more sympathetic toward the man? He'd lost his *twin.* An occurrence that would be so awful, I didn't even want to think about it.

So what was wrong with me? Why didn't I feel sorry for a man who'd clearly been through a horror in the past couple of years?

I was still thinking all this over the next day at work. I didn't have a lot of time to think, of course. When you're a temp in a CPA office, the closer you get to April 15, the more phones you have to answer. And the more paper piles up on your desk. I was so busy directing frantic callers to either Hazlitt, Horn, or McCombs, and at the same time, entering data onto electronic tax forms, that I hardly had time to breathe, let alone think about Crane and my reaction to him. My being so busy—and, yes, distracted—was probably why I didn't notice that I had a visitor until he was already standing at my desk, directly in front of me.

"Morning," he said.

I looked up from the Form 1099 I was typing on, and there was Detective Goetzmann. Just standing there, looking at me, not smiling or anything. In an office filled with ornate French Provincial furniture, Goetzmann—with his marine haircut, his oversized body, and his perpetual scowl—looked distinctly out of place.

"Detective?" I said.

He glanced toward the clock on the far wall. It was three minutes to twelve. "Would—"

That was all he got out before the phone rang again. While I answered it, Goetzmann shifted his considerable weight from one foot to the other as his eyes traveled over every single thing on the top of my desk. You might've thought he was playing that memory game, where they show you so many items on a tray, then take the tray away, and you have to write down what you remember. Watching Goetzmann's alert hazel eyes, always moving, never missing a thing, I'd bet he would win that game every time.

I turned away from Goetzmann a little, to transfer the call, and I could feel Goetzmann's eyes now studying *me*, just as he'd been studying the top of my desk.

I could also feel my cheeks getting warmer the longer he

stared. It always makes me nervous to be stared at. And when I get nervous, I begin to look as if I'd gone a little nuts with the blush-on.

When I could finally hang up, I quickly turned back around to face Goetzmann directly, so he'd stop staring. It didn't quite work. He just stood up a little straighter, his eyes still on my face. "You eat lunch?" he asked.

I blinked, not sure what his intentions were. Was he asking me to lunch? Or was he taking some kind of police survey?

Unfortunately, when I'm nervous, I not only turn several shades of red, I also have a bad habit of blurting out the first thing that pops into my head. "What do you mean by that?" I asked.

A wave of annoyance crossed Goetzmann's face, but was gone in an instant. "I mean, I'd like to take you to lunch." He raised his eyebrows, mutely asking the lunch question again.

I just looked at him while my mind raced. Why on earth did he want to take me to lunch? As soon as I posed the question, the answer came to me. Of course, he wanted to pump me about Nan and her new boyfriend. That was it. He'd tracked me down just to find out if Nan and Crane were serious.

Which brought to mind a question of my own.

"How did you find me?"

Goetzmann shrugged. "Got your current employer from the temp agency. Got the temp agency's name from the police report yesterday." He almost, but not quite, smiled, and for a second there, he looked exactly like Brian Dennehy, you remember, the burly actor I'd mentioned earlier who'd starred in *Cocoon*. "You want lunch, or what?" Goetzmann asked.

How could I refuse such a sweet invitation?

Actually, it didn't even occur to me to refuse. For all I knew, this was some kind of police summons. Not to mention, if Goetzmann intended to pump me for information, I had a few questions of my own.

At noon on the dot, I put the switchboard on automatic pilot, found my purse, and walked out with Goetzmann at my side. He stayed at my side until we got to The Food Factory, a new bistro-style restaurant that had just opened up on Breckinridge Lane only two short blocks from Hazlitt, Horn and McCombs. Goetzmann, believe it or not, was the perfect gentleman, walking between me and traffic all the way, and holding my elbow the entire time.

I would've enjoyed the walk more, and maybe even relished being treated like somebody who needs to be protected from the harsh emissions of passing vehicles, if he had spoken to me even once on the way. Or if he'd even glanced my way. As it was, after the first block, I began to feel as if I were on some kind of forced march.

At The Food Factory, Goetzmann did something that my ex-husband Jake never let me do during nineteen entire years of marriage. Goetzmann actually let me order for myself without criticizing what I chose. Giddy with newfound freedom, I ordered a BLT, a side order of grilled mushrooms, a chocolate milkshake, and a small Coke. Goetzmann didn't even look up from his menu.

Of course, he himself ordered two gigantic double cheeseburgers, two extra-large helpings of fries, a cup of coffee with real cream, and a chocolate milkshake—everything loaded, much like mine, with Carcinogens, Cholesterol, and Caffeine. The three vitamin C's.

I'd like to say that we made pleasant small talk before

the waitress finally showed up with our orders, but unless you considered, "These are good crackers" and "They sure are," fascinating conversation, I'd have to admit we mainly just sat there. Avoiding each other's eyes.

Once we started eating, though, Goetzmann seemed to relax. I only wished I could. My BLT certainly looked appetizing. It had been cut diagonally across, and each half had a little American flag stuck cheerily in the center. Unfortunately, I was barely aware of what I was chewing. I was steeling myself for whatever Goetzmann was about to ask me. I really didn't want to get into any long, drawn-out comparisons between Goetzmann and Crane Morgan.

I knew from past experience that "What does Nan see in him that she doesn't see in me?" was a topic I pretty much wanted to avoid. It never went well. You could tell the ex all night long that the new guy was not superior in any way, but the bare fact was that Nan obviously did not agree. After all, she was with the new guy, wasn't she? That was pretty much an inescapable value judgment.

The only way around this was to insist that Nan was totally deranged, incapable of knowing a good thing when she had one, but this last didn't always fly. Mainly because, amazingly enough, there were a lot of men who found the concept of dating the deranged pretty offensive in itself. They seemed to believe that the implication was, the only women who'd go out with them had to be insane.

When Goetzmann wiped mayonnaise from the corner of his mouth with a napkin and started to actually speak, I could feel myself tense up. "I thought," he said, "that you might want to know that I called up the Daviess County sheriff in Owensboro to get some more information about the murder of Marian Fielding."

I could feel myself relax a little. Oh. We were going to talk about *murder*. Well, then, that was different. Discussing murder would be a cake walk compared to discussing Nan's love life.

I took a large bite of my BLT. "So what did the sheriff say?" I asked.

Goetzmann had just inhaled half of one cheeseburger, and he swallowed before he spoke. "The whole thing went down about two years ago. Marian Fielding was only twenty-five when she died." He popped in a French fry. "Coroner's report said she'd been stabbed repeatedly. Her face was purposely slashed."

I put down my sandwich. So much for lunch. "How could anybody do such a thing? And why on earth would he do it?"

Goetzmann shook his head, studying his burger. "You'd have to ask Lane Morgan about that. One thing for sure, he was very, very piss—" He broke off, giving me a quick glance. "He was real *angry*," he said.

I almost smiled. Lord knows, I'd heard Nan say a lot worse than *pissed*.

Goetzmann hurried on. "Marian Fielding's death was over-kill, pure and simple. Everybody involved in investigating her murder realized that from the get-go. Clearly a crime of passion"—his eyes met mine—"and rage."

With him looking directly at me like that, I started feeling nervous again. If my cheeks weren't turning a little brighter red than a stop sign, I'd be surprised.

"According to the sheriff, Fielding's killer was seen by neighbors on each side of her apartment," Goetzmann went on. "Each neighbor reported seeing the murderer as he ran from the scene of the crime, and each said that it had been one of the twins. *Which* one of the twins, of course, is the sixty-four thousand–dollar question."

I all but caught my breath, staring at him. "Then Crane was a suspect?"

Goetzmann shrugged. "Not really, even though nobody in town could tell the twins apart. You saw those photos—could you?"

I shook my head. "Just because I'm a twin doesn't give me any better ability than you at telling other twins apart, Goetzmann," I said.

Goetzmann nodded, started to go on, and then apparently thought better of it. Taking a deep breath, he said very quickly, "You know, Bert, you can call me Hank. A lot of people do."

I just stared at him. I guess I'd always called him what Nan had always called him. And as I recalled, she'd never called him Hank. He'd always been Goetzmann, even when they were dating.

He continued his story without giving me a chance to say anything. "Crane wasn't a suspect because there were several witnesses who testified about a huge argument between Lane and Marian at a shopping center shortly before she died."

"Does anybody know what the argument was about?" I asked.

"You going to eat that?" Hank answered.

I stared at him blankly, and then realized that he was talking about the other half of my BLT, the part I hadn't taken a bite out of yet. I handed it to him.

He took a big bite, chased it with a sip of coffee, and then, just as I was thinking I'd better repeat the question, he said, "Nobody seemed to know what they'd fought about. They think it might've had something to do with Lane cheating on Marian, because Marian kept yelling, *I can't believe you'd do this to me!* Or something like that."

I frowned. "What a messy scene," I said.

Hank nodded, still swallowing. When he could speak, he said, "It got a lot messier. When an APB was ultimately issued for Lane Morgan, he committed suicide. The body was recovered from the Ohio River ten days later."

Hank seemed to have finished his story, but still, he continued to stare at me.

His hazel eyes were so intense. "What?" I finally said.

Hank took another sip of coffee before he answered. "Bert, would Nan lie about Crane being with her the entire evening, just to protect him?" he asked.

I didn't hesitate even a second. "No, of course not," I said, shaking my head. "Crane is still practically a stranger to her—she's just met the guy, for goodness sake . . ."

I thought I sounded pretty definite, but let's face it, the real question was, could Nan ever tell a lie under the right circumstances? That was like asking if the Pope could ever say the blessing. The more I thought about these particular circumstances, the more I wondered. Nan definitely wouldn't cover up for a murderer, no matter how handsome he happened to be. However, if Nan didn't believe the guy really *was* a murderer, that might be another story. Goodness knows, Nan and I haven't always trusted wholeheartedly in the opinions of the police. If Nan thought the police—in the person of Hank—was just persecuting Crane out of jealousy, she might say anything.

I looked Hank right in the eye. "No," I repeated emphatically, "Nan would never lie."

Hank frowned, and I wasn't sure he was buying it. "My

gut feeling," he said, "tells me that this Crane character is not what he appears to be."

I just looked at him. He was echoing my own sentiments, and yet, I wondered. Were Hank Goetzmann's personal feelings coloring his professional judgment?

"There's something about this guy I don't like," Hank went on.

I couldn't help mentally adding, You mean, other than him dating Nan?

"You watch yourself around him, OK? I don't want anything happening to you," Hank added. He reached across the table to pat my hand. "Or to Nan either," he added belatedly.

I stared back at him, realizing for the first time that Hank's eyes really were not so much hazel, as a light golden brown. And that his big, rough hand felt warm and protective, resting on mine.

Then, of course, it hit me.

Oh for Pete's sake.

I was surprised it had taken me this long to catch on. When it was *so* obvious what Hank Goetzmann was trying to do. He was trying to pull what back in high school Nan and I had called the Old Switcheroo.

It was where a guy who'd been going out with one of us tried to switch in midstream, so to speak, to the other one. Back in high school, the Old Switcheroo had never been successfully accomplished, it being a pretty tricky maneuver. In order to pull it off, the Switcher had to convince both of us that his first choice had somehow been an error in judgment. On both his and the chosen twin's part. Moreover, he had to do this without suggesting in any way that the twin he'd chosen first was somehow lacking.

An important Switcheroo principle was: Insulting one of

us was insulting both of us. Needless to say, the Switcheroo failure rate up to now was 100 percent. In every case, the Switcher had not only failed to land the new twin, he'd lost the twin he'd had in the process. The failure rate, however, could be explained by the maturity level of the boys who'd attempted it. The Old Switcheroo required far more finesse than the average high school kid possessed, no matter what TV shows like *90210* seemed to imply.

Hank Goetzmann had to be in his mid-forties.

That was in his favor.

What was not in his favor, though, was what I already knew about him and Nan. They'd slept together. Several times, according to Nan. So exactly what was I supposed to be—a rerun?

I pulled my hand away. "Well," I said, focusing now pretty much entirely on my plate, "of course, I'll be careful. I'm always careful." I waved my hand in the air. "You don't have to worry about me."

Hank just looked at me for the longest moment, his expression unreadable. "Bert, listen to me," he said, his face grim, "I don't want you or Nan to become another Marian Fielding. For all we know, the man we know as Crane is not Crane at all. Lane could have killed Marian and his brother, and then taken his brother's place."

I shook my head, still avoiding his eyes. "That's pretty far-fetched! I mean, the twins' family would've immediately realized that a switch had taken place, wouldn't they? I know mine and Nan's would know immediately. Sure, *we* can't tell the Morgan twins apart, but their family has got to know—"

Hank was already shaking his burly head from side to side. "I already asked about that. According to the information from the sheriff, the twins' parents are dead. The only family the sheriff is aware of are distant cousins, aunts, and uncles, most of whom live out of state."

"There's nobody?" I asked.

"In Kentucky, there's only a second cousin—a Miss Edna St. Charles," Hank answered. "The Daviess County sheriff only found out about her when she showed up at the funeral for Lane. He talked to her and got an address for her on High Street in Bardstown."

Bardstown is a small town about forty-five miles south of Louisville. Hank was shaking his head again. "The sheriff's guess is that Crane—or Lane—or whoever he is—hardly ever sees this second cousin."

I still couldn't believe that there really could've been a switch. "But what about fingerprints?" I asked. "Surely those would show if the killer was Lane or not."

Identical twins may have identical DNA, but unlike what a lot of people believe, they don't have the same fingerprints. Hank obviously knew that, too.

"Whoever killed Marian Fielding was smart enough not to leave behind any fingerprints on the knife that killed her," Hank said. "He was probably wearing gloves." He popped in several more French fries. "The same goes for Louise Eagleston's killer."

I stared at him, feeling an icicle go down my back. My God. Hank actually seemed to be implying that Marian Fielding and Louise Eagleston had been murdered by the same person.

Hank leaned forward, and for a second, I thought he might be about to pat my hand again. I put my hands in my lap.

Hank seemed not to notice. "I do have an idea, though, on how to find out if there's been a switch," he said. "I've found out that there are fingerprints on file for Crane, but not for Lane. Crane had his prints done as part of a college research project some years ago. So, if we could compare those prints with the prints of the man we now know as Crane, we'd know for sure if it really was him." He took a deep breath, and then added, "That's where you come in."

I swallowed. Well, what do you know. Maybe I'd leaped a little too early at the Old Switcheroo concept. It now looked to me as if Hank wasn't interested in me personally, after all. He was interested in what I might do to help him solve Louise's murder. I sat there, waiting for the big, teddy bear of a guy sitting opposite me to tell me what he wanted me to do, and I felt oddly disappointed.

"Since we have Crane's fingerprints on file," Hank went on, "all you'd have to do is to bring me something with the current Crane Morgan's fingerprints on it. Then I could run a match; and at least, we'd know definitely whom we're dealing with."

I stared back at him, thinking it over. It sounded simple enough. Get a few fingerprints, and get a pretty big question answered once and for all.

Hank's eyes had gotten intense again, looking unwaveringly into mine.

Courageous person that I was, I looked down at my lap.

On the other hand, if I did this and Crane really was a murderer, I would be putting myself in terrible danger.

And yet, if I didn't do this, and Crane really was a murderer, wasn't Nan already in terrible danger?

I lifted my eyes to Hank's. His eyes had the longest eyelashes. I'd never really noticed them before.

Then again, if I did this, and Crane *wasn't* a murderer, I'd be putting myself in the worst danger of all. From Nan.

Still, could I afford to take the chance that Crane wasn't exactly who he said he was? Could Nan?

I made up my mind. Before Nan got in any deeper, she needed some answers, whether she knew it or not.

"OK, Hank," I said, "I'll do it."

Oh dear. Maybe I was the deranged twin, after all.

Chapter 13

●

NAN

Bert was up to something.

I wasn't sure what it was, but she couldn't fool me. In fact, that's the bad thing about being a twin. You know the other one so well, you can tell right away when she's not being completely honest.

Or when she's faking it big time.

It's right there on our mutual face. Like, for instance, right after Goetzmann left, when Crane started being so sweet, actually apologizing to Bert and me about our having to stay up so late and to spend so much time talking to the police. Bert acted as if she agreed with me—that none of this was Crane's fault, so there was no real reason for him to apologize—but I could see that she was faking.

I could see, just as plain as the nose on our face, that Bert was looking holes through Crane and pretty much picturing just how *his* face would look on one of those wanted posters that are always hanging on the wall in the post office. I couldn't believe it. Bert was actually looking at Crane as if she were trying to make up her mind if he could be a murderer or not. *Crane.* Who at that very moment was going on and on about how guilty he felt about our missing our *bed times*, for God's sake. *This* was the man Bert thought could be a three-time killer.

Although how in the world Bert thought Crane could've killed Louise Eagleston was beyond me. I thought I'd made it abundantly clear that he'd been with me the entire evening.

I think Crane might've picked up on Bert's real attitude, too, because he seemed preoccupied when he walked me home. Not that he wasn't the perfect gentleman, because he certainly was. He walked me across the lawn, stood quietly on the porch while I unlocked my door, and then took me into his arms and gave me a good night kiss.

He was the perfect gentleman *par excellence.*

I don't think I've ever been so disappointed.

Crane didn't even *try* to come inside.

All of which goes to show you. Murder can really spoil a mood.

Oh my yes, if spending an hour or so discussing the murder of an acquaintance—with particular reference to the possibility of your having done the deed—well, if that doesn't cool your jets, I suppose nothing will.

Crane did ask if I was free tomorrow night, thank God. Otherwise, I would've worried that, since he'd found out tonight that I used to date the very cop who was now trying to implicate him in multiple murders, Crane's interest in me had cooled for good. Once I told him I was free, he didn't leave me hanging either. Unlike some other guys I've dated who shall remain nameless, Crane said, "Good. I'll pick you up at seven." That was it, though. He made the date for seven, and then he turned immediately and left.

No additional kiss. No hug. No nothing. Yes, indeedy, thanks to Goetzmann and Bert, this evening had taken a major nose-dive in the romance department.

I blamed Bert in particular. Bert and her big mouth. If she hadn't told Goetzmann every single thing Louise Eagleston had said, Crane would not be on Goetzmann's short list of suspects in Louise's murder. Like I believe I've mentioned before, Bert repeated a whole bunch of crap, and she didn't even know that any of the things that Louise had told her was really so.

In fact, as I watched Crane get into his Camry without turning around even once to look back at me, I had an almost overpowering urge to march right back over to Bert's and give her a piece of my mind.

I decided against it, though. As Crane had pointed out, it *was* late. I was far too tired to get into a lengthy debate over whether Crane happened to be homicidal or not.

The next morning, however, I realized I probably should have gone back to Bert's and had it out, after all. Because Bert and her stupid suspicions had been on my mind so much during the night that when my alarm went off, I felt as if I hadn't slept at all. Not to mention, I was still fuming about Bert and the way she'd treated poor Crane when I got to the radio station.

In fact, I was so distracted by the whole situation that I almost allowed dead air after the last Vince Gill song ended. I quickly back-announced the Vince Gill song—meaning I identified the song and the singer after the song had played—and slapped a CD into the CD player, smacking the *play* button with a vengeance. Apparently, the teeny-tiny noise I made was loud enough to go out over the air. It got amplified a little, I guess, so that it ended up sounding a lot like Shania Twain had kicked a metal trash can right before she started singing about any man of hers.

Through the large picture window that separated my con-

trol room from the news room, I saw Dale Curtis's head jerk
up. Dale is the WCKI news director, and usually, as far as
Dale is concerned, I can do no wrong. I am—and I'm quoting
Dale verbatim here—*a groovy chick.* Dale, poor thing, has
never quite gotten out of the seventies. He looks like a cross
between an aging hippie and Less Nessman of WKRP fame—
complete with the snazzy wardrobe—and he talks like a
Simon and Garfunkel lyric.

Even Dale, however, can't quite forgive a screw-up on
the air. When the trash can noise went out over the air, Dale
stared at me as if I'd just farted into the mike. I stuck out
my chin and glared at him, daring him to say one word to
me. Just one word. Dale instantly dropped his gaze.

I, on the other hand, drew a long, disgusted breath. I
could pretend to Dale that my mistake wasn't all that big a
deal, but I couldn't fool myself. Great, just great, I thought.
All this garbage with Bert and Crane was actually affecting
my work.

Not that it was absolutely necessary that Bert like every
guy I date. I mean, I'd known how she'd felt about Chuck—
or rather, Upchuck, as she so affectionately called him. And
Will, whom she'd always called Won't, for some odd reason.
I'd had a pretty good idea exactly what Bert's opinion was
of each of these guys, and it hadn't bothered me. I think Bert
has a perfect right to find the men I go out with unbelievably
nauseating. Lord knows, I'd felt that way about her ex-husband Jake for years before she finally divorced him. However,
bearing all this in mind, I still think that it's not too much to
ask if Bert would kindly refrain from accusing the current
man in my life of murder. Hey, I'm just picky that way.

I was thinking about calling Bert at the accounting firm
where she was working these days and explaining to her

exactly how picky I was when the phone rang. Or rather, it blinked on and off. Phones in the control room are hooked up to colored lights to let the announcers know that there's an incoming call. That way, we don't have the not-so-entertaining sounds of ringing phones going out over the airwaves.

I picked up the phone, not really thinking about it, still going over in my mind what all I intended to say to Bert, even as I said hello.

"Call on line four, Nan," Bambi, our receptionist, said. Bambi usually has the sort of voice you'd associate with hog-calling, but when she answers the phone, her voice becomes low, throaty, and as sexy as she can possibly make it. Hearing that voice, coupled with a name like Bambi, we've had more than one guy drop by the station, expecting to see somebody at the front desk who resembled, oh, say, a young Lauren Bacall. Or maybe even Kathleen Turner. Instead, they meet Bambi, six feet tall and weighing in at 250 pounds. Bambi considers sweatshirts and sweatpants in neon colors appropriate attire for the workplace, and nobody has ever had the guts to tell her any different.

"Thanks, Bam," I said and punched the button for line four.

"Oh God, Oh God, *Oh God!*" The woman's shrill voice on the line bordered on hysterics. "I just saw it in the paper! I just *saw* it! Oh God!"

Oh God indeed. This voice sounded appallingly familiar. "Excuse me?"

"Good gravy! Are you deaf as well as dumb?"

She pronounced the word deaf as if it had two *e*'s. *Deef.* Oh, yes, I recognized the voice, all right. It was Looney Tunes.

I can't say I was glad to hear from her.

"I *said* I just saw the paper!" she was saying. "And oh,

God, he's killed *her* too! Just for trying to help me! Oh, God, what have I done? I should never, *never* have dragged her into this!"

I was too tired to put up with much. "Lady," I said, "what in the world are you talking about?"

The woman stopped crying and took a deep, ragged breath. "Louise Eagleston's been murdered!" she said. *"That's* what I'm talking about! Oh, God, I can't believe Louise is dead!"

My mouth went dry. *Looney Tunes had known Louise Eagleston?* Could this be true? Or had this crazy woman just read about Louise's murder in the paper, and was using what she'd read to try to reel me in one more time?

"I should never have asked Louise to help me!" Looney was saying. "Because I knew—I *knew*—she wouldn't turn me down. On account of us being such good friends back at Daviess County High." Looney sounded as if she were suppressing a sob. "And now I got her killed! I knew Louise had moved to Louisville, so I'd thought she'd be perfect. And now, oh God, I set her up . . ." Her voice trailed off.

I gripped the receiver a little tighter. "Who exactly *is* this?" I asked. "If you want me to listen to you, you've got to tell me who—"

Looney cut me off. "Are you *nuts?*"

She was asking *me* this?

"He's killed Louise, and my sweet thing, and you want me to tell you who I am? Why, you'd tell him, I know you would, and then he'd know that I'm here in town. He'd come looking for me, he would, and . . ."

Looney sounded distinctly paranoid. And yet, as they say, even the paranoid have enemies. And let's face it, Louise really had been murdered.

"Ma'am," I said, trying to cut her off, "listen to me . . ."

The woman ignored me and went right on, her voice cracking a little with the effort. "Louise must've found out that he really is the one who killed Marian! Just like I said. And now he's killed her, too! Oh, God, oh, God, oh . . ."

I felt as if a cold wind had blown through the room. Had I heard this crazy lady right? "Did you say *Marian?*" I didn't really want to know the answer, but I had to ask.

"Of course, I said Marian," Looney snapped, wheezing a little now. "What did you think? I'm talking about my sweet baby. *Marian Fielding.* My poor, poor, poor sweet thing." The more she talked, the weaker her voice sounded. It was barely a rasp when she said that last word.

I put a hand to my head, rubbing my temple. I could feel a headache coming on. It wasn't terribly painful yet, but I could feel the pulse building beneath my fingers. The murder that Looney Tunes had been trying to get me and Bert to look into had been that of Marian Fielding. All this time she'd been talking about the murder that Lane Morgan, Crane's brother, had committed.

As soon as all this occurred to me, everything else fell into place. This, then, was the real reason that Louise Eagleston had introduced me to Crane in the first place. She hadn't been an amateur matchmaker, like she'd told Crane. Louise had introduced me to Crane because an old high school friend—Looney Tunes—had talked her into doing it. Hell, Louise had probably gone to have her portrait taken by Crane in the first place because Looney had put her up to it. Looney here had been making sure that I got involved in her murder case, whether I'd wanted to or not.

And whether I liked Looney's methods or not, it had

worked. I was involved, all right. I thought of Crane, his remarkable good looks, his sweet, gentle manner, his kind smile. Oh, yeah, I couldn't be any more involved. But not in the way Looney had envisioned. "Look," I said, "I want to know who you are and I want to know now."

"Are you crazy?" the woman said. "If . . ." She broke off and began to cough, a great hacking, wet cough that left her voice trembling. "If he knew who I was," she finally rasped, "I might as well just shoot myself and get it over with. Because he's going to kill me, too, he is, just like he killed Louise!"

Listening to this crazy woman, I tried to remain calm. "Ma'am, you keep saying he. Who is this *he* you're talking about?"

Her response, oddly enough, sounded like a cackle. "You know damn well who it is. You want me to spell it out for you? It's Lane or Crane or whatever his name is."

My heart actually seemed to stop. I swallowed, willing myself to sound almost casual, as if this awful woman had not just told a terrible lie about a man I cared about. "Ma'am, you're mistaken," I said. "Crane couldn't possibly have been anywhere near Louise Eagleston's house last night. I was with him all night long, so if—"

I was interrupted by Looney's racking cough. "Fool!" she finally gasped. "You're a damn fool!"

Remaining calm was getting more difficult by the moment. "Ma'am, I'm telling you the truth, I—"

"You're an idiot," Looney snapped.

I was determined not to lose my temper. After all, this woman, whoever she was, did sound ill. In more ways than one, in my opinion. "Ma'am, you need to know that the police think Louise Eagleston might've been killed by a burglar. Her purse was miss—"

Looney coughed again, drowning me out. The woman really should be in a hospital, although it would be a toss-up whether to send her to a regular one or one fitted with nice, soft, padded cells. "Ma'am? Ma'am," I said, beginning again, "regardless of what you think, regardless of what Louise must've led you to believe—"

"Idiot! Louise never led me to believe anything," the woman said. "It was *me* doing the convincing, *me* talking her into—into . . ." Her voice trailed off. There was a moment of total silence, during which I could hear her labored breathing. When she spoke again, her voice was choked with emotion. "Oh dear God in heaven forgive me, I got poor Louise killed!"

My headache was now pounding like a drum on each side of my head. I rubbed my temple again. "Look, whoever you are, listen to me," I said, almost yelling now. "The man who killed Marian Fielding is dead, understand? He's dead. It was Lane Morgan. Not Crane—"

"Lane, Crane, it don't matter—"

My head throbbed. "Of course, it matters. Lane is dead, and—"

"Are you sure?" Looney said.

With my head hurting, I wondered if I'd heard her right. "Am I sure? That he's dead?"

"No! That Lane was the twin that died!"

Oh, for the love of Pete. "Well, of course I'm sure."

At this point I believe, judging from the sound I heard, that Looney snorted. "Then you're a dang fool!" she said, and she slammed the phone down.

The banging of that stupid phone did nothing to help my head.

I just stood there, listening to the dial tone for a long

moment before I finally replaced the receiver. My God. How did you combat this kind of unreasoning rumor? If you couldn't face your accuser, how did you convince people that what was being said about you was nothing but lies?

Now I understood exactly why Crane had left Owensboro. It wasn't just because the place had reminded him so painfully of his brother. It had also been because there was no way to fight this kind of vicious gossip.

And now, what was so awful was that it looked as if all the rumors had followed him to Louisville. In the person of a woman crazy enough to insist that Crane had committed a murder at the same time he'd been with me, and at the same time, not crazy enough to reveal her identity.

As I hung up the phone, I realized my hands were shaking. In front of me, behind the large window, I could feel Dale Curtis's eyes on me, his expression concerned.

I looked away. I segued the next couple of songs, without speaking at all, unable to trust my own voice. This was crazy, that's what it was. What this woman was implying was absolutely nuts. And yet, what if she could make someone else believe what she was saying? She'd apparently made Louise believe it. I didn't for a minute think that Louise's death and Looney's gossip were in any way connected. What I did think, though, was that Looney Tunes could cause an awful lot of trouble for Crane. She could hurt his photography business, she could ruin his reputation, she could make his life miserable.

And the awful thing was, Crane had already gone through enough with the death of his twin.

The phone blinked again, and I jumped, as if I could actually hear the strident ringing sound. If this was Looney Tunes again, so help me, I had had enough. OK, sure she was sick and crazy, but I was going to give her a piece of my mind. A big piece.

"Now what?" I all but barked into the phone.

"Nan? Are you OK?"

It was Bert. All right, in the absence of Looney Tunes, Bert would do just fine. Before Looney had phoned, I'd been about to tell Bert a thing or three about the way she'd treated Crane yesterday. This seemed as good a time as any. "I'm fine," I answered, "but frankly, Bert, I'm really disappointed in you. You let me down. And you let Crane down."

"I couldn't agree more," Bert said. She actually sounded almost cheery. "I've been awful, and I want to make it up to both of you."

I was back to rubbing my temple again. Wait a minute. Had I just wandered into the Twilight Zone? Was my very own twin sister actually going on to say, "I really feel bad about the way I've treated Crane, when I had no reason whatsoever, and when he seems like a very nice guy . . ."

"Uh-huh," I said. Was I imagining things, or was Bert laying it on a little too thick?

"So what I'd love to do is have you two over for dinner. Tonight, OK? I've already started grocery shopping, so please say yes. I feel so guilty, Nan, about the way—"

"—you've been acting," I finished for her. "Uh-huh."

My finishing her sentence must've rattled her a little, because Bert stopped for a long moment, as if trying to remember what she'd been planning to say next. "Uh, yes, that's right. I feel guilty, and I want to make it up to Crane."

"You said that," I told her.

"Yes, so I did," Bert said cheerily. "And I meant it, too. So, Nan, what do you say? You two will come, won't you?

Around, oh, I don't know, around seven? So I won't feel guilty anymore?"

This was a novel approach. Evidently, *I* was to feel guilty if I didn't help Bert get over feeling guilty.

On the other hand, it was, after all, a free meal, and one I knew would be done to perfection. Unlike yours truly, Bert is a wonderful cook. I've, in fact, been sure for years now that when we were dividing up characteristics and genes and whatever between us, Bert got 100 percent of the cooking gene. I, on the other hand, got the looking gene. That is, the looking-up-the-nearest-carry-out-in-the-phone-book gene.

So, let me see, on the positive side, we had a free meal, good food, and the possibility that once she got to know him, she might stop mentally fitting Crane for handcuffs.

On the negative side, Bert's sudden willingness to social-ize with me and Crane did seem a bit suspect.

"It's just going to be the three of us?" I asked. Not that I didn't trust Bert, mind you, but I did want to protect her. From me. If, oh, say, Detective Hank Goetzmann or any one of Louisville's Finest happened to show up at dinner, I'd have to kill Bert.

I really didn't want that to happen.

Not in front of Crane anyway.

"Oh, Nan." Bert's tone was gently scolding. "Of *course* it's just going to be the three of us! I want to get to know Crane better. I couldn't do that if there were a whole bunch of people around!"

True, and Hank Goetzmann could qualify as a whole bunch all by himself.

"OK," I said. "Let me give Crane a call, and see if he'd like to."

I guess I was halfway hoping that Crane would say no,

he'd rather spend a nice, intimate evening alone with me, but he didn't. As luck would have it.

In fact, he actually sounded pleased that Bert had invited him. "Tell her I'm looking forward to it," he said, his deep voice booming over the phone.

When I relayed his message, Bert sounded every bit as pleased as Crane. "Great! I'm looking forward to it, too!" Bert said.

Uh-huh.

"This is going to be such fun!" Bert added.

Like I said before, Bert was up to something. Maybe at her little dinner, I'd find out what.

Chapter 14

●

BERT

If I do say so myself, the dinner party for Crane and Nan was absolute perfection. At least, it started out that way. For once, my apartment was sparkling clean, boasting genuine vacuum cleaner tracks on the carpet and smelling of Lemon Pledge furniture polish. And appropriately enough, my lemon steak main course came out just right—not too much clove and the round steak so tender, you could cut it with a fork.

I'd set the table with my Gorham silverware and my Lenox dinnerware. I even had sprigs of parsley to garnish each plate, and in the center of the table an arrangement of daisies, carnations, and sweetheart roses that I'd picked up at the Kroger supermarket on the way home from work. I was still not quite convinced that the flowers you got at a grocery were just as good as those you got at a real florist, but according to their TV commercials, Kroger had done the blanket of roses last year for the Kentucky Derby. If Kroger was good enough for Churchill Downs, I guess it was good enough for me.

Having been a housewife for almost twenty years before Jake left me for younger pastures, I wasn't surprised to find myself stepping right back into the role of hostess without missing a beat. It was kind of ironic really—the one job I'd done well, I'd been fired from. It would seem then that *housewife* is the only occupation in this country where it's legal to be fired for age discrimination.

Not that it's all that great a job, of course—the hours are lousy, and the pay even worse, particularly if your husband is a tightwad like Jake. And when you're acting as hostess for a dinner party, it can be nerve-wracking.

As a matter of fact, this last was the only thing about the Nan-and-Crane dinner that did not start out in the perfection category. From the moment Nan and Crane walked in my front door, I was—to use one of Brian's favorite phrases— a *rervous neck*. I wasn't sure why exactly. It could've been because I was sure that Nan had to suspect that something was up. I didn't often have sudden inclinations to cook for her and whomever she was currently dating. As a matter of fact, I'd never had the inclination before.

Even if her date somehow got the idea that I didn't like him, I'd never felt particularly anxious before now to mend fences. UpChuck and Won't both pretty much knew—long before Nan finally got around to dumping them—that they were not exactly on my list of favorite people. For one thing I'd avoided them like the plague. I'd never made either one of them so much as a sandwich.

Given all this as background, I knew Nan had to know there were ulterior motives at work here. That was no doubt why I was so rattled. It wouldn't have been so bad if she hadn't been my twin. Because, of course, Nan knew that I knew that she knew about my hidden motives. And I knew that she knew that I knew that she knew, etc., etc., etc.

Well, it's easy to see how keeping track of all *that* could drive a person berserk. It was no wonder I was a wreck. The instant Nan laid eyes on me, she'd be able to tell just how rattled I was. Which would make me even more rattled.

"Welcome, welcome, welcome!" I said as I waved Nan and Crane into my living room. "It's so nice of you to come!" My smile was already beginning to hurt.

Crane's smile was as wide as mine, but he didn't look as if he were in any pain whatsoever. "Well, it's so nice of you to invite us," he said. He was dressed perfectly for dinner at a friend's house—tan slacks, lightweight navy blazer, and a soft blue sweater that matched his eyes.

Nan, for once, was not wearing jeans. She had on an Ann Taylor silk print dress with a scoop neckline, cap sleeves, a wide belt, and a flowing, ankle-length skirt—a dress that I immediately recognized as my own. I'd been looking for the thing on and off for about two months. The instant I saw Nan walk up in it, I remembered that I'd loaned it to Nan on the strict promise that she'd return it to me as soon as she had it dry-cleaned.

Evidently, getting something dry-cleaned these days took months.

"What a lovely dress," I said as Nan glided by me.

"This old thing?" she answered with a knowing smile. "I've had it forever."

I couldn't argue with that.

"And for our lovely hostess, a little gift . . ." Crane's deep voice seemed to fill my entire apartment as he produced, with a flourish, a bottle of Cabernet Sauvignon.

"Why, thank you so much," I said as Nan's eyes seemed to say, *See? See how wonderful Crane is?*

The man was smooth, I'd give him that.

When I asked if anybody would like something to drink, Crane waited until Nan answered first. Then, when she asked for "just a Coke," he, too, nodded and said, "That's just what I was going to ask for."

Nan beamed. Her eyes this time said, *One more thing Crane and I have in common.*

I looked away so Nan couldn't see my own eyes saying, *Gag me.*

While we all drank our Cokes—I'd gone with the majority—Crane entertained us with amusing anecdotes about well-known people in Louisville whom he'd photographed—Denny Crum, the U of L basketball coach, Muhammad Ali, and Mayor Jerry Abrams, the man a local radio station—not Nan's—refers to as Mayor for Life. When our Cokes were gone, and we headed into the dining room, Crane held Nan's chair for her. He didn't make a big deal of it either. He just pulled out Nan's chair and held it for her just as if it were the most natural thing to do in the world.

He would've done the same for me except that I didn't sit down right away. I was trotting back and forth from the kitchen, bringing in food, and yes, whisking our empty Coke glasses away—like your basic good little waitress.

Nan's and my glasses went into the dishwasher. Crane's glass I carefully placed on the cutting board on top of the dishwasher—like your basic good little undercover detective.

One down, I thought, and several more to go.

I'd decided that getting just one glass with Crane's fingerprints on it would not be enough. I'd read somewhere that fingerprints smear, and that even on the most perfect surfaces, you can still end up with only partial prints. Then, too, I'm such a klutz, I've broken quite a few things, just carrying them inside from the car. Given my record as a klutz and the risk of partial prints, it seemed to me I ought to amass as many Crane-fingerprinted glasses as possible. That way, if I didn't dazzle Goetzmann with quality, I'd get him for sure with quantity.

Toward that end, I got four wineglasses out of my kitchen cabinet, and hurried back into the dining room. While Crane poured the Cabernet Sauvignon into the wineglasses, I served us all large helpings of lemon steak, asparagus tips, rice pilaf, and green beans almondine.

The whole time I was spooning all this onto our plates, I could feel Nan's eyes. Which, of course, made me an even worse *rervous neck*. I'd worn my navy blue Laura Ashley dress with the deep side pockets so that I could hide my hands if I got terribly nervous and my hands started shaking. And yet, how can you hide your hands when you're serving dinner?

Nan blatantly stared at my hands for a good minute before she reached over and took the serving spoon and fork right out of my grasp. "Here, Bert, let me do that," Nan said. Her voice was saccharine-sweet. "You've done *far* too much already."

I gave her a quick, sideways glance. Had she already caught on? Did she suspect that I was putting together a Crane glass collection?

I hurried back out to the kitchen to get a stainless steel pitcher of water I'd left chilling in the refrigerator. No, Nan couldn't possibly know. If she did, she'd be yelling at me. And maybe throwing things.

When I returned and began pouring water in the water goblets I'd placed to the right of each dinner plate, Nan had finished serving. "Do you want me to help you bring anything in from the kitchen?" Nan asked.

I, of course, immediately flashed on the glass sitting on

the cutting board. My luck, this would be the first time in her life that Nan would load the dishwasher without being told. "Oh, no!" I said. I guess I sounded a little too forceful because Nan's eyes widened. I quickly added, "Tonight I'm doing it all. I want you to stay right where you are—and just relax."

Nan didn't reply. She just looked at me, her eyes getting significantly smaller. Oh my, yes, she was suspicious, all right.

"Wow, this is really good," Crane said after we'd all sat down and he'd tasted the lemon steak. Looking over at Nan, sitting opposite him, he added with a teasing smile, "So I guess you're a good cook, too, since you and Bert are identical?"

Nan smiled, and took a sip of her wine. "Bert hogged all the domestic genes, I'm afraid."

Crane paused in the middle of eating another piece of steak, and looked over at me. Seated on Crane's left, at the head of the table, I smiled and shrugged.

"I, on the other hand, firmly believe," Nan went on, "that the only utensil you really need in the kitchen is a can opener. Or a phone."

Before I mention what I did next, I want to make it abundantly clear that I was very nervous. And that, when I'm nervous, I sometimes laugh a little too loudly. When Nan said what she said, I laughed far louder than I intended. The sound seemed to bounce off the walls around us. "Oh, Nan," I said, still chuckling, "you just *kill* me!"

The instant I realized what I'd said, I froze. I didn't exactly clap my hand over my mouth, but the silence that immediately followed was so awkward, I might as well have. As my cheeks burned, I tried to fix it. Like an idiot. "I mean, that is, what I meant to say was that you're funny, Nan. Not that other. I don't know why I said that even. And, Nan, you cook fine—you really do—you're a great cook!"

Nan, oddly enough, did not seem bowled over by the compliment. She was looking at Crane, her expression concerned.

I, on the other hand, was looking for a sharp object with which to cut out my tongue.

Crane took a deep breath. "You know," he said slowly, his eyes on my face, "you are very sweet. But you don't have to watch every word you say around me, OK? I'm pretty tough, I think I can take it."

I just looked at him. He was obviously trying to put me at ease. Could it be that he really was just a nice guy?

"We don't have to avoid certain subjects either," Crane went on. "In fact, I think it would be a relief for me to be able to talk freely. OK? Is it a deal?"

"It's a deal," I said.

Crane's grin grew even wider. He picked up his fork again and pointed it at me. "Oh, and Bert? You are one *killer* cook."

At that, I had to grin back at him. "Why, thank you," I said.

Crane took another bite of his steak, and looked across the table at Nan.

She was still looking concerned.

Crane smiled at her. "Nan, don't look so worried, OK? If I weren't pretty tough, how do you think I could've gotten through that little interview last night with the police? That guy actually seemed to think I'd murdered poor Louise Eagleston."

Nan immediately jumped on that one. "Nonsense, Crane. Goetzmann was just being a pain in the neck. I don't think he seriously suspected you for an instant. How could he? He knew you were with me."

I didn't say a word. In fact, I chose that particular moment to begin buttering a dinner roll.

Crane shook his head. "I don't know. If he didn't seriously suspect me, he sure could've fooled me."

Again, I said nothing. Of course, by then I was taking a bite out of my dinner roll so it looked as if I was just being polite and not talking with my mouth full.

"I think what Goetzmann suspected was that you were going out with me. *That's* what he suspected," Nan said. Frowning, she bit into an asparagus tip.

I continued to say nothing.

"I'm still in shock about poor Mrs. Eagleston. I can't believe anybody would hurt that nice woman," Crane said.

Finally, somebody was saying something I could agree with wholeheartedly.

"I can't believe it either," I said.

Crane turned toward me as soon as I spoke. "It must've been awful for you. Finding her like that."

Nan, of course, was now staring directly at me, her eyes eloquent once again. They all but yelled, *Does this guy sound like somebody who could commit murder?*

I turned away from Nan, and concentrated on Crane. "It was pretty terrible."

Crane took another bite of his steak, chewed it thoughtfully, and then said, "You know what bothers me is that if the police really are looking at me as the one who did this, then whoever really did it is getting away. He's out there somewhere, and he's dangerous."

Nan, of course, was nodding agreement with everything Crane said.

Crane took another bite, swallowed, and then went on, "I wonder if it really was a burglar, or somebody Mrs. Eagleston knew." He turned again to look at me. "Of course, I guess if it was somebody she knew, she would've said something to you."

I shook my head. "She wasn't saying a whole lot, regardless. In fact, the only thing I remember her saying was one word. *Too.*"

Crane frowned. "Too?" He looked over at Nan, and then back at me again. "What do you mean, *too?*"

I just looked at him for a moment, wondering. Should I be telling him all this? Crane had been right; he *was* a suspect. Hank Goetzmann clearly thought Crane might've hired someone to kill Louise.

And yet, if Crane was guilty, what good would knowing what Louise had said do him? And if he wasn't guilty, maybe this was something he ought to know. Maybe it might explain to him why Goetzmann had homed in on him.

"Well," I said, "it could be too, as in *t-o-o.* Or it could've been two, as in *one, two.* Louise didn't really make herself clear, and right after that she lost consciousness." I took a deep breath, and tried not to think of poor Louise's last moments. "Also, I'd just told her that the paramedics were coming, so she could've just been telling me that they were going to get there too late." I swallowed against the lump in my throat. "Because, well, that was what happened. She was already dead when they arrived."

Nan's eyes now held nothing but sympathy. "Good heavens, Bert, it must've been just terrible."

Crane looked sympathetic, too. As he reached for the salt shaker, he said, "It sounds like a nightmare." He was reaching across the table right in front of me, and as he did so, his sleeve slipped up, to a point just above his wrist. I could see a small tattoo on his left arm, just above the wrist. It was a bright purple flower—a forget-me-not. I couldn't remember precisely, but it sure seemed to me like the same flower I'd seen in the photographs Louise had given me.

I couldn't help staring at the little flower. Maybe, when Louise had said "two," she'd mumbled the first part. Maybe what Louise had actually said was "Tat-*too*."

Crane salted his steak, returned the shaker to the center of the table, and then said, "What I don't understand, though, is how Mrs. Eagleston came by all that information about me and Lane. I really didn't know her at all. So how did she find out all that?" As he said this last, he looked straight at me, as if he fully expected me to offer an explanation.

I didn't have one. "It's a mystery to me."

I glanced over at Nan, and oddly enough, she wasn't looking at me for once. Instead, she suddenly seemed preoccupied with cutting her lemon steak into small pieces. When she lifted a bite to her mouth, her eyes remained on her plate.

I wasn't about to draw attention to her by staring, but if I didn't know better, I'd say that Nan knew something about where Louise had gotten her information. And she did not intend to discuss it at the moment.

Which left me, of course, with the question: Did Nan want to avoid discussing it in front of me? Or in front of Crane?

Crane was now working on his asparagus tips. "You don't suppose," he said between bites, "Mrs. Eagleston could've been one of those people who get obsessed with famous murder cases. What happened two years ago in Owensboro didn't make national news, but it was all over the paper down there for a while. Maybe that's where Mrs. Eagleston got all her information. After all, it seemed to me that everything she told you, she could've gotten from the Owensboro *Messenger-Inquirer* or television."

I stared at him. Could that be true? Had Louise Eagleston been some kind of murder groupie? I remembered reading in the newspaper about how Jeffrey Dahmer and Ted Bundy had received fan mail in jail from all these women who'd become fascinated by them.

Still, the idea of Louise Eagleston, of all people, obsessed with a sensational murder seemed pretty far-fetched.

Across the table from me, Nan continued to dissect her lemon steak, saying nothing.

The subject was pretty much dropped then, to my relief. We talked of books we'd read and movies we'd seen, and the food in front of us quickly disappeared. At one point Crane reached over and sort of patted my hand. "You know," he said, "it's really nice to be here. Lately I've come to realize what a privilege it is to be invited to somebody's house."

He was smiling, but I could see the sadness in his eyes. Had he been shunned by a lot of his former friends after the deaths of his brother and Marian Fielding?

I returned his smile, but I felt a little sick inside. In my mind's eye I could see Crane's glass sitting out on the cutting block in my kitchen. All ready to hand over to the police.

I was a first-class jerk, no doubt about it. Because even after Crane said all that, even after I really did feel sorry for him, I still watched until he'd drunk all his water, and then hopped up to refill his glass. And once I was out in the kitchen, I still put the glass he'd just drank out of right next to the one already sitting on the cutting board, and I got him a brand new one out of the cupboard.

Oh, yes, I was a total jerk. I continued to be one as I served the strawberry shortcake with ice cream, and I brought Crane another glass of wine. And one more glass of water.

As Crane and Nan were leaving, Crane took a moment to kiss my cheek and say, "Thanks." He started to go past me—Nan had already gone out the door, and was standing out on the sidewalk, waiting for him—and then, he stopped. Leaning close to me, he said, "I guess you know I was pretty nervous when I first got here. I know you're an important person in Nan's life, and—well—I wanted to make a good impression. Thanks for making me feel so welcome."

I wasn't sure what to say. I continued to smile, but my mind went totally blank. "Good," was finally all I came up with.

That didn't seem like enough so I added, "Glad you came by."

That seemed pretty lame, so I added to *that*, "It sure was fun, wasn't it?"

Oh God.

Crane still wasn't on his way. As a matter of fact, he was actually taking a step closer and lowering his voice. "You know, Bert, you and I have something in common. You love Nan, and—well, so do I."

I did my best to look pleased to hear this, but let me tell you, it was not easy. Mainly because I was thinking the entire time, *Wait a second, this man is saying he's in love, and he's only been going out with Nan for three days?* It wasn't quite as unbelievable as love at first sight, but it was close. Love at first *week?*

I waved at Nan and Crane as they started across the lawn toward his Camry, and then I went back inside, closing the door firmly behind me.

I headed straight for the kitchen, and yes, the cutting

board with the glasses sitting on top. There were six of them now, six glasses with Crane's fingerprints hopefully all over them. Holding each glass by its edge, I slipped them, one by one, into separate plastic baggies, and then I packed the baggies in a nice lidded wicker basket. In between the glasses I stuffed old newspapers for cushioning.

That done, I phoned Goetzmann.

Goetzmann sounded surprised and pleased. "My, that was quick. Well, bring them on over."

I wasn't sure I'd heard him correctly. "Bring them over?"

"Sure," Hank said. "It's not too late for you, is it?"

I was losing the thread. "You want me to bring the glasses to you right now?"

"Is that a problem?" Hank asked. He sounded amused.

"Oh, no, no problem at all," I said. "Do you want me to meet you at the police station?"

"No, bring them to my place. I don't live too far from you," he said.

I hesitated. I knew very well that I was probably the last woman in America who still felt the way I did. Be that as it may, from the time we were thirteen on, Mom had drilled it into Nan's and my heads that nice girls never, never, *never* go alone to a gentleman's apartment. When you're thirteen, three *never's* really make an impression. Unless, of course, you're Nan. Nan had told me recently that she'd always interpreted what Mom had said to us back then to mean that you could not go alone to a guy's apartment if he was a gentleman. If he had no manners whatsoever, you could drop by his place anytime you wanted.

This could possibly explain some of the men Nan has seen fit to date.

Unlike Nan, wouldn't you know, I took what Mom had

to say to heart. Even now, at almost forty, I still felt more than a little strange agreeing to meet a man all by myself at his place. However, I couldn't help remembering that crack Hank had made about my being a woman of the world. With the definite implication that I was *not* one. I could only imagine what he'd say if I told him about Mom's three *never's*. I took a deep breath. "Sure," I told Hank, "I'll bring the glasses right over."

Hank gave me his address, told me directions, and I got off the phone as quickly as I could before I could change my mind. Grabbing the wicker basket and my purse, I headed out the door.

I was halfway to my car when I noticed something that stopped me right in my tracks.

Crane's Camry was no longer parked at the curb in front of my apartment. It was now sitting in Nan's driveway.

Obviously, Crane had not gone home after he'd walked Nan over to her apartment.

He was still over there with her right this minute. And unless I was hallucinating, I didn't see any lights on.

Oh dear.

Chapter 15

●

NAN

Crane and I had intended to go out for a drink after Bert's little dinner party.

It's true. That had been the original plan.

As soon as Bert closed her door, Crane had turned to me, smiling. "Your sister is wonderful," he'd said.

I can't say I'd been thinking the same thing. All through dinner, in fact, I'd thought that Bert had been acting awfully strange. Even for Bert. If I hadn't known better, I'd have sworn that she was wearing a wire. Or that she'd had the police come in and bug her entire apartment. So that every word we said was being recorded somewhere in the hopes that Crane would mutter something incriminating between the entree and dessert.

Of course, I knew all that was just my imagination talking. Bert would never really do such a thing. She may have been a little suspicious of Crane at first, but after tonight, when she'd seen firsthand how sweet he was, I was sure he'd won her over. She'd actually looked a little guilty several times during dinner.

The dinner, to give credit where credit was due, had been a pretty big success. As far as I was concerned, there had been only one really bad moment. That was when Bert and Crane had started talking about how Louise could've possibly known all that she knew about what had happened in Owensboro. I was well aware, of course, that I could've mentioned Looney Tunes right then, and I could've repeated everything she'd said about how she'd persuaded Louise to look into Marian Fielding's murder for her. Looney Tunes might have indeed played a big part in getting Louise the information Crane and Bert were talking about, but I didn't want to bring it up. We were having a perfectly nice dinner, and there was no real reason to spoil the evening.

Besides, I wasn't even sure Looney really had known Louise. Looney might just be, well, *looney*. And even if she was for real, what did I know about her? I didn't know her name, or where she lived, or anything else. All I knew was that she sounded ill, and that she said she'd known Louise back in high school. Hell, she'd also sounded totally convinced that Crane had killed Louise, and I knew for a fact that was impossible. So why tell Crane that there might actually be somebody out there who believed him so guilty, she wouldn't even let a little thing like *facts* change her mind? It had been so nice to see him smiling and looking carefree for a change. As if, for the moment anyway, a shadow had been lifted from his face.

Now, on the way to the car, Crane was still looking almost carefree as he reached over and took my hand. We continued walking toward the car, hand in hand, like two teenagers going steady.

I was sure I had never felt so comfortable with anybody before. It was hard to believe I'd only met Crane three days earlier. How had I come to feel as if I knew him better than anybody else I'd dated, in such a short time? How had that happened?

When we were only a few steps from Crane's Camry, he said, "You know, this has been such a nice evening, I don't want it to end just yet. Would you like to go and get a nightcap somewhere?"

I didn't even hesitate. "I'd love to." Crane put his arm around my shoulders as we approached the passenger side of his Camry. I couldn't help shivering a little. I wasn't sure whether it was Crane being so intoxicatingly close, or the chill of the night air cutting through the thin fabric of Bert's dress.

Crane evidently voted for the night air theory. "You should get a coat," he said. "Come on, I'll drive you to your front door, so you don't have to get your shoes wet, walking through the wet grass." He opened the passenger door, and held it for me until I got inside.

Then he pulled the Camry into Bert's driveway, made a T-turn, and then pulled into mine.

That, then, is how Crane's car ended up parked in my driveway.

How the rest of it happened, though, I'm still not quite sure. Crane and I headed into my apartment, talking about where we'd like to go for a nightcap. We decided on The Brewery, a late-night spot only minutes away down Bardstown Road, and while I looked through my living room closet, trying to find my lightweight tan wool coat, Crane just stood there, leaning against the wall, watching me. Oddly enough, his watching me made me shiver even more than I had outside.

It also made me so rattled, I couldn't locate my damn coat.

"Do you want me to help you look?" Crane asked, moving to stand next to me.

My heart was pounding so loud, I could barely hear him, but I turned to tell him no, I'd probably loaned the coat to Bert, so maybe I'd just wear my trenchcoat. That's what I *meant* to tell him anyway. I'm not sure I got out even one word, though, because the second I turned toward him, Crane pulled me into his arms.

"You are so damn beautiful," Crane said.

I just looked at him. I have never in my lifetime ever thought that I was beautiful. No offense, Bert. She and I are attractive enough, I suppose—we probably wouldn't frighten dogs or small children—but beautiful, we most definitely are not. I know this, and yet, hearing Crane say it made my breath catch in my throat.

His eyes were so intense, I could hardly bear to look at him. "Crane—"

Before I could say anything more, Crane kissed me.

Long and slow and deep.

Until whatever I'd been about to tell him went right out of my head.

Until I actually felt as if I were falling into his kiss, down, down, down to a place where there was nothing in the world but the dizzying sensation of Crane's lips on mine.

His hands moved down my back, pressing me closer, and somewhere in the back of my mind, a small voice said, *Whoa, slow down, girl, think this over.* And yet, with each kiss, each caress, that voice got fainter. And fainter.

By the time Crane carried me over to the couch, leaning away from me for just a moment to snap off the lights, I couldn't hear anything—except the ragged thunder of our breathing and the pounding of our hearts.

Chapter 16

●

BERT

Hank Goetzmann was right. He really didn't live very far from Nan's and my duplex. His apartment was in Mosswood, one of several very nice apartment complexes just off Breckinridge Lane. Which was only a ten-minute drive from Napoleon Boulevard, if you took a shortcut through Cherokee Park.

It was a good thing that Hank's apartment was so close. Not just because I didn't have so far to drive either. Although I would be the first one to admit that I've never been any too crazy about driving in the dark.

No, his apartment being close was a good thing on this particular night because it meant that I only had about ten minutes or so to worry about everything. *Everything*, of course, being Nan and Crane, and whether or not—to be blunt—they were at that very moment doing what my son so delicately calls "the wild thing."

I wanted to believe that Nan would never go to bed with somebody she didn't know any better than she knew Crane—that surely she'd put her libido on hold until she found out for certain if Crane could possibly be a murderer. I decided, however, just as I was turning into the entrance to Mosswood, that if I really did believe such a thing, Nan probably had a bridge she wanted to sell me.

And when you come right down to it, who was I to say that Nan was in the wrong here? At least, she had the courage to jump right in and take a chance. Me, I was so cautious, it was beginning to look as if I might be spending the rest of my life on the sidelines, watching other people have a love life.

True, Jake's suddenly taking off with a girl only a year older than our daughter had been a bit of a shock. It had left me wondering if I'd ever really known the man—after living with him for over nineteen years. It had also left me seriously questioning how good a judge of people I really was.

Still, there was such a thing as being too cautious. The number of dates I'd had since Jake and I were divorced, I could count on one hand. And I'm just talking *dates* here— going out to eat, or going to a movie, but certainly not going anywhere even close to bed.

I might as well face it. My love life would not change one iota if I joined a convent tomorrow.

As I mentioned earlier, thank heavens I didn't have much time to pursue this cheery line of thought. I'd just passed a sign marked POOL, and Hank had told me that his apartment was the fifth apartment building past the pool entrance, on my left. I started counting buildings.

I'd planned to just hand the basket of glasses over to Hank and then get out of there. However, when he opened the door, he immediately handed me a glass filled with Coke and ice.

"What's this?" I said.

Hank just shrugged. "Well, I knew you and your sister seem to be crazy about Coke, so as soon as I heard you pull up, I fixed you one."

I stared at him. What a sweet thing for him to do. "Why,

thank you," I said. As I took the Coke, I handed Hank the wicker basket.

It would've been awkward to continue to stand outside on his porch while I drank the Coke he'd fixed for me, so I moved past him into his apartment.

Trying, of course, to put Mom's three *never's* right out of my mind.

For a bachelor pad—as Mom, no doubt, would call it—Hank's apartment was a big disappointment. I don't know, I guess I expected to see mirrors on the ceiling, nude pinups on the wall, and empty beer cans all over the floor. Instead, everything was as tidy as my own apartment. Hank's wall-to-wall carpet sported fresh vacuum cleaner tracks, and unless my nose deceived me, that was the unmistakable scent of furniture polish in the air.

I tried not to look surprised, but it wasn't easy. No wonder Hank Goetzmann and Nan had not exactly hit it off. I would imagine that if Hank ever saw Nan in her natural habitat—also known as her apartment—he might've gotten the hint that they were seriously incompatible. Furthermore, if he'd tried to suggest that she tidy up a bit, he might've also realized that Nan did not respond well to any sentence that contained the phrases *you should* or *you ought*. How she responded to sentences containing *you'd better*, I believe, goes without saying.

Actually, this is one of the things about Nan that I've always admired. She doesn't let anybody boss her around. I've often wished that I could be more like her, in this respect. I certainly wouldn't have spent so many years taking orders from Jake.

"So what's this?" Hank had followed me into his apartment, closed the door behind us, and he was now peering into the wicker basket. "You bring me a picnic?"

When he looked back up at me, he was actually smiling. I hadn't seen Hank smile too many times before. Somehow what few times I'd run into him when he was dating Nan, he'd usually been scowling—a thing which, I guess, should have also given me a hint as to how their relationship was going.

When Hank smiled, it took ten years off his face.

I smiled back at him. "Well, I wanted to make sure I got at least one good fingerprint, and I was afraid that some of them might be smeared. Or that, rattling around in that basket, the glass might get broken." I was beginning to feel a little foolish. Hank was peering into the basket again. "So I brought you, uh, more than one glass that Crane handled."

Hank was hefting the basket with one hand, as if weighing the thing. "More than one?" he repeated.

I took a long sip of Coke before I answered him. "Six," I said. "I brought you six."

Hank's eyes widened. "What did you have him do, unload the dishwasher?"

I took another sip of Coke. I was no longer feeling a *little* foolish. I was feeling a *lot* foolish. I mean, my God, why didn't I just go to the nearest mental health facility and turn myself in? Apparently, I was obsessive-compulsive to the max, a textbook case. I needed help. Or I was just thorough.

I cleared my throat. "Well, I wanted to make sure, you know, that I got you what you asked for."

Hank nodded. "Right," he said, putting the basket down on top of his gleaming coffee table. He must've picked up on what an idiot I felt like because right away he started going on and on about what a good job I'd done. "That was good thinking," he said. "You never know what could happen. So it's always a good idea to cover your bases." His voice trailed off, as if maybe he'd run fresh out of words. Apparently, however, after just a moment's pause, he found a new batch. "In fact, Bert, you did absolutely right. Hey, I only wish I'd thought of it myself."

I just looked at him. Was I imagining things, or was he laying it on a bit thick?

Hank was nodding again. "Oh, yeah, I wish I'd just asked you in the first place to get me—"

"Six," I finished for him.

Hank cleared his throat. "Right," Hank said. "Six."

He looked at me for a long moment.

I looked at him.

And then we both grinned.

"OK," I said, "so maybe I was a little overzealous."

Hank shrugged, still smiling. His eyes crinkled at the corners, and for a moment, I could see the little boy he used to be.

The little boy who'd grown up to be a cop.

"Here, let me take your coat," he said.

I sort of hated to give up my coat. It would make it that much more difficult to leave. His apartment was warm, however. He had a fire going in his fireplace, for God's sake. And short of just telling him, "No, I'd like to keep my coat with me in case I suddenly feel the need to bolt for the door," I couldn't think of a good reason not to let him take it.

"Thanks," I said. There was an awkward moment while Hank helped me out of my coat, and I more or less juggled my glass, passing it from hand to hand, trying not to dump Coke all over his freshly vacuumed carpet.

I had my coat off before it occurred to me that I could've

just put the glass of Coke down. On an end table or something. And yet, for some stupid reason, I'd gotten so rattled, having Hank stand so close as he helped me, that I hadn't even thought of it.

I watched Hank as he walked over to the closet right next to his front door, took out a wooden coat hanger, and draped my coat over it. What was it about this man that made me so nervous? I mean, I knew he was a cop and all, but I didn't think he was going to give me a ticket for Coke spilling.

"By the way, I've talked to Bentley Shepard, Crane's partner," Hank said. His back was still toward me as he finished hanging up my coat and closed the closet door.

"Oh?" I said.

"Yeah," Hank said, turning around. He looked a little surprised to see me still standing. Waving toward his living room at large, he said, "Sit down."

I was sure that was supposed to be an invitation, rather than a direct order. I looked over the room, trying to decide where I should sit.

Now that I had a moment to really look the place over, I recognized the decorating scheme immediately. It was Contemporary Divorce. According to Nan, it's a style you see in a lot of men's apartments these days. After a divorce, the man is often the spouse who ends up with the worst furniture that the couple had owned together.

After a time of living on his own, he starts adding a few nice pieces here and there. What he ends up with is, well, exactly what Hank's apartment looked like. There was probably some formula that could be applied, which would involve counting the total number of nice pieces in this entire apartment, the total number of beat-up pieces, factoring in Hank's salary, and you could figure out exactly how long Hank had been divorced.

The sleek walnut bookcase with beveled glass doors, standing on my left, looked relatively new, but it didn't match at all the frayed Queen Anne chairs and the scarred Early American coffee table. He had two table lamps and a floor lamp, but none of them went together. There were mismatching end tables, one Early American and one Danish Modern. His sofa, however, was obviously the best piece in the room—a glove-soft beige leather sectional, just a little older than the bookcase—and it didn't look as if it went with anything else in the room.

I headed for the luxurious sofa.

He sat down on the other end of the sectional, allowing enough room between us for a Sumo wrestler to make himself comfortable. Even with Hank all the way over at the other end of the sofa, I still felt as if he were sitting right next to me.

I guess I don't have to mention that I still felt rattled.

Hank looked a little rattled himself. He tried to lean back against the sofa cushions and cross his legs, as if he couldn't be any more relaxed, but he didn't quite pull it off. He looked too wooden. And he kept shifting positions as he talked, as if he couldn't quite get comfortable. "So, like I said," he went on, "I talked to Bentley Shepard. And to the Vice guys downtown. According to Vice, since he got here from Owensboro, our friend Bentley has been a very busy man."

I nodded, as if I knew exactly what he was talking about, but I really had no idea. Hank was looking straight at me. I looked away, and took a long, long sip of Coke.

"Yeah. It seems old Bentley has been doing a little illegal photography on the side," Hank said.

I was still sipping, but I glanced sharply at Hank. *"Illegal?* What do you mean, illegal?"

"Illegal like pornography." Hank scowled. "Looks like our boy Bentley has been doing a pretty good trade in porn. That is, in addition to all his nudie *art."*

My mouth actually went dry. *"Pornography?* Does Crane Morgan know about it? Is he involved?"

"Don't know, and don't know to both of your questions. Vice is still trying to find out who all is implicated in Shepard's little sideline."

Hank went on, telling me all about how Vice had managed to tie Bentley Shepard to a web page peddling pornography over the Internet. Still shifting positions on the couch, Hank was going on and on about web servers and newsgroups and modem hookups, and I sat there, nodding, as if I were hanging on his every word. The truth was, I'd pretty much stopped listening right after he said the word *porn.* In fact, all I could seem to think about was Nan, and how she might very well be in bed right this very minute with a porn king.

I guess it goes to show you just what a prude I really am, but somehow, being a porn king seemed even worse than being a murderer.

Although, let's face it, neither one was exactly something you'd want on your résumé.

Hank kept on talking, and I kept on not quite listening. One thing I did notice was that he seemed to be going out of his way not to mention Nan. Realizing this, I felt—what else?—more nervous. Because this little maneuver, even *I* knew about. It's the same gambit that married men always use just before they make their move. Suddenly, they're talking a lot, but the names of their wives never seem to come up.

In this case, Hank seemed to be making a deliberate effort not to remind me that once upon a time he and Nan had been a thing. An item. Whatever you call it, if Hank Goetzmann thought I was going to forget, he was out of his mind.

Finally, Hank seemed to wind down a little, and I noticed that my glass was empty. I got to my feet.

Hank looked a little startled.

"I guess I'd better get on home," I said. "I've got to be at work early tomorrow."

I wasn't sure why I said that. I really didn't have to be at work any earlier than usual. What's more, the second I said it, I thought, *Lying to a cop? Are you nuts? He can probably spot a lie a mile away. For sure, he can check up on what you've told him and find out that you're lying.*

Can you believe, all this was going through my head as Hank followed me to his front door.

There I turned to face him, expectantly.

Hank just stared back at me for a long moment, and then he seemed to realize that I was waiting on him to do something. He cleared his throat. "You know, you really do look nice tonight," he said.

I still had on the navy blue Laura Ashley dress I'd worn at dinner. It had a high neck, long sleeves, and a skirt almost to my ankles—just what everybody is wearing at the convent this year. If Hank thought I looked good in this, he didn't get out much.

"Thanks," I said. I was still looking at him expectantly.

He held my eyes, and what do you know, for a moment there, he actually looked almost as nervous as I felt.

How cute.

"Hank?" I said.

He moved closer to me, but this time I didn't immediately

move away. In fact, realizing that he was ill at ease had made my own nervousness evaporate.

I leaned toward him a little, and I said, "I'll need my coat."

The man actually reddened. "Oh, of course," he said, "let me get it for you. What was I thinking?"

I stood there, watching him. He was doing an almost perfect imitation of me, pulling at the hanger with my coat on it, getting it tangled in the hanger next to it, having to shove the other hangers away in order to get my coat out.

It was adorable.

Once he'd extricated my coat, Hank helped me put it on. If I hadn't known better, I would've sworn that his big hands lingered longer than necessary on my shoulders.

I turned to face him. I had meant to say, "Well, I appreciate the Coke," but suddenly, he seemed awfully close.

So what I said was, "Wel-l-l-l-l . . ."

Hank reached toward me, and I immediately stiffened.

He noticed, too, because he said, "I was just going to open the door for you." His voice sounded a little hurt.

"Oh," I said. I was now trying to act as if I hadn't just looked like a rabbit frozen in the headlights of an oncoming car, that in fact if he thought he'd seen me do that, he was terribly mistaken. "Well, thanks so much. For the Coke, and—and everything." I was trying to sound breezy, but I was pretty sure I just sounded airheaded instead.

Hank got his front door open, and I started to move past him out onto the porch. "Let me know about the fingerprints, OK?"

"Sure. And, uh, Bert?"

I stopped and turned to look at him. My silly heart had actually started to pound. "Take care, OK?"

His hazel eyes were deep and unreadable.

"OK," I said.

I only looked back at him once before I got to my car. He was standing there in his doorway, watching me, and yes, there was that old expression I'd seen so often on his face when he'd dated Nan.

Hank Goetzmann was scowling.

I waved, smiled as if I didn't see the expression on his face, and I got in the car. Once in the dark, where he could no longer see me, I took a deep breath. He'd said that he was just getting the door for me, but I wasn't sure. I could've sworn he'd been going to kiss me.

That in itself was a surprise enough. What was really surprising, however, was something else.

The fact that I'd wanted him to.

Chapter 17

●

NAN

Crane didn't stay the entire night.

I was a little surprised that he didn't, but I really couldn't decide if I wanted him to or not. On the one hand, I did adore waking up in the morning, reaching across cool sheets, and finding a warm man at my fingertips.

On the other hand, Bert lived next door.

I already knew that, if she'd noticed that Crane's car had been in my driveway for more than an hour, I was going to be in for the Twinquisition. That's what I call when Bert sits me down, and in the name of all that's holy, forces me to answer every one of her questions. I even knew exactly what her questions would be.

1. Did you sleep with him?
2. Did you practice safe sex?
3. What the hell were you thinking of?

The answers to the first two questions were going to be easy. Yes and yes. The answer to number three, I was pretty sure Bert didn't want to hear.

In fact, standing on my porch, kissing Crane good night, the things I was thinking could make even me blush.

"You're wonderful," Crane whispered against my hair.

I leaned against him. I felt wonderful, that was for sure.

He kissed me again, lightly on the mouth, and then he turned to go.

That, unfortunately, was when we both saw Bert's car coast to a stop right in front of the house, and then pull slowly into her driveway.

Crane looked back at me, and I guess he could see right away that I wasn't exactly overjoyed to see my beloved sister at this particular moment. "Is there a problem?" he said, glancing over at Bert, who was now getting out of her car.

And naturally, looking this way.

I shook my head. "Oh, no, of course not," I said.

Silly boy, Crane believed me.

I was standing in my doorway, clad only in a silk robe, kissing him good night, and Crane actually seemed to buy it when I said that there wasn't a problem.

In fact, he smiled, and kissed me one more time. "Did I mention that you are wonderful?" he said.

"No, I don't think you did," I said, smiling.

"Remind me to tell you tomorrow," he said, and then he was gone, heading toward his Camry.

Bert did have the decency to wait until Crane had started his car and had actually pulled away before she came running over.

"Did you sleep—" she started to ask, but evidently, my silk robe answered the first Twinquisition question for me. Bert broke off to gawk at my robe for a second, then with a quick glance at the darkened houses around us, she said, "Nan, come on, let's go inside. The whole neighborhood can see you."

"The whole neighborhood is asleep," I said, but I did as I was told.

Bert followed me into my living room and, frowning, plopped herself down on my sofa. "Well, did you at least practice safe sex?"

I closed the living room door, and tried to smile. So far, I was two for two in the Twinquisition.

"We didn't have to *practice* safe sex, he was very good at it already."

Bert frowned. "Nan, I'm not joking. You did make him wear a—"

I held up my hand. "Bert, I am not a total idiot, OK?"

Her second question answered, she immediately moved on. "Oh yeah, well, if you're not a total idiot, then why couldn't you have waited a little while longer?"

OK, so I got two out of three. "What do you mean, why couldn't I have waited? Is there a clock running? Is there some kind of a record I'm supposed to beat?"

Bert heaved a sigh that I was positive was identical to our mother's. "Nan, you don't know anything about him." Her tone was long suffering.

Like Mom's.

"I know I'm crazy about him," I said. I couldn't help smiling, remembering the events of the evening.

"Oh brother," Bert said, rolling her eyes. "I can't believe the second I'm gone . . ."

As soon as she said this last, Bert looked as if she wished she hadn't. I knew why, too. Because it reminded me to ask her a few Twinquisition questions of my own. "Now that you mention it . . ." I began.

Bert looked pained.

"Where the hell were you?"

Usually after having people over for dinner, Bert begins immediately doing her very own personal rendition of Mrs. Clean. The Bert I knew had never been one to leave a dirty dish unwashed. Or a soiled napkin unlaundered. Or a leftover un-Tupperwared. So, with all this work waiting to be done, where exactly had she gone?

Sitting on my couch, Bert blinked at me, obviously thinking fast. "Why, I just needed to take a ride, that's all," she said. "I just needed a little fresh air."

I just looked at her. Was she serious? Did she expect me to actually believe that? "You're telling me that you suddenly got a craving for fresh air so you got into your car and drove nowhere?"

Bert got to her feet. "Well, I drove somewhere, of course, it wasn't nowhere, I mean, everybody has got to be some—"

I cut her off. "Where did you go?"

Bert was now suddenly in a big hurry to leave. Fumbling in her purse for her keys, she walked over to my front door. "Look, Nan, it's really getting late, and I'm beat," she said over her shoulder. "Why don't we talk about this tomorrow?"

I put one hand on each hip. "You've got the time to come over here and jump on me about Crane, but you don't have the time to tell me where you went?"

I was beginning to get a bad feeling about all this. Where would Bert have gone that she wouldn't want to tell me?

Bert flung her hands in the air. "That did it," she said. "I will *not* be cross-examined."

I had to hand it to her. She did a very nice dramatic exit, stomping over to my front door, flinging it open, and stomping out.

I would've applauded, but I was right behind her, trying

to grab her arm. "Wait a minute, Bert. Answer me. Where have you been?"

Bert picked up speed, and all but sprinted toward her apartment. I knew she thought I'd never run after her, dressed in just a flimsy robe.

She thought wrong. Hell, I've thrown up on top of a flag-pole, for God's sake. I have no pride.

I got to Bert's door a couple seconds after she did, but she had to take the time to stop to unlock it. So we pretty much went through the door at exactly the same time.

Once inside, she stopped, turned and faced me. "OK, Nan, what do you want? I've got to go to bed, you know."

From where I was standing, I could see the dinner table in the dining room, still covered with all our dirty plates. "I'm not leaving until you tell me where you went."

Bert ignored me, walked into the dining room, and started clearing the table.

I sighed, and headed into the dining room after her. There I picked up a plate and some silverware, intending to help her clean up.

Bert took the plate and the silverware out of my hand.

"I'd rather do this myself, thank you." Her tone was clipped.

I just looked at her. I'd never seen Bert act so un-Bert-like. The Bert I knew would never leave dirty dishes all over the place. The Bert I knew would never refuse help cleaning up a big mess like this. And the Bert I knew was never this touchy.

Unless the body-snatchers were in town, I'd say the Bert I knew was up to something.

She'd piled her arms up with dishes and silverware, and she was now heading out into the kitchen.

I followed her.

"Are you still here?" she asked.

"Bert," I said, "you have been acting weird all night."

Bert turned her back on me, and started running water into the sink. "I most certainly have not been acting weird. I've been a little nervous, maybe," she said, "but I heard a lot of things about Crane from Louise. And then her dying like that, well, I think that kind of thing could make anybody nervous."

I folded my arms across my chest. "Nonsense."

Bert turned off the tap, and turned to face me. "Nonsense? Nan, you know nothing about Crane! Nothing!"

She was beginning to irritate the hell out of me. "I know a lot about him," I said.

"Oh, yeah?" she said, crossing her arms over her chest. "What do you know about him? Where did he go to school? Who are his relatives?"

"You know that yourself," I said. "He had a twin brother."

"I mean other family," Bert said. "You've had exactly—what? Three dates with this guy and what has he told you about his family? Where are they from? Where are they now? What do they do for a living? What are their names?"

"Well . . ." I drew out the word so I'd have more time to think.

Bert cut me off. "Who were his parents? His cousins? Aunts? Uncles? Name a few." Bert stared at me, arms crossed. "Name one."

I threw up my hands. She was beginning to infuriate me. "Come on, this is ridiculous. He's not hiding his background from me—it just hasn't come up. It's very painful for him to talk about. We talk about other things."

Bert turned her back on me, and squirted lemony-smelling

dish detergent into the water in the sink. "Like what? His work? What do you know about his business partner?"

The way she said it was odd. As if she knew far more than she was saying.

"Associate, not partner," I corrected.

"OK, associate. This Bentley Shepard—where's he from?"

"You know that." I shrugged. "He's from Owensboro, too."

Bert turned to look at me. "And what does he do for a living?"

I shrugged again. "You know that, too. Photography, just like Crane."

Bert put her hands on her hips. "No, Nan. He sells dirty pictures on the Internet. He's some kind of e-mail porn king."

I blinked. *"Porn* king? How do you know that? Who have you been talking to?"

Bert blinked, and turned back to her dishes. "I haven't been talking to . . ."

It dawned on me then.

Of course.

"You've been talking to Goetzmann."

Even with her back to me, I could see that I was right. Bert stiffened for just a moment, and then said, "I most certainly have not been—"

"Can it, Bert," I said, cutting her off.

I stared at her, trying to understand what was going on. Had Goetzmann been filling Bert's head with more lies about how Crane might be a murderer? Was Goetzmann really that jealous?

No matter what I said to the contrary, I found the idea of Goetzmann doing all this out of jealousy hard to believe. For one thing, I'd thought that he and I had parted, maybe not amicably, but at least we'd both agreed it wasn't working.

Hell, we had nothing whatsoever in common. Unless you count a healthy sex drive.

Had I been wrong? Had Goetzmann cared a lot more than I thought? And now was he trying to get to me through Bert?

"OK," Bert was saying. "OK. But whatever I did, I did because I'm worried about you. And Crane . . ."

I was listening to what she was saying, and yet, at the same time, I was looking at all the pots and pans and dishes on the sink. And in the sink. Everywhere but on the cutting board above the dishwasher.

Wait a minute. Pots, pans, plates, silverware. A couple of glasses, taken from mine and Bert's places at the table. So where were Crane's?

There should be at least a couple glasses from him, because he'd had wine and water throughout dinner.

I turned to look at Bert.

And as soon as I looked at her, I knew. Later, I would try to figure out what really made me think of it, but at that moment, it seemed almost as if I'd seen it in Bert's eyes. All our lives we've had a hard time keeping a secret from each other. Things like this, believe it or not, have happened to Bert and me before. Over the years I'd grown accustomed to never thinking of what I'd gotten Bert for Christmas or for her birthday when I was around her; or I swear, she'd guess it, for sure. Back when we were in high school, we called it our twin mind-meld, like the Vulcan mind-meld that Spock always used to use to read other people's minds on *Star Trek*.

Tonight my twin mind-meld was telling me exactly what Bert had done with Crane's glasses.

I took a deep breath. "So. Where are Crane's glasses?"

"What?" Bert actually stammered. "Why, why—they're

right there." She pointed at our two glasses on the cabinet top.

"Nope. You just got those from our places at the table. Where are Crane's?"

Bert tried to bluff. "They're in the dishwasher."

I started toward it, but she stepped in front of me.

And I lost it.

"I cannot believe you did this!" I yelled. Right in Bert's face. "What an unbelievably shitty thing to do! You gave those damn glasses to Goetzmann so he could get fingerprints, didn't you?"

"It was for your own good!" Bert yelled right back. "If Crane had nothing to hide, what could be the harm? And Hank said—"

"Hank?" I snapped. "Oh, so it's Hank now? You had a choice between Hank and me, and you chose Hank?"

Bert shook her head. "No! I had a choice between Hank and Crane—"

Oh, that was nice to hear. I was suddenly so angry, I actually thought I might throw something. I glanced around Bert's kitchen, breathing hard.

I'm ashamed to admit that, as a child, I was indeed the twin who threw things. Unfortunately, sometimes things that I really liked. The day I finally broke a favorite figurine of mine—a white bone china Pegasus—that pretty much cured me.

Bert, though, must've recognized the look in my eyes. She stopped talking, and started snatching up every one of her prized Lenox dinner plates and saucers, clutching them against her chest, dirty food and all.

That did it.

If Bert could do a dramatic exit, I could do her one better.

I stormed out of her kitchen, through her living room and out of her apartment, slamming the front door so hard, the window panes rattled.

The sound actually made me feel a little better.

It did not, however, stop me from thinking about what Bert had said. Hurrying home through the cold night, the wind cutting through the thin silk of my robe, I could still hear her asking, "What do you really know about Crane?"

What *did* I know about the man who'd just made love to me?

Chapter 18

●

BERT

I woke up the next morning, feeling miserable. There's nothing like a knock-down, drag-out with your sister to really lift your spirits. I fixed myself a Coke and stood at my kitchen sink, staring at nothing. Oh, sure, Nan and I had argued before—in fact, sometimes it seemed as if we quarreled all the time—but usually, our quarrels don't result in my smearing food particles all over a Laura Ashley dress. Oh, yes, last night's fight had been a beaut.

I was going to have to try to clean the dress myself, too. I couldn't face taking the dress into the dry cleaners and trying to explain how it was that a grown woman had managed to get into a food fight.

I took a long, self-pitying drink of Coke. Nan's cool-down period was at least twenty-four hours—sort of like a nuclear reactor—so I couldn't even approach her until tomorrow. Unless, of course, I wanted to precipitate a melt-down.

Besides, I didn't know yet whether I should apologize to her or try to get her to listen to reason. I wouldn't know the answer to that until Hank got the fingerprint results back. The worse thing was, Kentuckiana Temps hadn't scheduled me to work anywhere today. Usually, a day off was cause for celebration, but today I would've welcomed something to take my mind off Nan. And Crane. And Nan and Crane together.

I only wished I knew more about Crane.

As soon as I thought this, I realized that Hank had already told me exactly how I could find out more. I was showered, dressed, and already in my car without knowing precisely where I was going. That is, I knew I was headed for Bardstown, but I didn't have any idea where High Street was.

Still, Bardstown was not all that large a town. High Street couldn't be too hard to find. I knew that the exit off I-65 to Bardstown was about thirty miles south of Louisville, then you drove about twenty miles east, and you were in historic Bardstown, home to The Old Kentucky Home of Stephen Foster fame. And more importantly, home to Edna St. Charles, Crane Morgan's cousin.

As soon as I pulled into Bardstown, I found a telephone booth with an actual telephone book still dangling from its chain. This raised Bardstown in my estimation tremendously. A city in which phone books are safe on the streets? My goodness, it was an example to us all.

I looked up Edna St. Charles in the phone book, and what do you know, she was actually in there. Score another one for Bardstown.

Edna St. Charles's house turned out to be one of those 1940s red-brick monstrosities, with a square-pillared porch, and all glassed in. It looked for all the world like the house Archie Bunker had lived in for the duration of that old TV series. The outer door to the glassed-in porch was unlocked, and when my knock brought no immediate response, I let myself in. Sitting in large plastic planters all over the porch were an assortment of wilted and dying plants, with huge hunks taken out of their leaves. If they'd had an infestation of leaf mites, I sure didn't want to see one of those mites. For a mite, those things had to be enormous. I stared at the plants, suppressing an almost irresistible desire to find some potent insect spray and baptize the woman's plants with it.

I rang the doorbell and, after a few moments, heard rustling from inside. When the door slowly opened, I almost did a double take. This couldn't be Crane's cousin. She was far too old. As a matter of fact, the woman's face was so lined, she looked as if she had a hairnet stretched over it. She had a bun of blue-white hair perched precariously on top of her head and an enormous widow's hump. It was cruel of me, I know, but I couldn't help thinking fleetingly that this woman made Quasimodo look like he just had bad posture. I took a deep breath. This had to be Edna's mother. Or her grandmother. Or even her great-grandmother.

"I'm looking for Edna St. Charles?" I said. "Is she home?"

"Ye-es?" She made the word sound as if it had two syllables.

It took me a moment to realize the crone was indicating that she was Edna. I blinked at her. "You're Crane Morgan's cousin?" I blurted.

Edna beamed at me. "Why, yes, dear."

I guess I looked positively shocked, because Edna laughed, covering her mouth with a bony hand. "You were expecting somebody his age, weren't you?" At my nod, she smiled. "A lot of people make that mistake. I'm actually Crane's second cousin, twice removed. On his mother's side."

"No kidding," I said. I had no idea, of course, what she was talking about.

Edna nodded her gray head emphatically, opening her door wider. "Well, come right in, dearie, any friend of Crane's is, well, you know." She spoke haltingly, in a near whisper, as if speaking out loud was not something she did very often, and she was still getting used to it.

I followed her into the dark shadows of her living room, noting a strange odor on the way. The house smelled musty and stale, like an attic closed off for far too long. There was also another smell in the air that I couldn't quite place.

Edna immediately arranged herself, hands in her lap, legs crossed primly at the ankle, on an old red velvet settee, and indicated with a nod the other settee positioned at right angles to the first.

In the gloom of the ill-lit room, I could barely make out a faded oriental rug on the floor between the two settees. I headed for the settee Edna had indicated. There was a white rabbit-fur pillow in the corner of this one, and when I sat down, I leaned a little against the pillow.

"It's always so nice to meet a friend of the family, you know," Edna was saying, but to tell you the truth, my mind was elsewhere.

Because the pillow I'd just leaned against moved.

I let out a little shriek and jumped to my feet, turning around to stare at the fur pillow, as it gathered itself and jumped to the ground.

Now I could clearly see that the thing was a rabbit, an enormous Godzilla-sized bunny who stared at me with malevolent pink eyes and a twitching nose.

"Oh, there you are, Bugsy," Edna said, extending a gnarled hand toward the animal. "I didn't see him there, my eyes are getting so bad."

I was breathing hard, trying to get my heart to stop pounding. "You have a rabbit," I said. "Running around loose."

"Well, yes, I certainly do," Edna said. She sounded proud. "Bugsy's a wonderful pet, don't you know."

Upon hearing his name, Bugsy waddled over and proceeded to leap into Edna's lap. Actually, he half-leaped and half-climbed, clutching at her shirt with his little front paws and then dragging his ample rear over and up. When he settled himself in her lap, his legs hung over on all four sides. From the looks of him, old Bugsy had better get started on a Weight Watcher's program very soon, or else one day he was going to leap on poor Edna's lap and cut off the blood circulation in her legs.

If, indeed, he wasn't already.

"He's just like a little puppy, don't you know," Edna said. "I even take him for walks on a leash—well, not walks exactly, more like hops, I suppose . . ." That should give the neighbors pause, I thought. Not to mention, blowing a lot of kiddies' dreams of the Easter bunny right out of the water. Looking at Bugsy, they'll figure he's already eaten all their candy—and the basket, too.

Edna began scratching Bugsy behind the ears, right above his little rhinestone collar; and he closed his pink eyes, a look of bliss on his face. I sat back down, checking first, of course, to make sure there were no Bugsy relatives lying in wait. Bugsy certainly explained the huge holes in the plant leaves out on the porch. Judging from the size of him, Edna was lucky she had any plants at all.

"It's so nice of one of Crane's friends to visit me," Edna was saying, still scratching Bugsy. "Especially since Crane himself doesn't come around to see me anymore."

"He doesn't?"

"Well, you know all about what happened, don't you? Well, of course you know. Everybody knows. Those boys, they were so close, before they met that—that awful girl. Just like two peas in a pod, they were."

Edna took a deep breath, scratched Bugsy some more, blinking hard, and then hurried on. "When Lane did that to himself, I guess Crane couldn't bear to see any of the family anymore. He just cut all ties with his people. Never sees any of the Morgans anymore, and nobody on his mama's side neither. Once upon a time, those boys would come visit me all the time. Now, I guess, Crane can't stand to be reminded of Lane. And all the times the two of them came here to visit."

I shook my head sympathetically. "Did you ever meet Marian Fielding in person?" I asked, eyeing a particularly suspicious-looking clump of brown nuggets in the corner. Apparently, Bugsy was not as housetrained as one might hope. I began to realize what that other smell might be.

"Oh my, yes. Marian came out here with one of the twins to visit several times. A pretty little thing, of course; but no good, you know. Still, you'd have never known from looking at her. Blond, blue eyes, and butter wouldn't melt in that girl's mouth. But she was a *party girl.*" Edna leaned a little toward me, and whispered the last, as if she were calling Marian a dirty name.

I wasn't sure I'd heard her right. "Excuse me?"

"You know." Edna gave me a pointed look, thumping Bugsy on the head for emphasis. Bugsy opened his pink eyes and glared at me, as if these raps on his noggin were all my fault.

"Marian partied a lot," Edna explained. "She liked to go out with a lot of different men. Why, Crane told me at Lane's funeral how Marian had tried to break him and his brother up. She just loved to watch men fighting over her. She even tried to get Lane and Crane to take her places where they would run into some old boyfriend of hers—that's what Crane told me." Edna drew herself up, and sniffed. "Well, Marian should've known better than to try to split those twins up. Blood is thicker than water, you know."

Edna again tapped Bugsy's head for emphasis. The animal actually bared its teeth at me. Really, I could hardly believe my eyes. Was there such a thing as a vicious rabbit?

"And Marian was such a liar," Edna said. "Why, Crane said Lane never knew if she was telling the truth or not."

I nodded, as if I believed everything Edna was saying, but I wondered. It sure sounded to me as if Edna had gotten all her information about Marian's bad character from Crane himself. "You say that Crane told you all this? Did you ever see Marian acting the way he described?"

"Well, yes, of course I did," Edna said. "I actually saw Marian making goo-goo eyes at them both, right in front of me. She'd come out here one day with Lane, and then the very next day she'd be out here with Crane. Kissing and hanging on to whichever one she was with. Calling both of them "honey" or "sweetheart." It was scandalous. Just scandalous. It's no wonder that Lane did what he did. She was enough to drive a man crazy." Edna's chin went up.

"She sounds pretty awful," I said.

Edna was pounding Bugsy's head again. "Oh, she was terrible, just terrible. Lane wasn't really to blame at all." She paused and clucked her tongue. "Such a shame, too. And now all that's left is poor Crane."

"I'm sorry I never met Lane," I lied. "Especially since I know Crane so well. I suppose they were a lot alike. Although I'd guess you could tell them apart pretty easily," I said.

"Oh, yes, of course, *I* could tell which was which," Edna

said, beaming. "Before my eyes got so bad about five or six years ago. But there were lots of people who couldn't, you know. Some of their aunts and uncles got them mixed up all the time. Even their late mama and papa got confused sometimes."

"I guess that tattoo of Crane's helped some," I said, "I'll bet a lot of people told them apart that way."

"Oh, no," Edna said, looking surprised. "That was Lane."

I just stared back at her. "What?"

"Lane—he was the twin with the tattoo," Edna said.

My heart started beating wildly. Keep calm, I told myself. Maybe she was talking about another tattoo, not the purple forget-me-not I'd seen on Crane's wrist at dinner last night. "The tattoo was a flower of some kind?" I asked.

"Oh, yes. A forget-me-not. All in purple. It was the boys' favorite flower—on birthdays they'd bring me bouquets of it surrounded by baby's breath, tied up with ribbons and—"

I couldn't help it. I had to interrupt. "You're sure it was Lane who had the tattoo?"

Edna looked a little irritated to be challenged. "Well, yes, my dear, it was Lane. He got it when he was just barely eighteen. Right at his wrist." She showed me where it had been by pointing at her own wrist with a gnarled index finger.

Where Edna was pointing was exactly where I'd seen the tattoo on Crane's wrist.

Edna was now blinking again, staring fixedly at the place on her wrist she'd just indicated. "I—well—I think it was Lane. Oh, yes, it was Lane all right. Except"—she paused for a long moment, and then rushed on—"well, my memory isn't quite what it used to be. But still I'm almost positive it was Lane."

If Edna was almost positive about that, then I was almost

positive that Crane could really be Lane, just as Hank and poor Louise Eagleston had said. The thought made me feel a little sick inside.

Lane had killed Marian and then his own brother, and had somehow taken Crane's place. That's why he wasn't visiting Edna here anymore. He was afraid that, even with her eyesight failing, she'd be able to pick up on something and find out the truth.

And then he'd have to kill her like he'd killed Louise when she'd found out.

Oh my God. Could all this really be true?

If it was, then Nan had just gone to bed with a monster.

I rose, my mind whirling, as I thanked Edna for the visit and for telling me so much about my dear friend Crane. I started to put out my hand to shake hers, when Bugsy bared his fangs at me again. Rabbits were not supposed to be carnivorous, but I decided not to put that to the test.

I told Edna I'd let myself out and for her not to get up— under the weight of her gargantuan Easter bunny, it looked as if it might take her a while.

Then I drove straight home.

In the car, with nothing else to think about but what I'd heard, I had to fight rising panic. Oh God, oh God, oh God. Nan might be in terrible danger, and I didn't have the slightest idea how to get her out of it.

She was most certainly not going to take my word for anything.

What's more, after last night, it was going to be difficult for me to get her to listen to me for five minutes.

The phone was ringing when I unlocked my door. I rushed over and snatched up the receiver before my answering machine could pick up. "Hello?"

"Bert? It's Hank."

"Oh, Hank." I was actually relieved just to hear his voice. "I'm so worried. I think Crane might really be Lane. I—"

"Hold it, Bert," Hank said. "I've just gotten the results back from the fingerprints you got on the wineglasses."

"And?" I asked. My heart was pounding so loud, I could hardly hear him.

"The fingerprints matched what we had on file." Hank paused, evidently to let this news sink in.

It didn't.

"I don't understand," I said.

I could hear Hank take a deep breath. "Bert," he said, his tone infinitely patient, "they belong to *Crane* Morgan. Without a doubt."

Chapter 19

●

NAN

OK, I admit it. I wasn't in a good mood before Bambi, the receptionist at WCKI, called to me. "Nan! *Nan!* Just a sec!"

I didn't have to turn around to know who was bellowing at me. Our receptionist, Bambi, believed an intercom could never measure up to the raw power of her own vocal cords. She yelled at me just as I was leaving the control room at the end of my shift, heading for the production studio to record some spots—radio-ese for commercials. I turned around, mentally gritting my teeth.

After the exhausting argument I'd had with Bert last night, all I wanted to do today was get my work done and get out of here. I was not in the mood for surprises. Especially in the form of extra assignments from Charlie Belcher, P.D., short for Program Director. Or for Prevailing Dickhead.

Bambi was holding the door to the front office open as she called down the hall to me, "Nan, there's someone here to see you. Can you—*hey!*"

As Bambi yelled and tried to grab his arm, Crane, of all people, pushed past Bambi—no easy task, believe me—and all but sprinted toward me.

I stared at him as if he were some kind of mirage. He was wearing a dark blue designer suit, so he'd either just come from his studio—or he was on the way there. So why had he come by here? Last night we'd talked about getting together again tonight or maybe tomorrow. He'd been supposed to phone me, though, not drop by the radio station. Even from this distance, I could see that the expression on Crane's face was not exactly cheerful. His blue eyes looked slate gray with anger, and his mouth was set in a tight, thin line.

"We have to talk," was all Crane said when he reached me. His tone was grim, his glance very, very cold. I stared at him, trying to get some kind of clue from his eyes. He seemed to be staring back at me from a very great distance.

I didn't get it. What on earth was the matter?

Crane took my elbow, starting to steer me on down the hall, away from Bambi's earshot.

"Hey! What the hell—? Let go of her this minute!" Bambi had left her post at the door and was now hurrying toward me and Crane, her footsteps sounding like thunder in the narrow hallway.

Let's face it, Bambi might not be all that great as a receptionist, but as a bouncer, she was formidable.

Before she could tackle Crane, I stepped in front of him, holding out my hands, gesturing her to stop. "It's all right, Bambi. He's a friend of mine."

I looked back over my shoulder at Crane as I said this last. At least, I thought he was a friend. From the way he looked right this minute, I suddenly wasn't so sure.

Bambi actually looked a little disappointed that she wasn't going to get to manhandle Crane. Muttering under her breath, she turned on her heel and walked back toward the door. She didn't open it and go on back to her desk until she'd flashed Crane a final reproachful glare over my head.

I turned back around to face him. "What *is* wrong?"

"Not here," Crane said, his expression still remote. "Is there someplace we can talk? In private?"

I stared at him, found it impossible to decipher the look on his face, and then shrugged. "Sure." I tried to act casual as I preceded Crane down the hall, but my heart had started to pound. Last night this man had been warm, and wonderful, and loving. Just a few short hours ago. What could've happened to have changed that so quickly?

I opened a door that said C-ROOM. Most visitors to WCKI generally thought that meant "Conference Room." Around the station, though, we called it the Coaxing Room. It was the room used by our salespeople to make presentations, to play recorded spots, and as much as humanly possible, to coax our clients into buying more and more air time. The room contained a large conference table surrounded by chairs, a wet bar, and a couple blackboards on stands. In case our clients ever forgot why they were there, every square inch of the room's walls were covered with mammoth posters of country music stars. Right now, all I cared about was that the room was empty. "In here," I said. "We can talk in here."

Crane brushed past me without even looking at me, and sat down in one of the chairs.

I closed the door behind me, and walked slowly into the room, still staring at Crane. I'd slept with this man only last night, and right now it was as if I didn't even know him.

What could've happened?

Then, of course, it hit me.

Crane had somehow found out about Bert getting a set of his fingerprints and sneaking them to Goetzmann. That was why he was acting this way. That had to be it. Well, I certainly didn't blame him for being mad. Hell, I was mad about it, too.

I went around to the other side of the table, and Crane didn't even acknowledge that I was there. Good Lord. Was it possible that he thought I'd been involved, too? Did he actually believe that I'd known what Bert was up to, and I'd helped her by telling him nothing about it?

The very thought made my stomach hurt.

"Look, Crane, I know you're mad," I began, sitting down across from him, "but—"

Crane cut me off with one raised hand. "Stop right there. I want to know what you were doing out at my cousin's house," he said.

I blinked at him. "What? What are you talking about?"

"Don't bother denying it," Crane went on. His expression had still not changed from that remote, cold stare. "My cousin Edna just called me. It seems that she was just delighted to meet you this morning. Edna said it was so nice to visit with—how did she describe you?—the lovely new girlfriend of mine."

I spread my hands. "Crane, I don't know what—"

He cut me off with that raised hand again. Like he was some kind of conversation traffic cop. I stared at his hand, beginning to feel a little irritated.

Crane went on. "Cousin Edna was so happy that I was putting the past behind me, she said. And getting on with my life. She wants you and me to come visit her soon—just like I used to do when Lane was alive." Crane paused, and I could see a muscle jumping in his jaw. "Now what I want to know," he said, "is why? Why did you feel it was necessary to sneak around, quizzing my relatives about my past? Why couldn't you have just asked me what you wanted to know?"

Crane looked straight at me as he finished, and for the first time, I could see the pain in his eyes.

"Crane, I am so sorry, but I didn't—"

That damned hand shot up again. "Nan, I can't believe you'd do this. I really can't."

He looked so unhappy, I reached across the table to touch his arm, but he pulled away.

Focusing on a poster of Clint Black, Crane said, his voice deeper even than usual, "There's one thing I feel very strongly about. You should be able to guess what that is. When you think about everything that's happened to me, I think you can understand why it's so important." He took a deep breath. "It's *trust.* T-R-U-S-T."

Oh, for the love of Pete. The man was spelling to me. Like I was a preschooler.

I sat back a little in my chair, and took a long look at Crane—Lord, the man was unbelievably good-looking. Anger, if anything, had accentuated his features—his face looked almost sculptured, and his eyes were so dark, they looked navy. I felt drawn to him, even now, but wait a minute. Spelling to me? Oh, please, that was a bit much.

"Crane . . ."

His hand went up still again.

I felt anger wash over me like a wave. The least he could do was let me get a word in edgewise.

Crane cleared his throat. "I came all the way over here even though I really should be at work, because I wanted to talk to you about it in person. I—"

OK, he'd interrupted me. Apparently, then, he felt that was acceptable behavior. "Crane," I said, cutting him off this time, "why go to all that trouble to talk to me in person if you're not going to let me talk?"

Crane looked straight at me, his eyes darkening even more. "I can't believe you'd go behind my back. I really feel bad that you felt you couldn't trust me."

I touched his arm, but he pulled away as if my hand were red-hot. "Crane," I said, "will you listen? I did not—"

The hand jerked upward one more time, but this time I grabbed his wrist, trying to pull his hand down while he tried to yank it back up. For a few minutes there, if anybody had walked in, they would've probably thought that Crane and I were arm wrestling. "Listen to me," I said through my teeth, tightening my grip on his wrist. "I wasn't there. OK? I don't know your damn cousin. I've been on the air all afternoon. If you'd have turned on your damn radio, you'd have heard me." I let go of his hand.

Crane raised an eyebrow. "Come on, Nan, I know there are ways you can get away from the radio station, if you want to—you know, like tape your show ahead of time and play it back, something like that."

I wished I could say it wasn't true; but actually, he was right. I do play a taped show every once in a while. "You're right," I said.

There was a brief flash of victory on his handsome face. I felt another not-so-brief flash of anger.

"But Crane," I went on, "I did not play a tape today." Hell, if he could spell to me, I could spell right back at him. "That's not. N-O-T. As in, I did *not* visit your cousin Edna."

Crane, though, was already on his feet. "She described you perfectly," he said. "Hair color, eye color, height, weight . . ."

As he was saying this, I suddenly knew exactly who Crane was talking about. The minute I realized who had talked to Cousin Edna, I found myself wondering why on earth I hadn't thought of it immediately. "Now think, Crane, if it wasn't me, but it sounded like somebody who looks just like me, who do you suppose that possibly could be?"

Crane had been walking toward the door, but he stopped, turned, and looked at me. "You're not trying to push this off on Bert."

I shook my head. Now I wasn't just angry. I was furious. And when I get furious, it's all I can do to keep from crying. "You asshole," I said.

Crane's head went back as if I'd slapped him. "Now just a—"

That's all he managed to get out, before I drowned him out. "You're a fine one to talk about trust! I tell you exactly who really did talk to your cousin, and you don't trust me!"

Well, at least he didn't put his stupid hand in the air this time. He just stood there, staring at me, as if trying to somehow make sense out of what I'd just said.

Apparently, though, he hadn't really heard any of it.

He turned and walked out of the room.

I was so stunned that he would just walk out, without saying anything more, that I stood there for several more minutes, expecting him to come back.

He didn't.

So was this it? Had I met a wonderful man who was exciting and passionate, and we were splitting up because he thought I'd done something I hadn't?

I stood there in the conference room, staring at the poster of Tammy Wynette, as if Tammy knew the answer.

Then I lost no time leaving the radio station, and heading for home as fast as I could.

Bert's car was in her driveway, and I leaned on her doorbell for what I hoped was an obnoxiously long time. When Bert opened the door, she had the gall to actually smile at me.

"Nan!" she said. "You're here! And you're speaking to me!" Her voice sounded delighted.

"I'm not speaking to you for long!" I said, heading past her into her apartment. Once inside, I turned to face her, hands on my hips. "Why did you do it?"

"I'm so glad you want to talk about it," Bert said. She was still sounding delighted. "Because I wanted you to know that I did it for you. I was just so worried about you. I was just trying to make sure that none of the awful things Louise Eagleston had said about Crane was true. That's why I took Crane's glasses—"

I held up my hand, imitating somebody I'd seen do this recently. Hey, I knew exactly how irritating this little gesture could be. "Bert," I said, "we're way past the glasses."

"We are?" Bert was trying her best to look totally baffled, but she'd begun to look a lot like Lucy always did when Ricky yelled, "Lucy, you got some 'splainin' to do!"

"As if you didn't know, I'm talking about this morning," I went on, "you remember, when you went to talk to Cousin *Edna.*"

Bert had the good grace to look guilty. Guilty and caught. "How did you find out?" she asked.

"I had a little visit from Crane. For some odd reason, he thinks it was me who went to visit his cousin, and can you believe, he's so mad, it looks like he never wants to see me again."

In the middle of my speech, Bert's hands had gone to her mouth, her eyes becoming very large O's. "Oh dear," she said. Taking a deep breath, she hurried on to say, "First of all, I did not tell Edna I was you." She must've noticed my eyes starting to blaze, because she quickly changed her tune. "Of course," Bert stammered. "Edna must have just assumed—"

"Assumed?" I asked. "Oh, yeah, she assumed, all right;

and now Crane has assumed he can't trust me any farther than he can throw me." I went over to Bert's sofa, sat down on it, and took one of her pillows onto my lap. I couldn't remember when I'd ever felt so utterly defeated. I wanted to smack Bert silly, but what good would that do?

I wanted to smack Crane for being such an idiot, but that would be pretty pointless, too.

I hugged the damn pillow in sheer frustration.

Bert sat down beside me, patting my arm.

Taking another cue from Crane, I pulled away and glared at her.

Bert, to give her credit, did look appropriately miserable. "Nan, I am really sorry," she said. "I've been a total idiot about Crane. I don't know what got into me. Please forgive me, please? I'm sure he'll get over it soon, and—"

I gave her a pointed stare that pretty much had "you've *got* to be kidding" written all over it.

Bert brightened. "OK, I've got it. I'll go and explain to Crane that it was me. That I was the one who talked to Edna. Because I was just protecting you."

I looked at her, still strangling the pillow. "Do you think he'll believe you?"

Bert nodded. "I'll make him believe me." She picked up her car keys. "Come on, show me how to get to his studio, and I'll do the rest."

The way I saw it, I didn't have a whole lot of choice. Obviously, Crane didn't believe me. I might as well let Bert give it the old college try.

Then, of course, if she didn't convince him, I could always strangle her instead of the damn pillow.

Chapter 20

●

BERT

Lord. The things you have to do when you've been a jerk.

Standing outside the door with the words MORGAN PHOTOG-RAPHY elegantly stenciled on the smoked glass door, I took a deep breath, steeling myself against what was undoubtedly not going to be a pretty scene.

Across the way, there was another glass door that read "Bentley Shepard, Photographer." That office was dark, but the Morgan Photography office, wouldn't you know, was brightly lit.

Beside me, Nan was taking a deep breath, too. I glanced over at her, gave her what I hoped was a confident smile, received a pitying look in return, and pushed open the door.

Crane Morgan was sitting right in front of us, at a desk piled high with photo mailers. His eyes immediately widened when he saw us walk in. Then he looked first at Nan, then over at me, and then back again at Nan. Frowning, he got to his feet. "Nan, I thought we'd said all—"

I interrupted him. "I asked her to bring me here, Crane. I've got something to tell you."

I was all prepared to start doing heavy groveling, but the door in back of Nan and me opened just then. I turned to see who had come in behind us, and I caught my breath.

This guy looked an awful lot like Turtlehead, the guy I'd seen running away at Louise Eagleston's house. He wasn't dressed the same, of course, and I had seen Turtlehead at a distance, so it was hard to be absolutely sure. Instead of a three-piece suit and a bow tie, he was wearing jeans, a blue Chicago Bulls sweatshirt, and sneakers. The balding turtlehead sure looked familiar, though. I stared at him as he walked toward us.

Nan was now poking me in the side. "Bert, don't you have something you want to tell Crane?" she said. Her eyes were saying other things, all of them threatening.

I turned, so that my back was to Crane. "Nan, I think that's Turtlehead!"

Nan, oddly enough, did not seem to get the significance of this. She was giving me a Twin Whammy that looked as if she might be on the verge of bursting a blood vessel.

Turtlehead walked right past Nan and me as if we weren't even there, and headed straight for Crane. "You got the mail sorted yet, Crane?" he asked.

Crane shook his head. "Not quite yet."

As Crane spoke, Turtlehead glanced over at Nan and me, his eyes doing the twin-bounce, going back and forth from my face to Nan's and back again.

"Twins, huh?" Turtlehead said. "Here to get your portraits done, I reckon." He said the word "portraits" as if it were spelled *pore-trayts*. "Lookers like you two ought to get glamour shots taken. For the boyfriends. You know."

Crane cleared his throat. "These women are friends of mine, Bentley," he said.

Bentley grinned. "Hey, I knew that," he said, winking at Crane. His eyes returned to Nan and me, traveling slowly from our heads to our toes, and missing nothing in between.

I was pretty sure I could assume he was not looking at us so closely in order to be able to tell us apart. "I'm a friend of Crane's, too—Bentley Shepard, at your service."

"Bentley is my *associate*," Crane corrected. Evidently, Crane wanted to make it clear that he didn't consider Bentley a friend, but I was barely listening. I was too busy staring at Bentley and trying to make up my mind. Was this Turtlehead, or not?

Bentley shook Nan's hand, saying, "Glad to meet you, doll," and then he turned to me. The second his hand touched mine, I don't know, I guess I had a moment of temporary insanity. It flashed through my mind that my hand was now getting itself squeezed by the extremely moist hand of a porn king, and then I heard my mouth blurting, "It *was* you, wasn't it?"

Bentley blinked a couple of times. "What do you mean, it was me?"

I just stared at him, hardly daring to believe what I'd just said. If Bentley really was Turtlehead, he might very well be a murderer. So what in the world did my mouth think it was doing?

I swallowed. On the other hand, I'd already come this far, I might as well go the distance. "At Louise Eagleston's house," I said. "Wasn't that you that I saw, running by her house, on the day she was killed?"

Bentley's reaction was immediate. His eyes got about six sizes larger, and he began waving his hands, as if warding off a horde of flying insects. "No way, baby doll. Wasn't me." As he said this, Bentley glanced nervously at Crane, then at Nan, and finally back at me. Bentley looked so scared, it gave me courage.

"Sure it was," I said. "I saw you come out of the open garage next door while I was phoning the police."

The word "police" seemed to cause Bentley to kick into reverse. He started backing up. "I don't care what you think you saw, baby doll. You're mistaken. It was not me. Got it?" His eyes darted to Crane, and then back to me once again. "You'll be sorry if you spread any lies about me, too. I mean it, girlie. I'll sue you for slander."

I just stared at him. *Slander?* For saying somebody had run past a house?

Bentley turned back to Crane. "I've got an appointment, Crane—I'll come by and get the mail later."

"Just a minute, Bentley—" Crane said, moving around the desk.

But Bentley had backed up all the way until he sort of banged against the frosted glass door. When that happened, he turned, opened it, and was gone. He was through the front double doors and down the steps, before the rest of us even got out on the porch.

A minute later, Shepard sped by us in a bright red Corvette, peeling rubber.

Crane's face was grim, as he stared after the rapidly disappearing Corvette. "Are you sure it was Bentley you saw?"

To be totally honest, I wasn't sure. I shook my head. "It sure looked like him, though," I told Crane as we all moved back inside. "And if it wasn't him, why did he leave in such a hurry?"

Crane frowned. "Maybe he just didn't like being accused of something he didn't do," he said quietly.

I held up my hand. "Hey, I wasn't accusing anybody." I could feel Nan's eyes, as she directed yet another Twin Whammy my way.

I took another deep breath. OK, OK, it was obviously time to do some heavy groveling.

"Look, Crane, I certainly didn't mean anything by visiting your cousin. I was just trying to find out a little more about the new man in Nan's life." At this point I gave Nan a glance I hoped looked fond. "I was being overprotective, of course. I realize that now. But after hearing all the things that Louise Eagleston told me, well, I'm sure you can understand where I was coming from."

I glanced at Crane this time.

He looked back at me with dark navy eyes that were completely unreadable.

Nan's eyes, on the other hand, might as well have had print running across them. They said, *Tell him some more.* Good Lord, what else could I say? That I'd give him my firstborn child? Come to think of it, considering what tuition costs were these days, Crane would no doubt consider my making a present of Brian something else I'd need to apologize for.

I continued. "Like I said, I was terribly out of line. Terribly. I shouldn't have gone to see your cousin. I'll never do it again. And I really hope that you won't continue to be angry with Nan for something that I did. I'm sorry I did it. I really am. Really. I do apologize."

So there. I wasn't sure what else I could do, short of signing up for a public flogging.

Of course, judging from the look on Nan's face, I'd say she'd vote for the flogging.

I looked over at Crane. "All right," he said slowly. "I accept your apology."

That's all I wanted to hear. "Great!" I said. I was anxious to get out of there. "Well," I said, beginning to sidle in the general direction of the door, "thanks for listening, and we'll—"

Crane's hand went into the air in a gesture that was oddly familiar.

"I can take Nan home," Crane said, cutting me off. He glanced over at Nan, and judging from the look he gave her, taking her home was not exactly what he had in mind.

Oh my yes, I was now more than anxious to get out of there.

Nan was now returning Crane's look with a steamy one of her own. "I guess I've been acting like an idiot, haven't I?" he said, his eyes never leaving Nan's face. "I should never, ever have thought that you would do a lame-brained thing like that."

I winced a little at the term "lame-brained," but I really didn't want to stay and argue the point.

"We need to talk," Crane told Nan, moving toward her.

I gave up on subtlety, and headed for the door. "See you later, Nan." I said it pretty loud, but neither Nan nor Crane seemed to know I was still there.

It was just as well. I had a little errand of my own to do.

When I left Crane's office, I noisily closed the frosted glass door. I made as much noise as I could, walking toward the front copper doors. There I opened them and let them slam shut.

While the noise was still dying down from the doors slamming, I moved quickly on tiptoe, to stand against the far wall in the hallway so that if either Nan or Crane looked this way, they wouldn't be able to see me.

After a moment, I saw through the frosted glass of the front door, the shadows that were Nan and Crane merge into one. Oh, yeah, they needed to talk, all right.

While they were busy talking, I intended to be busy, not talking. In fact, being extremely quiet in general.

I tiptoed to the door opposite Morgan Photography, staring at the name on the frosted glass. BENTLEY SHEPARD, PHOTOGRAPHER. I didn't care what the guy said, I knew I'd seen him at Louise's house. So what exactly had he been doing there? Had he first met Louise at Crane's office when she came in for her portrait to be taken? I could hardly bear to think it, but could Bentley—the man who'd just touched my hand all over—could he actually have been the man who'd killed poor Louise?

He'd looked rattled. Maybe, if he wasn't guilty himself, he'd seen the killer.

I tried the door. Locked. Of course. Still, I wasn't going to let a little thing like a locked door throw me off. After all, hadn't I seen Magnum PI or Jessica Fletcher or any number of TV detectives get past a lock with little or no trouble at all?

I started looking in my purse for the thing the TV detectives always use for just this purpose—a credit card. On TV it had always looked easy. You slide it between the door thingie and the door jamb, and you wiggle it a little, and open sesame! It was a snap.

I came up with my Marathon gas card, and I took yet another deep breath. What I was about to do was called breaking and entering, something I do believe that Hank Goetzmann could arrest me for. And yet, I wondered if he really would. He had to be as anxious as I was to find out more about Crane's associate.

I shoved those worries right out of my mind. And I shoved the Marathon card between the door whatsit and the door jamb and started wiggling. It was a snap, all right.

The card snapped cleanly in two. I sincerely hoped I wouldn't need to get gas on the way home.

I glanced back over at Morgan Photography. The two shadows were still locked in a clinch. I riffled in my purse one more time and found my VISA card. This puppy had so many charges on it, it had to be made of steel. I stuck it in and jiggled it against the doowhahickey a couple of times, and—would you believe it? The catch actually gave way, and the door swung silently open.

Jessica Fletcher would've been proud.

The front area in Shepard's office was a waiting room, just like a doctor might have. It occurred to me that the decor was sort of appropriate since apparently Shepard seemed to encourage his clients to play doctor quite a lot with each other. There were a few vinyl-covered chairs and dog-eared magazines scattered around on beat-up wood-look end tables. Surely a successful photographer could pop for better office furniture for his clients. Of course, if what Hank had said really was true about Shepard, I'd guess someone running a pornographic establishment wouldn't really care a lot about decor. On the opposite wall, the inner door turned out to be—as luck would have it—unlocked.

The door led right into Bentley's postage-stamp-sized office. A desk, a chair, couple of metal filing cabinets—that was it. His scarred oak desk pretty much begged me to look inside. I immediately complied, only to find that there wasn't anything in the stupid thing except junk like ballpoint pens and paper clips and stationery. And lint. Lots of lint.

Next, I tried the file cabinet closest to the desk. The top two drawers were filled with receipts and statements and canceled checks. The third drawer down, though, was stuffed with manila file folders. I pulled one out, and a photograph fell to the floor. Even standing up, I could make out what definitely looked like an ultra close-up from the waist down of legs and pubic hair. Definitely female. And in a rather unusual pose.

I flipped through the rest of the photos in the file. They were all similar to the first photograph I'd seen. Definitely female, definitely unusual poses. In fact, some of these women had to have had a real backache the next day.

There were also several truly amazing photographs of women doing rather unusual things to themselves. Sometimes alone. Sometimes with battery-powered objects. Sometimes with cucumbers and, strangely enough, celery. The photos I'd found at Louise's were fast beginning to look as if they could've been featured in a children's book, compared to these.

I found myself wondering if these women really wanted to do this for the camera. I studied the expressions on their faces to see if I could tell. I'd certainly heard about exploitation of women as sex objects, of course—like in the Miss America pageant. But worrying about women parading around in bathing suits seemed pretty tame compared to this degrading portrayal.

The lower file drawers and the other file cabinets contained even more photographs. Some of these added a male to the scenario—sometimes, more than one male. Generally, though, it was couples doing things to each other with or without the aforementioned objects. In one's wildest imagination—which certainly seemed to be actively at work here—none of these photos could possibly be described as art.

I opened the bottom file drawer, leafing through the files. The thin one in front, though, did not seem to have photos in it, and I pulled it out. When I saw what was inside, my heart seemed almost to stop. Numbly, I stared at the driver's license and four credit cards.

All made out in the name of Louise Eagleston.

Oh my God.

My heart was pounding in my ears as I picked up the telephone and called Hank. "I've found them," I said, my voice sounding strange even to my own ears. "I've found them all." The license and cards were the things missing from Louise's house the day she was killed. Things that would have been in her purse. Finding Bentley's pornographic photographs seemed to be almost an anticlimax, no pun intended.

Of course, I'm sure that Hank did not believe me when I told him that the doors to Shepard's office had been standing ajar, and that I'd gone in, looking for a bathroom. "His file cabinet drawer was standing wide open, and all I had to do was look in and see the stuff," I said.

I was sure Hank didn't believe a word of it, but he didn't say anything except, "I'll be right over." I hung up and went back next door.

Nan and Crane jumped apart as I opened his door.

The good news was they were still fully dressed.

The bad news, apparently, was me.

"Bert! What are you doing back here?" Nan threw me a sour look that definitely repeated Greta Garbo's famous line. She wanted to be alone. With Crane, that is.

"Hi," I said. "I thought I'd better warn you that the police are on their way."

Nan gaped at me. "The police? What, *again?*"

Crane got to the point immediately. "Why are the police on their way?"

Crane's expression grew darker and darker as I told them what I'd found in Bentley's office. Nan actually gasped when

I got to the part about Louise's belongings. I couldn't make out if Crane was more shocked by the items belonging to Louise being found in Bentley's office or by the pornographic photographs I'd found.

"I can't believe it," he kept saying, and probably would've gone over there to look for himself, if Nan and I hadn't convinced him that the police ought to find it just like I had found it.

Naturally, I deleted vivid descriptions of the subject matter of the photos I'd found—I really couldn't bring myself to relate that kind of thing to a member of the opposite sex. Nan, of course, I'd tell in meticulous detail later. It would be another Twinquisition if I didn't.

I was trying to find an appropriate euphemism for the vegetable detail in the pictures when Hank walked in without knocking. I, of course, wouldn't have noticed the lack of formality except for what Crane said.

"Don't you policemen ever knock?" Crane said.

Goetzmann did his usual shrug for an answer and took me by the elbow, nodding briefly at Nan. "Show me," was all he said.

I showed him.

He frowned at the file with Louise's belongings and then began flipping through the photographs in some of the other files with the end of a pencil. I tried not to look directly at Hank as he did so. Mainly because I'd just as soon not be staring into the eyes of a guy who was looking at pubic hair, spread legs, and bare breasts, with assorted fruits and veggies, right in front of me.

It made me feel terribly uncomfortable. I had no doubt I was actually blushing—something I'd hoped I'd left behind long ago in high school. Studiously looking at my hands, I suddenly had a very strong desire to go wash them.

While Hank studied porn, I glanced around Bentley's tiny office and headed for the nearest door. The room it opened into was dark, and I felt for a light switch inside the door. I flipped it on.

Oh, my goodness.

A rumpled king-size bed pretty much filled the room. That, and the video, lighting, and camera equipment that surrounded the bed. It didn't exactly take a rocket scientist to figure out what had been going on here.

Behind me, I could hear Hank making a phone call. I heard words like "warrant" and "judge" and figured Hank was arranging to search the place. Then I could feel him looking over my shoulder at the bed beyond. When he completed his call, I turned around, avoiding his eyes. "I, uh, was looking for the bathroom," I said.

"Again?" he said, just looking at me. "Well, that ain't it," he said. "Besides, I don't want you adding more fingerprints to the ones you've already left."

Goodness, I hadn't even thought of that.

While we waited for the search warrant, Hank went back next door to talk to Crane, me following him like a puppy afraid to be left alone. I certainly did not want to be in Bentley's office when he came back. *If* he came back. Something told me he would not be in his best mood. And if the evidence was to be believed, this guy had already killed one person.

"I don't know anything about how Bentley got Mrs. Eagleston's credit cards," Crane insisted to Hank. "I also don't know anything about those photographs. We're not partners, we just share offices—how many times do I have to tell you?"

Hank shrugged. "I guess until I believe you," he answered.

I winced, waiting for Nan's explosion. She didn't disappoint me.

"How dare you!" Nan said. "How can you just automatically assume that Crane was involved in all this just because Shepard was?"

"How can you automatically assume he wasn't?" Hank replied.

Nan actually began to sputter at that one. "It seems to me that, once again, Hank Goetzmann, you're letting your personal feelings run away with you! You're letting spite and jealousy color your professional judgment!"

Hank glanced at me, then turned back to Nan. "Nan, you couldn't be more wrong," he said quietly.

I wondered, though. Not necessarily about Hank's lack of prejudice. But about how clear everything was.

I mean, this whole thing with Bentley looked just a little too contrived. Certainly, I couldn't deny that Bentley did look stupid, turtle-head that he was, but could the man really have been so dumb as to put the items he'd stolen from Louise in his own file cabinet? He might as well have filed them under LAST MURDER. Why not just throw them away?

Of course, maybe old Bentley didn't realize anybody was going to be searching his file cabinets anytime soon. But then again, why was he at Louise's in the first place? Had he added burglary to his pornography pursuits?

By this time, Crane had already given Bentley's home address to Hank, and Hank had put out a BOLO. According to what Hank told me, that was cop talk for "Be On the Look

Out"—for Bentley. "We will catch him," Hank told Crane pointedly. "Then we'll just see what Shepard has to say."

When the rest of the police contingent arrived, Hank took statements from all of us, while his lab people crawled over Bentley's office with their fingerprint powder and tweezers and plastic baggies, picking up evidence. I'd seen this whole act before—once when my own apartment was burglarized—so it had pretty much lost its charm for me. With Nan still planning to be driven home by Crane, I made my escape as soon as I possibly could.

I noticed Hank purposely caught my eye as I headed toward the door, but he merely nodded at me, before he turned back to one of his cop-helpers. I couldn't tell if his customary frown was one of irritation at my sneaking away or of concern.

I was still trying to decide what that look had meant, as I'd pulled onto I-65 south, heading for the Watterson. Sometimes, I actually thought there was something in Hank's eyes when he looked at me, and then other times, I was sure it was something in mine. Like, oh, say, a speck of dirt.

I'm not sure why I glanced in my rearview mirror—maybe I'd seen some motion out of the corner of my eye—but I spotted the car coming up fast behind me when it was still several car lengths behind. It was late afternoon by now, but I could still tell in the waning light that the car heading toward me was red. When it pulled up alongside me on the passenger side, I could see that it was a Corvette.

My heart started to pound. Where was a cop when you really needed one? Goodness, they were looking hard for Bentley Shepard, weren't they, and apparently, here he was, big as life. So where in God's name were they? I pressed on my gas, trying to pull away from him and, at the same time, saw the green highway signs overhead for the Watterson come into view. The red Corvette kept right beside me, matching my speed.

My God, what was he going to do? I raced onto the ramp, just as the Corvette veered sharply to the left, banging against the side of my Festiva. I screamed at the sound of scraping metal, yanking at my wheel to keep my little car from flinging itself headlong into the ramp's guardrail.

It's amazing to me that, when something life-threatening happens, everything suddenly slips into slow motion. Very slowly, one second at a time, I felt my car smack into the side of the red Corvette one more time, metal screeching, then clip the edge of the guardrail as it sailed past, whipping around like a pinwheel.

As I spun around, I caught sight of the driver of the Corvette—his face a brief flash before I spun away. Then, for a long, long sickening moment, I was airborne.

Chapter 21

●

NAN

Crane said very little as he drove me home from his studio. I knew he was upset, with the police being in his life again and all. After all that had happened with his brother, this had to be a horrible reminder. And yet, he didn't say a word about it. He just drove, his eyes focused stonily on the road ahead.

If he hadn't reached over and placed my hand against the side of his thigh, a gentle reminder of our first date, I would've felt completely shut out.

When he did that, though, I looked over at him and smiled.

He gave me a quick, sad smile, and held my hand a little tighter.

At that moment, I was sure I was in love at last.

To show you just how delirious I was, when Crane pulled into my driveway minutes later, I didn't notice anything wrong at first. I was still looking at Crane, wondering what I could say so that he'd know that I did have some idea what he must be going through.

He was holding the door open for me and I was getting out of the car when I finally noticed. *Across the way, Bert's driveway was empty.*

I looked toward the curb, looked around back. Bert's little turquoise Festiva wasn't here.

But it should be. Bert had left Crane's studio way before we did. So why on earth wasn't Bert home yet? I know it sounds strange, but seeing Bert's empty driveway gave me a sudden hollow feeling inside.

Bert and I have always said that if anything terrible ever happens to either her or me, the other one will somehow feel it. I've never told her, but I really believe that I will somehow feel it when she dies. Or if I'm the lucky one, she will feel it when I do. I really mean that about being lucky, too. I think I'd rather die than feel the way the world is like when Bert's not here anymore. I glanced toward Crane. I didn't know how he could stand it.

Because I certainly didn't like the feeling I was having right now.

"Bert left at least an hour before we did, didn't she, Crane?" I asked as he closed the passenger door after me, and we walked toward my front door. "So where *is* she?" I knew I was asking myself more than him. I stood for a moment on my porch, hugging my elbows and looking up and down Napoleon Boulevard, as if by doing so, it could cause Bert's little turquoise Festiva to suddenly appear.

Crane knew immediately what I was feeling. That was one of the great things about him—he knew what it was like to be a twin. What was scary to me was that he also knew what it was like to be a twinless twin. He was living proof that it could really happen. You could actually lose the part of yourself that had been your sister.

Crane came quickly up the steps, stood right next to me, and put his arm around my shoulders. "Come on, Nan, don't get all upset. I'm sure she's fine," he said. "She probably just stopped off at the grocery or something. She'll be here in just a minute."

"Sure," I said without much sincerity. "That's it, all right." I tried again. "Bert is always saying, *When the going gets tough, the tough go shopping.* That's Bert, all right. She's probably in Wal-Mart right now." I said all this, and I still didn't believe me.

Bert had been acting too strange lately. Even for Bert. I certainly didn't like the myriad directions in which she appeared to be tearing off these days. Finding Louise dying and reacting to that had been one thing—that one had basically been all my fault for getting her into it. But going off and searching Bentley Shepard's office? Not to mention interrogating Cousin Edna? Those had been purely Bert's decisions. As far as I was concerned, I really didn't think the entire pattern Bert was establishing these days boded well for her safety.

Nobody had to remind me that Shepard was still on the loose. Nor that Bert was the one person who could place him at the scene of Louise's murder.

I shivered involuntarily, leaning against Crane. He tightened his arm around me. "Let's go inside and I'll phone Goetz . . ." I began when the sound of an approaching car made me turn around.

My stomach twisted when I realized what was approaching was not Bert's car. It was, in fact, a dark brown car pulling into my driveway behind my car. There was a uniformed policeman at the wheel.

Suddenly my knees felt as if they might not support me. I sagged against Crane, and he held me tight. Don't let him be here about Bert, I silently begged. Please, please, don't let it be about Bert.

I actually felt dizzy when the cop's rear passenger door slowly opened, and Bert herself climbed out. She was an unbelievable sight, her gray wool slacks torn down one side and little pieces of shrubbery sticking out of her cuffs and even her hair. She looked as if she'd been trying out for a part as the scarecrow in *The Wizard of Oz*.

I don't even remember running to her, but I must have because I was suddenly there by her side, picking the twigs out of her hair and brushing off her clothes. "Good God, Bert, what happened? Are you OK? Where in hell have you been?"

"I'm fine. Really," Bert began, looking down at herself. She seemed to notice the state she was in for the first time. She began to brush off the cuff of her coat. "I just had this little car accident—"

"Not an accident. Someone ran her off the goddamn road," Goetzmann interrupted, his tone grim. I hadn't even noticed him getting out of the other side of the squad car. "Happened on the I-65 ramp, just entering the Watterson. She ended up having to climb out of the ditch. On the other side of the guardrail."

"Oh my God, Bert." I think it was perfectly natural that I would grab her right then and start feeling her arms up and down for fractures. "Have you been to the hospital? Is anything broken?"

"Just my pride." Bert was already batting my hands away. "I'm fine, all right? All right? I just wish I could say the same for my little Festiva."

"The turquoise roller skate?" I glanced at Goetzmann, my question apparent even to him.

He shook his head, his eyes grim. You might've thought he was conveying the news of the death of a friend.

"Totaled," Bert said sadly. "Sailing over a guardrail does that to an automobile. Not to mention what it does to the human body." She pressed her hands into the small of her back, wincing as she did so. "Actually, the sailing wasn't the problem. The landing was the problem. I've just got to lie down before everything I own begins to really ache." Bert started walking slowly toward her house, and the rest of us walked with her. She moved as if every step was an effort.

Crane moved up beside Goetzmann. "Who did this to her?" Crane asked.

Bert opened her mouth to answer, but Goetzmann interrupted. "She got a fleeting glimpse of the bastard as he sped away. But it was a red Corvette. Bert's sure about that."

I stared at him. A red Corvette? Like the one driven by Bentley Shepard? *Shepard* had forced Bert off the road? My God, he really was trying to silence her. "Haven't you caught that guy yet, Goetzmann?" I began, but Bert shot me The Look.

The Look was the one our mother gave us at church every Sunday when we were about six and began to whisper to each other during the sermon. At Bert's look, I automatically did exactly what I'd always done when Mom gave me The Look. I closed my mouth.

"We'll get him," Goetzmann said, more to Bert than to me.

At her front door, Bert handed her key to Goetzmann, and he unlocked her apartment just like he'd done it, oh, maybe a thousand times before. Of course, now that I thought about it, he'd opened mine for me now and again; and let's face it, the doors were identical. I looked away, suddenly feeling uneasy. I guessed I was just experiencing a little déjà vu, that was all.

That little thought made me pause again. Déjà vu? I glanced over at Bert and then back at Goetzmann and then back at Bert again. Well, what do you know, was it possible that Goetzmann was trying to pull the old Switcheroo?

I continued to stare at Bert, wondering. If Goetzmann really was trying for a Switcheroo, how did she feel about it? I wasn't sure myself how I'd react. It had never happened before so I just didn't know. For a second, I tried to put myself in her place. Being a Bert rerun? It didn't sound appealing. One thing for sure, I'd have to make very, very certain that Goetzmann knew exactly which twin I was.

Goetzmann flipped on the light switch just inside the door and ushered Bert inside. She naturally made a beeline for her wing sofa, and lowered herself gingerly into it as if she were made of spun glass.

"Here, let me." Goetzmann began piling pillows behind Bert's back. I just stared at him. He had never piled pillows behind my back. Of course, I'd never particularly liked being fussed over, but that was beside the point.

"I suppose the two of you have been together ever since you left the Crane studio?" Goetzmann asked, over his shoulder. His tone was ultracasual, but it didn't help. A stunned silence hung in the room as that little question sank in.

"My car had to be towed," Bert piped up, changing the subject ever so subtly. "It isn't even drivable."

I could tell a diversionary tactic when I heard one. I ignored her. "Yes, Crane and I were together," I said, glaring at Goetzmann. "What exactly are you trying to say?"

Goetzmann shrugged. I'd always hated those damn shrugs of his. I mean, he had a voice box, didn't he? And a passing acquaintance with the English language? So speak, already.

Say goodbye to the animal kingdom, and join us humans, OK?

"I'll go get Bert a Coke," Goetzmann said and headed out to the kitchen. Crane followed him. Before the door closed behind them, I could hear Crane asking, "I'd like to know exactly what you were implying by asking that question."

When the men were out of sight, Bert leaned toward me, wincing as she did. She whispered, "I—um—didn't get a good look at the man who ran me off the road, but for a second I thought—well . . ."

Something about her manner made me immediately on guard. She didn't see who had run her off the road. Was that what she was telling me? So she didn't see him, why whisper? "What are you talking about?" I asked.

"Well, for a second, I thought . . ." Bert rushed on, still whispering. "But then, of course, I knew it couldn't have been Crane. He was with you. I knew that."

Bert actually tried to smile at me.

I didn't know whether to smile back at her or not. "Bert, what are you saying?"

Bert closed her eyes for a moment, and then hurried on. "I'm trying to explain why Hank asked if you two had been together. He was just checking out all the possibilities. Believe me, I'm not surprised I wasn't seeing straight. And that I got confused. I *was* scared to death. And it *was* getting dark. And I really only saw the other driver for a split second."

I stared at her. Bert actually believed that she'd seen *Crane*. It was written all over her face. And she'd told Goetzmann that she'd thought it was Crane.

Oh my God.

I sat down in the chair opposite her, suddenly very weary. If Bert had felt better—and she hadn't nearly died—I might've killed her. But now? I couldn't possibly be angry with Bert now—good Lord, she'd almost died in a traffic accident.

"Bert," I said carefully, "Crane really has been with me ever since I saw you last. So help me, God." I raised my right hand to swear.

Bert gave a little shrug, wincing as she did so. I just looked at her. Was that a shrug for an answer? Now where could she have picked that little trait up?

Bert didn't even seem to notice she'd done it. "Well, my eyes were playing tricks on me, that's all. Anyway, the car *was* a red Corvette. When Hank came, he got on the police radio and found out that they still hadn't located Bentley. So it had to have been Bentley—I guess he's on the run for sure now. With a few dents in that red Corvette."

About that time, the two men rejoined us, Goetzmann bringing both Bert and me a Coke. I took a big sip before peeking over at Crane. I felt I might need the extra strength, if Crane was standing over there next to the wall, tight-lipped and altogether pissed. But apparently, whatever Goetzmann had said to Crane had soothed Crane's troubled waters. He just looked bewildered, more than anything.

"I can't understand it," Crane said, sitting down in a wing chair right next to Bert's sofa. He ran one hand through his hair. "This is like a nightmare. Why, I've known Bentley Shepard since high school. That's why it seemed so right for me to share studio space with him. I could trust him. I knew all about him. His family. His friends. How could I have been so wrong about the guy?"

I went to sit on the arm of Crane's chair, leaning a little against him, touching his arm. As one who has certainly had plenty of experience in being wrong about men, I was pretty sure I understood exactly what Crane was going through. He reached over and took my hand.

It felt good just having his fingers intertwine with mine.

"Any idea where Shepard would go?" Goetzmann asked. He was still standing, leaning against the wall closest to Bert, watching all three of us.

Crane shook his head. "He's still got some family in Owensboro—maybe he's gone back there." He looked over at me. "Do you think Bentley was just getting back at Bert for revealing his sleazy operation to the police?" He looked at Bert. "Do you think that could be it?"

"Maybe Louise found out about it, too," Bert suggested.

Crane nodded, thinking it over. "Maybe when Mrs. Eagleston was digging into all that crazy business about Lane, she found out about what Bentley was doing. That's why Bentley killed her—trying to keep it all from coming out. But my God, now he's tried to kill Bert, too. He—he's a psychopath." Impulsively, he reached out to touch Bert's cheek lightly.

Evidently, Bert had never considered that Bentley might actually be trying to kill her. She stared at Crane, her face blank. Bert started to say something, but the reality of what had happened seemed to suddenly dawn on her. Her eyes were fixed on Crane's wrist and that tattoo of his—the one of a light purple forget-me-not—but Bert didn't react. She just froze, like somebody in a horrible dream.

"Bert, hon, don't think about it now," I told her, patting her hand. "You're too tired to worry about all this. Hank will make sure that Bentley won't ever hurt you again."

I meant to just say that and move on, but Crane didn't pick up on my trying to get off this subject once and for all. He ran his hand through his hair all over again. "I can hardly bear to think of what he's tried to do. I mean, my God, Bentley must be insane. You"—he turned to include me in his glance—"you both have got to be very, very careful until the police pick him up."

"Don't worry about us," I said, glancing over at Bert. "We'll take care of each other—"

"He's right," Goetzmann interrupted, his gruff tone saying he'd rather swallow nails than admit that Crane was right about anything. "You two shouldn't take any chances. We're going to get this guy, but until then . . ." He let his voice trail off.

Until then, what? Keep the wagons in a circle? Hire a night watchman? Did Goetzmann expect Bert and me to stay put in our apartments until this guy was caught? I could feel a wave of irritation rising within me—it was the same reaction that I eventually always ended up with when I was around Goetzmann for more than a very few minutes.

"Just hurry up and bring this guy in," I said, trying not to say it through clenched teeth.

"Please," Bert added softly.

"You know, there might be something in some old papers at home," Crane said, standing up. "From when Bentley and I first signed the lease downtown together. I think I have some old business records of his. Maybe something in there will give us a clue as to where Bentley might go. I think I'll go take a look and give you a call, Goetzmann, if I find anything helpful."

I walked Crane to the front porch, closing the front door behind us.

He gave me a quick kiss, and then before he hurried off, he added, "Be extra careful, OK? Don't let anyone in but me."

I nodded. "You be careful, too." I stood watching him, noting the slump in his shoulders as he walked to his car. All of this *was* reminding him of the time his brother had been in trouble with the police—right before poor Lane died. It had to be agony for Crane, far too much like reliving the horrible nightmare before Lane's suicide.

When I opened the door to go back inside, I glimpsed Goetzmann bending down to speak to Bert. Or at least, I thought he was about to say something to her. The look I caught on his face, however, I'd seen there before. A few times, a long time ago. If I hadn't known better, I would've sworn that Goetzmann had not been saying something to Bert, after all.

Instead, he'd been about to kiss her.

I recognized the look on Bert's face, too, as she gazed up at him. Tempted, confused, panicky. Oh, and pretty damn fascinated. I figured Bert had been trying to make up her mind whether she was going to let Goetzmann kiss her or not. When she saw me, though, she made up her mind pronto. She grabbed for Goetzmann's hand and started pumping it as if she were congratulating him for winning the state lottery. "Thanks for everything, Hank," she said. "I really appreciate, uh, the ride home."

I tried not to smile.

"I'll be going along now," Goetzmann announced, standing up straight again. He leaned down and touched Bert on the nose. "Stay in bed and rest. Take two aspirin and I'll call you in the morning."

Bert gave him a dazzling smile, as if that was the wittiest thing she'd ever heard. I, of course, was thinking, *Gag me.*

"Thanks for everything, Hank," Bert said again. Her eyes sparkled as she looked at him. Oh, yeah, she was smitten, all right. She was smitten, and I wasn't even sure she knew it yet.

I opened the door and waited as Goetzmann lumbered through it. "Good night, Goetzmann," I said, smiling at him.

He stopped and looked at me. Then he leaned toward me, glancing over at Bert. "You staying here tonight or what?"

I lifted my eyebrows. Did Goetzmann, perhaps, want to know Bert's sleeping arrangements for the evening?

I showed excellent restraint by refraining from making an inappropriate comment. "Yes, I'll stay over tonight—"

"Ooh, no you won't," came Bert's voice from behind us. "I don't need a nurse maid. I'm fine."

We ignored her. "I'll stick around, at least until Bert goes on to bed. And I'll be right next door all night if she needs anything."

"Good," Goetzmann growled, glancing back at Bert. "Take care of her. And *you*, too." With that, he was gone.

Wow. Goetzmann seemed every bit as worried about us as Crane had been. Although I would imagine that Goetzmann's interest was much more directed toward Bert. Which was fine by me.

I thought about that for a second.

Yeah, it really was fine by me. I could certainly recommend Goetzmann as a lover, and I could even take his interest in Bert as a sort of compliment to me, since Bert and I were in many ways alike.

On the other hand, Goetzmann's overbearing, pushy manner drove me up the wall. Of course, Bert would probably describe that trait of his as being considerate and helpful. Even sweet.

Sweet, in fact, was not a word I'd ever use in connection with Goetzmann. Bossy. Nuisance. And Asshole. Those were the words that I would use. I peeked out the window, to watch Wonder Man drive away—and frowned at what I saw.

I walked back over to Bert. "You know, Goetzmann is plenty worried about Bentley coming back. I think he really cares about you."

"Me?" Bert asked, saying it as if the idea had never occurred to her. "Oh, no, he's worried about both of us. Besides, Hank's a cop. He just wants to catch the bad guy." She reached down to arrange the cream-colored crocheted afghan around her feet, wincing at the movement. I took the thing away from her, tucking it around her legs.

"He may want to catch the bad guy, but I think he also wants to catch the good girl," I said. Bert shot me a look, but before she could say anything, I added, "At any rate, he's definitely worried. I really do think he's expecting Shepard to show up here."

Bert frowned this time. "How on earth do you know that?"

"Because he's sitting outside right now in his car."

"He is?" Bert's dark eyes blinked at me. She glanced at the front windows as if she could see through the miniblinds. "But why?"

I rolled my eyes, and reminded myself to be patient with the patient.

"Bert, he's staking out our house."

My God, did I have to tell her everything?

Chapter 22

●

BERT

Getting up off the couch was a new adventure in pain.

Even my hair seemed to hurt. They'd given me a couple of painkillers in the emergency room when they'd looked me over, but I didn't want to take them. For one thing, if Shepard really did show up, I didn't want to be so doped up, I couldn't run.

Nan was still over at the window, peering through the slats of the miniblinds. I joined her, peering through slats about a foot under hers.

"Nan, it really does look like Hank has staked out our house."

Nan stepped back and looked at me. "No kidding."

I peered through the slats again, trying not to groan with the effort. "I don't like it."

I was serious. Being staked out was an invasion of privacy, for one thing. If he sat there long enough, Hank could get a pretty good idea of the kind of dull, humdrum, monastic life I led. And how few gentleman callers actually called.

Mostly, though, I didn't like what his staking out our house told me. Hank's stakeout pretty much yelled from the rooftops, loud and clear, that a cop—a very nice one, by the way, but a professional crime fighter, nonetheless—had

decided that Nan and I were likely crime victims. That we
were in danger. That a murderer might be dropping by for
a little visit.

None of those situations sounded like something I
wanted to admit could be true.

Nan had left the window, and plopped herself down on
the far end of the sofa, leaving plenty of room for me to lie
down again. I decided to do just that, moving back across
the room to the sofa, and feeling an entire muscle group
shriek in protest.

I eased myself down on the couch, and then I glanced
over at Nan.

She was staring into space. I couldn't tell if she was just
exhausted, or if she was lost in thought.

Either way, there was something I had to ask her. "Nan?
Don't take this the wrong way, OK? But was Crane really
with you all night long? Or were you just protecting him?"

Nan sighed and turned toward me. Considering my question, her tone had only a trace of irritation in it. "What do
you mean, don't take the question wrong? How could I take
it wrong? The absolutely *right* way to take it is that you're
asking me if Crane could have run you off the road. You're
asking if Crane could've tried to kill you tonight."

I could see her actually shiver at the thought.

She leaned toward me, her dark eyes on mine. "Look at
me," she said. "Bert, I swear that I told Goetzmann the truth.
Other than leaving me a couple of minutes to go to the can,
Crane never left my sight. All night long."

After thirty-nine years of reading Nan's face, I knew for
a fact that she was telling the truth.

I should've felt better, but I didn't.

"Oh, Nan, I'm sorry," I said. "I should never have told

Hank that I thought I saw Crane. I mean, I was in the middle of totaling my car, so I wasn't exactly paying a whole lot of attention to other drivers. And now that I think about it—well, I guess that Shepard and Crane do resemble one another a little. In the dark, I guess."

Nan just stared at me. "Oh, sure, they do," she said. "Shepard is bald and short, and Crane is dark-haired and tall—why, they're practically twins!" She turned away from me abruptly, and stood up.

And she began, inexplicably, to pace.

Up and down, up and down.

It was making my eyes hurt, watching her.

Thank God she finally stopped. "OK," she said. "I have to admit it. Whether I like it or not."

I was still staring at her, wondering what in the world she was talking about.

"A lot of terrible things have been happening. And they all seem to have something to do with Crane." Surprisingly, her eyes filled with tears all of a sudden, but she brushed them angrily away. "I don't know what any of this means. But I need to find out." She sighed, adding in a very small voice, "Because I think I'm falling in love with Crane Morgan, and I need to know before I'm in so deep, I'll never get out."

It was a voice, I have got to tell you, I rarely hear from Nan.

"I am going to prove to myself," Nan went on, a little louder this time, "as much as to anybody else, that Crane is exactly what he seems to be."

Then she stood there and just stared at me again, her eyes narrowing. I really was beginning not to like the look in her eyes. "Nan," I said, and believe me, I hated to ask, "what are you planning?"

Nan walked over and peeked out of the window again. "Well, I know it's not the nicest thing in the world to do."

"What? What isn't the nicest thing to do?"

Nan let go of the blinds and turned toward me. "I'm going to run over to Crane's studio and have a quick look-around. All by myself."

"What?"

Nan, of course, was already heading up the stairs to my bedroom, making straight for my closet. In spite of aching muscles, I hauled myself off the couch, and hurried after her.

She'd pulled my Anne Klein black jeans and my Liz Claiborne black turtleneck out of my dresser and tossed them on the bed by the time I came into the room. "These will do fine," she said as she pulled out a pair of black high tops from the closet floor that my son Brian had left here since his last visit. "They'll be a little big on me, but . . ." Her voice trailed off.

I stared at the clothes, as Nan started getting dressed.

Let me see now. I believe I'd seen this little getup worn by several people in the classic movie *To Catch a Thief.* Nan was dressing up like a cat burglar. Next, she'd be looking for a ski mask and black leather gloves.

"Are you out of your mind?" I asked.

"You don't mind if I borrow these, do you?" Nan paused, one leg in the jeans. "Just for a couple of hours?"

I shook my head. "No, you cannot wear my clothes to break into Crane's office. No. Absolutely not."

"Thanks," Nan said, and continued to dress. She zipped up my black jeans and, opening a drawer, pulled out my black leather belt. She threaded it through her belt loops. At my frown, she added, "Come on, Bert—you did the same thing to Shepard's office. I want to see what's in Crane's."

"Then tell the police to look," I said.

"Uh-uh. Besides, they can't. Cops need something like reasonable cause to search Crane's studio. I don't." Nan yanked the black turtleneck over her head, tucking it into her jeans, and then sat down, pulling on a pair of black trouser socks she'd gotten from my bureau drawer. She started lacing up the shoes.

"You'll be going to Bentley Shepard's studio, too, you know," I said, "I mean, think about it, Nan. It's right next door—what if he's there?"

Nan fluttered her hand, like she was waving away a pesky fly. "He's long gone, and you know it."

I must've been more tired than I thought. I couldn't think of anything to say to stop her. "All right, then let me go, too," I said. "Or better still, let me go instead of you. You're way too close to this thing—you're not thinking straight."

To that, Nan gave me a pointed stare that said, *Like you are?* "I'm clearly the one to go, Bert," she said. "You're too banged up. And I'm more familiar with Crane's studio—I can sneak past any police that might be watching Shepard's place to go in the back way. Besides, I need to see things for myself."

I must've looked panic-stricken, because Nan paused on her way out of the room. "Don't worry, Bert—I'll be fine." She started to leave again, and then definitely eased my mind by adding, "But if I'm not back in two hours, go outside and tell Goetzmann where I am. OK?"

My eyes probably looked like they might pop out of my head. She really had gone nuts. Nan knew this could be dangerous, but she was doing it anyway. What in the world was she thinking? Her mentioning Hank, however, made me remember something.

"Nan, you can't go." I actually felt a surge of relief. "Hank is right outside. He'll see you leave in your car."

Nan just grinned. It was the same grin she used when she had me take her place in the senior school play, so that she could neck behind the curtains with Curtis Ledford, the prompter. He also happened to be the guy voted Most Likely to Succeed that year. *I'll* say.

"I've got a plan to get around Hank," Nan said. "It'll be easy. All you have to do is be me."

Right away, a pretty sensible question leaped to mind. "Then who's going to be me?"

Nan grinned even wider. "You are."

Oh, dear.

Chapter 23

●

NAN

I was *out.*

I felt like a teenager again, sneaking out of our parents' house to meet friends after Mom and Dad had gone to bed. Come to think of it, Bert had stayed home back then, too— absolutely refusing to break the rules about our curfew. Bert has always said I must've gotten all of the rebellious gene. Personally, I like to think of it as getting all the courageous gene.

Even now, part of me thrilled at the idea of sneaking out. Past an actual honest-to-God cop, no less. My heart pounded as I climbed out the back kitchen window of my apartment. I noticed across the way that Bert was, at the same time, climbing out of hers. Right on schedule.

She only grunted as she passed me, but I gave her a cheery little wave. Bert frowned her reply, refusing even to acknowledge that I had indeed come up with a fool-proof plan to cover my absence. She was climbing into my window, still not even looking at me, as I ran away.

So all right, already, her opinion of my foolproof plan was duly noted.

It was also duly ignored.

I stopped on the other side of somebody's shrubbery a

couple of lawns away from our duplex. Before I got too far away from Bert's and my duplex, I figured I'd better sneak a look back at Goetzmann. Just to make sure he hadn't caught on, and everything was going exactly the way it was supposed to. I pulled apart the shrubbery branches, like that German guy did on that old sixties' television show *Laugh-In*.

Nothing was very interesting.

Not even Goetzmann. I could tell his keen cop eyes hadn't seen a thing. He wasn't even looking in my direction; his peepers, instead, seemed to be fixed first on the windows of Bert's apartment, then back at mine. I repressed an urge to yell "Gotcha!" at him and took off at a dead run, crouching low until I felt it was safe to stand up.

I'd told the cab I'd called at Bert's to pick me up at the corner of Napoleon Boulevard and Douglass, a few blocks away from the duplex. I cut across well-manicured lawns, blending into the shadows like some kind of guerrilla fighter, to come out finally at the proper location. The cabbie who pulled up didn't even seem to notice that he was picking up a woman dressed all in black, wearing skin-tight black gloves, even. Maybe he thought I was in some kind of cult, or better yet, that I was a Johnny Cash fan.

More likely, however, he didn't think about it at all. Over-weight, in his late fifties, and chewing on an unlit cigar, he looked as if he'd seen it all, and seeing it again wouldn't surprise him. He barely glanced at me before he pulled down the little flag and started it ticking. I smiled even wider and tried to act like driving me to still another darkened street corner surrounded by businesses closed for the night was the sort of thing I asked cabbies to do every night of the week. Driving Miss Crazy was, no doubt, what Bert would've called it.

"You want me to wait, or what?" It was the first thing the cabbie said to me. I thought for a second, looking around. Probably I could phone for another cab from Crane's studio.

I shook my head and paid the man, feeling a little pang as I watched him drive away. There went my last chance to call this whole thing off.

When the cab was out of sight, I hoofed it down Main Street toward Crane's studio, staying in the shadows and keeping a lookout for Louisville's Finest. They really could be staking out Shepard's studio in case he came back. Apparently, though, the cops felt the same way I did—that this was the next to the last place Shepard would turn up, the last place being the Jefferson County Jail. There didn't seem to be a cop car in sight. Or even an unmarked vehicle that might harbor a watchful eye.

In fact, Main Street was deserted this time of night.

And quiet.

Brian's black sneakers made soft little thuds as I ran. I'd started to breathe a little heavily by the time I got to the remodeled Victorian building that was Crane's studio, cutting in about a block down to approach the building from a rear alley. When I got there, I bent at my waist, my hands on my thighs, trying to catch my breath. I really was going to have to start some kind of exercise program soon. Lifting six or seven Coke cans to my lips every day just wasn't going to get it.

When my heart rate slowed to only about 200 beats a minute, I climbed the wrought iron fence around the rear of Crane's building, missing those little iron spears that, my luck, would certainly tear Bert's favorite jeans. I ran across the yard and started trying windows on the ground floor in the rear of the building.

Damn. Everything was locked up tight. I really didn't want to go around front and jimmy the lock to get in, because anyone driving by could see me, brazenly committing a crime. Not that I really thought that Crane would press charges against me, but it would certainly ruin our love life. I remembered how upset he was earlier when he thought I didn't trust him—and all that just because Bert had visited his cousin, asking a few questions. Searching Crane's studio could certainly be construed as a definite indication of a lack of trust.

I didn't care, I told myself, as I tried another window latch. I had to know if Crane was involved in any of the things that had been going on. Were he and Shepard partners? In every sense of the word? Did he know anything about who had killed Louise Eagleston? I needed to know the answers to all of these things. So I had to get inside, that was all there was to it.

Bert had told me she'd used a credit card to do her own breaking and entering of Shepard's office, but I really didn't know how that would work on an outside door. Especially an old door. Usually doors as old as this one had those heavy metal locks that didn't exactly give way to plastic.

So far, the front door was beginning to look better and better. I stooped down, trying the casement windows of the basement, the shadows around me still hiding me pretty effectively. One of the windows, its metal frame red with rust and grimy, finally allowed me to push one of the glass panes out. Just one little shove and the dirty rectangle of glass teetered and then began to slowly fall forward. I quickly reached under its bottom edge, through the opening made by the falling glass and caught the pane flat on my palm before it crashed to the floor and broke.

I could feel sweat popping out on my forehead as I gently maneuvered the glass out of its frame toward me. When it was finally out, I laid it beside the open window on the ground. Then I reached through the opening, turned the latch, and lifted the basement window toward me to climb in.

I'd actually remembered to ask Bert for a flashlight, but all she'd had was one of those tiny key ring things which lights up maybe your thumb, and that's it. Still, it was better than poking around in total darkness.

The basement ceiling was pretty low, and I bumped my head against a couple of really hard cylindrical things—pipes probably—before I found the stairs going up to the first floor. A closed wooden door stood at the top of the landing, and I prayed the stupid damn thing would be unlocked.

The stupid damn thing turned out to be locked tight, wouldn't you know. I shined the thumb light on the door jamb. It looked fairly new.

Hell, I figured I might as well use Bert's tried-and-true method. I rummaged in my wallet for a credit card, cursing to myself until I found one. I stuck the plastic rectangle into the door jamb and slid it upward, pushing steadily on the door at the same time.

As it happened, the credit card wasn't even needed. The push alone popped the door open. Apparently, the door frame didn't quite fit the new door—which was still locked—but with the door not fitting tight, it really didn't make much difference.

I was through the door, closing it softly after me, and tiptoeing down the hallway.

I'd turned a corner when I heard the voices.

Deep male voices.

Sounding upset. And angry.

The nearer I got, the more positive I was that the man speaking was Crane.

I stopped, listening. What was Crane doing here so late? *He works here, dummy*, I could almost hear Bert answering me.

But who was Crane talking with? A client? I stood very still, trying to make out the words, but the sounds were still muffled. It seemed to be a heated conversation—urgent and agitated. Could Crane have found Bentley? Or worse, could Bentley have found him?

Before I could consider that, I heard a door open, somewhere down the hallway. My stomach turned to lead. Whoever Crane was talking to, his voice was growing louder.

Both men were heading straight toward me.

Chapter 24

●

BERT

Talk about feeling like an idiot.

I raised my leg onto the ledge of the window in my kitchen, hoisting myself up with about as much grace as a three-legged gazelle. I winced as I pulled inside my other leg, then eased my whole body through.

I'd just left Nan's apartment through the open back window in her bathroom. I'd tossed Nan's full-length pink chenille bathrobe on the floor, too, as I exited. It really went against my grain to just dump clothes on the floor, but what could I do? I sure couldn't wear the thing over here at my place. Besides, this was Nan's asinine idea—it served her right if her robe ended up filthy. And believe me, I'd seen her floor. At Nan's apartment, the robe was going to get filthy.

I, of course, was playing the part of both of us, all for the benefit of Hank sitting out front in his unmarked car. Nan's brainstorm was sort of the opposite of what they do when they need a baby in sitcoms. Instead of having twins play one baby, I was playing twins.

"It'll be so simple," Nan had said, her eyes sparkling at the very idea of our pulling this off. Just like her eyes had sparkled when we'd tried idiotic tricks like this, as kids. Her eyes had been sparkling up a storm the day we'd both ended up in the principal's office, after "Sharp-Eyes" O'Leary, our second-grade teacher, caught us switching with each other. As I recall, my eyes had been sparkling, too. With unshed tears.

Nan had gone on to explain in more detail than was really required, how she was going to simply sashay over to her apartment wearing her raincoat over her cat burglar suit and go into her bathroom. Never mind what Hank might think, watching her wear her raincoat into the bathroom.

There she'd shed the coat and put a bathrobe over her cat burglar suit, again out of Hank's sight. She'd come out and walk around her apartment, turning lights on here and there, like she was preparing to settle in for the night. Then she'd go back into the downstairs bathroom, close the door, where Hank still couldn't see inside. Never mind what he might think about her having to visit the bathroom so often. In the bathroom, Nan would lose the robe, climb out the window, and come get me.

All this climbing in and out, of course, would be done in the rear of the house—away from Hank's snooping eyes, as Nan so charmingly referred to them. All I had to do was go into my own kitchen, close the door, and then climb out my own window. When I climbed in Nan's bathroom window, I'd slip on her bathrobe, and come out of the bathroom, just like I was Nan in the flesh. Or rather, in the robe. I'd then walk around in front of her windows, acting Nan-like.

After a little while, I'd do the reverse, going into her bathroom, shedding her robe, climbing out of her window and into my own. Hank would never realize he was only seeing one twin at a time. Even if he caught on, it still gave her time to slip away.

I believe Nan's exact words were: *Piece of cake.*

Slice of hell was what I called it.

Nan, of course, had forgotten that I'd just been in a not-so-small auto accident that had totaled my car. Every muscle I happened to have—some I'd never even known were part of my body—had begun to ache. Climbing in and out of windows wasn't exactly an activity I'd been hoping to do in the near future. Not without a strong shot of morphine. Or a strong shot of *something.*

The first time I climbed into Nan's bathroom, I thought I might just faint from the pain. OK, so maybe I could be exaggerating just a little. But if the pain didn't do me in, the strong case of nerves I was suffering from might easily have pushed me into unconsciousness. Nevertheless, I put Nan's robe on, opened her bathroom door, and stepped out, walking in full view of the front windows. I just stood there, waiting for Hank to turn on the sirens, or come banging on the door, or write me a ticket for impersonating an impersonator.

Nothing happened.

Then it occurred to me that I was just standing there, in front of the windows, motionless, practically begging Hank to notice that something weird was going on. I looked around Nan's apartment, trying to act natural. Which was pretty difficult since Nan's apartment, to put it kindly, was a pigsty.

Newspapers and books were piled on every horizontal surface, including her sofa and chairs, and old magazines littered any bare spaces left. It wasn't like Nan didn't have bookcases or magazine baskets in which to put these things either. I'd personally given her a very nice wooden magazine rack for Christmas last year. I spotted the thing in the corner of the living room—she had several pairs of shoes stacked in it.

In addition to the papers and books, empty glasses and dinner plates were scattered throughout the room, a couple actually on top of the TV.

I would've tried sitting down on Nan's sofa, but the newspapers kept getting in the way. I would've turned on the TV, but I couldn't locate the remote control with all the litter. I know, I know—you can turn on a television set with your actual fingers—but not finding Nan's remote only made me that much more aware of the mess around me. And that Nan wasn't here to clean up or find the remote for me—she can always put her hands right on the thing as if she has some kind of internal radar for it.

Goodness, I wished she was here. I really wished she wasn't doing what she was doing. I just knew I shouldn't have let her go. Once I started worrying, I couldn't stand it any longer. I started stacking Nan's magazines on the coffee table, sorting them by date. I carried the books back to the bookcase along the wall, ignoring my aching muscles as I moved. I stacked the newspapers next to the magazines, finally cleaning off enough space on the sofa to sit down. The remote peeked at me from between the cushions. I switched on the TV, and while I listened to it in the background, I carried Nan's dirty glasses and dishes out into the kitchen. The yawning window there reminded me that it was about time to switch and revert to being me for a while.

Oh, boy. Another trip through the window. If I got really good at it, maybe I could find work as a tooth fairy.

I sighed.

Then, of course, like the dummy I am, I climbed out the window.

Chapter 25

●

NAN

Hearing Crane and whoever was with him coming closer, I turned all the way around, looking for a place to hide. For a brief panicky moment, I felt as if I were spinning in circles. The walls on both sides seemed to stretch out before me— clean, white, and unbroken by doors, windows, or escape hatches.

Crane would be turning the corner any minute—his voice was growing even louder. Bert had told me that this was a crazy idea—why, oh why, hadn't I listened to her? I shined my thumb light around, frantically, retracing my steps. Any second now, Crane would be rounding the corner of the hallway, spot me, and my dream date would instantly become a nightmare.

There was no way I could explain my way out of this one. I could hear me now. "I just happened to be passing by, so I thought I'd climb in your window." And I didn't even want to think about what could happen if it was actually Bentley here with Crane.

I tried the door I'd come in—and wouldn't you know it? Now the damn thing wouldn't budge. And oh yeah, it was still locked tight.

I was royally screwed.

I started up the hallway beyond the door, growing more and more frantic as the voices grew louder behind me. The tiny beam from my thumb light played upon an indention in the wall up ahead. A door. I darted toward it, praying the damned thing wasn't locked, too.

Thank the dear Lord in heaven, it wasn't. I ducked inside.

The pungent smell of chemicals hit me like a splash of cold water. I shined my thumb light around. Five gray rectangular trays full of liquid stood on countertops lining the far wall. In the gloom, I could see a sink and, on the counter, a large black contraption standing on a squarish column mounted on a white almost-square base. A metal rectangular frame sat on the base. Overhead, hung with plastic clips on a clothes line, were several eight-by-ten photographs. The clothes line swayed a little as I moved around the room.

What do you know? I actually knew where I was. That contraption over there was an enlarger, and the rectangular trays held developer and other fluids to produce photographs. This was Crane's darkroom—he'd showed it to me the first time he'd brought me here. Lord, was that really only four days ago?

Outside, the voices were coming even nearer. Again, I heard Crane's voice, but this time I could almost make out what he was saying. ". . . cannot believe the . . . got to think what . . ."

I pressed my ear to the door, straining to hear.

I still could not hear the actual words, but one thing I could tell, though. I guess I could be wrong, but it certainly seemed to me that the conversation I was hearing came only from Crane. He *was* here alone, after all. The "voices" I'd kept hearing all belonged to Crane—I'd recognize that deep, sexy sound anywhere. And let's face it, he was apparently having a lively talk with himself, his voice taut and angry.

OK, so Crane talked to himself. I kind of understood that. We've all got our idiosyncrasies, and we've all developed coping behaviors when we get overstressed. Maybe Crane talked to himself—out loud, no less—when he was all by himself and very upset, just to ease the tension. Maybe he did it because he no longer had Lane to talk to now.

"I just wish you had . . . then it wouldn't have been . . ."

Hell, occasionally I bite my fingernails when I'm nervous. When I have a really bad day at work, my nails don't need trimming for months. Actually, talking to yourself isn't so unusual. Especially when you're upset. And Lord knows, Crane had reason to be upset.

I could hear footsteps in addition to the voices now. Coming closer. They seemed to stop almost right outside my door. And suddenly, Crane's voice boomed crystal-clear.

"I thought it was agreed," Crane said, "that neither one of us does anything without discussing it with the other one first."

I froze. What on earth?

Crane went on, "You never, never think it through. Now look at the mess we're in."

I felt as if my heart had stopped beating. Good God, he was talking crazy. Did he have some kind of split personality? Had the trauma of everything that had happened unhinged his mind? Was that what Louise was trying to tell Bert? Too, she'd said. Had she meant *two?*

"Calm down. Besides, what was I supposed to do? That bitch kept nosing around," Crane said, "and she was going to find out everything. Something had to be done—and it had to be done right away."

My mouth went dry. Could Crane be talking about Louise Eagleston?

"But running her off the road? What were you thinking? What were you trying to do? Ruin us both?"

Running off the road?

Bert? Was he talking about *Bert?*

I actually went cold. As if ice water had just replaced every drop of blood in my veins. My mind was reeling— what was going on here? Was Crane insane? He was actually talking as if he were two people.

Two. That *had* been what Louise had tried to tell Bert. She'd meant there were two of him.

Oh my God.

"Well, something had to be done—and you sure weren't doing anything. Except chasing after Nan."

I stifled a gasp, hearing my name. He'd been chasing after me? Outside my door, the footsteps continued on past. From the sound, I would almost swear there was more than one person out there. I heard the creak of a door opening farther down the hall.

"Just listen to me for a second, would you? It was stupid. If you'd wrecked Bentley's Corvette with that fool incident, you'd have had to leave the car behind. Then how would we have staged his accident? Tell me that, Lane. How?"

Oh my God.

I actually felt faint. *Lane.* He'd said Lane.

Louise had meant two, all right. But she'd meant there were two of *them.* She'd been trying to tell Bert that Lane was still alive.

"You'd have thought of something; you always do," Lane said. "Hell, I don't know what you're so upset about. When the cops finally do find Bentley's body in that wreckage in the river, they'll figure they've got their man. No prob. Finito. End of story. The perfect ending."

Bentley? Bentley was dead? I closed my eyes, willing none of this to be true. I didn't even want to think where Bentley's body could be right now.

"I'm just saying you should think first," Crane said, his deep voice calmer now. "You didn't have to eliminate Louise Eagleston—that was idiotic, too, Lane. She was no threat to us."

"Like hell she wasn't," Lane said. "That fat crone would've poked around until she found out everything. She wasn't about to give it up. Once she'd contacted Bentley, asking him questions about you, it was just a matter of time."

"It was stupid."

"Stupid? I'll tell you stupid. Stupid was sharing offices with that weasel Bentley in the first place. He actually thought Louise Eagleston was interested in *him*. He'd have told her everything she wanted to know if she'd have let him into her rich britches. Bentley actually thought she liked him—that she was interested in his dirty pictures, not us."

"How do you know that?"

"He told me. That idiot would've told me anything to keep me from killing him. He met Louise at some restaurant on Bardstown Road to give her the photographs he'd taken, along with those of us, too. Of course, Bentley just sat there, drooling, watching this society dame look at his dirty pictures. He couldn't imagine that the ones she really wanted were those of us and Marian. The stupid asshole. You can't tell me killing him was stupid."

"Yeah, well, I guess you're right there," Crane said. "I should've killed him myself when that cop told me what Bentley had been up to. I would have, too, if Nan hadn't been here when Bentley came back. His little sideline has brought the cops crawling down our throats."

I closed my eyes, fighting nausea. Oh God. How could I have ever thought this man was perfect?

"I'll tell you what else was stupid. Chasing after Nan Tatum. A twin? Come on—that was just asking for trouble."

"I thought she'd understand about us." Crane's voice actually sounded sad, and the nausea I felt grew worse. "But that's why killing Bert would be dumb. If Bert's murdered, Nan won't ever give up until she finds out what happened. Believe me, I know her. We'd end up having to do them both—and that'll bring that fucking homicide cop down on top of us. He's suspicious already."

"But we're going to have to kill Bert," Lane said. "She *knows*. I can feel it when I'm around her."

I felt numb. The voices were less loud now—they'd apparently gone into a room nearby, leaving the door open.

"You'd better not do a thing, until we both decide. Now tell me about the photographs you've finished. What needs to be mailed out tonight? And what's due tomorrow?"

I didn't know what was worse, hearing them talk about killing people or hearing them discuss photographs and meeting business deadlines. They used the same matter-of-fact tone whether they were talking about business or about the deaths of Bentley and Louise Eagleston. And Bert. It was all the same thing to them—business as usual.

I was certain now that I was going to throw up. I shone my thumb light around, looking for a trash can. Hell, I'd just barf all over their floor—it would serve the bastards right.

"There are still some photos drying in the darkroom," Lane said. "I've got the mailers for them already addressed."

I froze.

Oh my God.

Footsteps headed my way. Before I could move, the door to the darkroom opened, and the light switched on.

I found myself, staring at Lane and Crane Morgan, their identical mouths dropping open.

Oh, shit. Oh, double shit.

And I'd told Bert to wait two hours.

That could be very poor planning.

Chapter 26

●

BERT

Climbing out of Nan's window and into my own, I almost forgot to take off the robe, remembering it only when it snagged on the bush right beneath my kitchen window. I would have to remember to bring the darn thing with me when I went to Nan's, or else I'd have to come back for it.

I came out of my kitchen and walked into my own living room. I sat down in front of my own television, which I'd cleverly left on when I'd climbed out before. I'd left it on so that Hank would see the thing flickering, and think that I had to be somewhere still in the apartment, listening to the sound of the television.

I couldn't concentrate on what was on the screen in front of me, though. My goodness, where on earth *was* Nan? What was taking her so long? I really should have insisted on my going with her. After all, Bentley Shepard had already killed one person.

The very thought of Louise and the way she'd looked the day I'd found her made me shiver. I remembered the photographs she'd pressed so urgently into my hands. "Too . . ." she'd said. "Too . . ."

I thought of the two brothers smiling into the camera, so alike. The remarkable beauty of Marian. Two of those smiling faces were gone now—Lane and Marian. And now Louise, too.

I suddenly sat up straight. I saw in my mind's eye those photographs again. The two men, so identical—same clothes, same hair, same good looks, even the same forget-me-not tattoo.

I was just sitting there, staring into space, sorting it all out. Could it be?

Could it really be?

All at once, I knew what I had to do.

Chapter 27

●

NAN

I didn't even think.

While the Brothers Grimm just stood there, shocked motionless at the sight of me, I turned, grabbed a pan of chemicals, and threw it in the face of Lane—or was it Crane? Whoever it was shrieked and grabbed his eyes, while the other one turned toward him, apparently trying to help. I darted past both of them and ran.

I'd have made it, too, if I'd cut my shoulder-length hair like Bert and I had often talked about doing. As it was, the one not holding his eyes took a quick grab at me as I passed him by. He jerked me back by the hair.

I, of course, screamed.

Until one of them got me by the throat, his long fingers squeezing, his other hand still rubbing at his red, swollen eyes. The other one held me tightly by the hair, pulling me closer to them both. The fingers around my throat tightened, and I began to choke, gasping soundlessly for air. I started to black out, but Crane said, "Stop it, Lane. Not here—we can take her somewhere safe."

But Lane was still rubbing at his eyes, his other hand loosening just a little around my throat. He brought his face close to mine, grinning. "You know, it's really a shame it has to be this way. I really enjoyed the time we spent together."

"So did I," Crane said. I turned to look at him. Oh God. His ugly grin was identical to his brother's.

I stared at him, and then over at Lane. I felt sick to my stomach all over again. Because I finally understood. I'd been dating *both* of them—Lane and Crane—unable to tell one from the other.

"Unfortunately," Crane said, "just lately you've begun to remind us both a lot of Marian."

I was not delighted to hear it.

Lane tightened his grip on my throat. "Yes, that's right," Lane said, his breath so close, I could feel it warm on my cheek. "In fact, you're just like Marian—a damn sneak. Always sticking her nose in where it didn't belong. And you know what we did to her, don't you?" A switchblade had appeared from nowhere. He waved it in front of my face, no doubt enjoying the sudden fear I knew had to be in my eyes.

"Don't be a fool, Lane," his brother said, taking Lane's wrist and pulling it away. I looked over at Crane, thinking that maybe he was actually trying to help me. His face, however, was that of a complete stranger. His expression was cold, impassive.

"*I said*, not here. We can't make the same mistake we did with Marian," Crane said. "We can't let *me* get charged with murder, too. Mine is the only life we have, for God's sake. Nan's going to have to end up with Bentley. It's got to look as if he kidnapped her—to use as a hostage, or whatever, and then he had his car accident while he was trying to escape with her. We'll have to take Nan to the river, where we left Bentley. The cops have *got* to blame all this on him."

Staring at them, I realized then what Bert and I have

always suspected. When it comes to identical twins, there is no such thing as an Evil Twin and a Good Twin. All those dumb movies and books were wrong. Dead wrong. If one identical twin is evil, they both are.

It hadn't been Lane who'd killed Marian Fielding. Both of the twins had killed her. The neighbors on each side of Marian's apartment who'd recognized Lane leaving the scene of the murder had probably seen both of them. One had seen Lane, and one had seen Crane.

"Let go of me, Crane," Lane said, through his teeth. "You're always telling me what to do."

"Because you act stupid," Crane shot back.

Great, while they were working out their sibling rivalry, I was trying to keep from passing out, or from throwing up, or both. My eyes bounced between the two of them, like I'd so often seen people do with me and Bert. God, they were so identical. More so, even, than Bert and I were.

What had he said? Crane's was the only life they had. God. With Lane presumed dead, they'd actually been sharing the one life. And evidently everything else.

My stomach retched.

What a perfectly revolting idea.

"I do not act stupid," Lane whined.

"No?" Crane told his brother. "You want to leave evidence here for the cops to find? Nan'll be a lot easier to get to the river if she's alive—or did you want to carry a body down to the car? Remember Marian? And all the blood we had to deal with?"

I studied Crane now—too late, I was actually learning to tell them apart, now that I saw them together—and he looked back at me with eyes that mirrored his brother's. They held no remorse. And no compassion.

I shuddered when I recalled that I'd actually thought I was falling in love with this monster.

And when I thought of the other things I'd done with him. Oh God, I really was going to be ill.

"You're right," Lane said, suddenly showing that ugly grin again. He stuck the knife in his pocket and grabbed my left arm, twisting it behind my back. He'd released my throat, but still kept a firm hand on my shoulder. Crane took hold of me around the waist, almost lifting me off the ground as they forced me toward the door.

I twisted around and bit Lane's hand, and was rewarded with a stinging slap across the face. Stars danced in front of my eyes, and I tasted blood in my mouth.

"You hateful bitch!" Lane hissed at me.

"You'd better believe it," I hissed right back.

He would've taken another slap at me, but Crane grabbed his arm again. "Later, I said. We'll take her and put her in the trunk, and then she and Bentley can have their little accident together," Crane said. "When we get her out to the river, we'll have all the fun we want with her."

I actually groaned, listening to him.

They forced me down the hall, and through the front office door, me dragging my feet and fighting every step of the way. Until a punch in the stomach from Lane took the fight right out of me.

When the twins opened the heavy door to the outside, though, with me limp and all but falling between them, I felt them both go rigid. I looked up.

Detective Hank Goetzmann stared back at the twins, his gun drawn. In back of him were two more of the sweetest policemen you ever saw with their guns also drawn. Behind them, was Bert.

Simultaneously, Crane and Lane let go of me and slowly raised their identical hands.

And I finally did what I'd been wanting to do for a long time. I turned around and puked all over their identical pairs of shoes.

Later than night, when I was finally back at Bert's apartment, with a Coke in my hands, and my heart no longer beating like it was going to spring right out of my chest, I calmly sat on her sofa, staring at Bert. OK, I had to ask her.

"Why?"

Bert frowned at me, and looked puzzled. "Why what?"

"Why on earth did you come early? You were supposed to wait two hours. Good God, I thought I was a goner, for sure. I mean, I'm not complaining. Far from it. But how on earth did you know to come? And don't tell me our twin vibes have gotten better."

"*Your* twin vibes have gotten better," said a deep voice over my shoulder. I looked back, and Goetzmann grinned at me. I couldn't help it—I grinned back at the jerk. The man had saved my life—maybe he wasn't exactly the mate for me, but he could be a cop in my life any old day.

Goetzmann reached over the back of the sofa and handed Bert a Coke, twin to the one he'd just given me. I don't know how she'd done it, but somehow in Bert's part of our house, Goetzmann seemed to have suddenly become very well trained. He actually waited on us, for Pete's sake. Brought us Cokes, fixed with his own stubby gargantuan hands. What a fantastic lesson for the guy to learn.

And was it just my imagination or did Bert's eyes seem to glow a little brighter as she took the glass from him? "Thanks, Hank," she said, turning quickly back to me. She took a quick sip of Coke. "To answer your question, actually, it was that darn tattoo."

"Tattoo?" Goetzmann and I asked the question in unison.

"That tattoo—you know, the purple forget-me-not. I couldn't get it out of my mind. When I'd seen it at the dinner party I'd had for you and Crane, that tattoo, I was sure, had been a nice, bright purple. But later, when the person I thought was Crane touched my cheek, I could've sworn the tattoo was a lighter color. As if it had been on his hand for years and years and had faded. The tattoo at dinner seemed to be a lot more vivid—as if, maybe, it had just been done, oh, say three years ago, so that Crane and Lane could be really identical. When I remembered that tattoo and how they were different, I knew I had to go get Hank."

"Yup. Tattoos fade," Goetzmann said, nodding solemnly, as if this pronouncement was one of the wiser deductions he'd made during the case.

Bert nodded, too, looking enthralled. Hey, I didn't see it, but who was I to argue?

"Well, if you two are all right now, I guess I should be getting along," Goetzmann said. He nodded at me, but his eyes strayed to Bert.

"I'll walk you out," Bert said, popping up from the chair as she were spring-loaded. I watched them, Bert's eyes sparkling, her face turned to his with interest as he mumbled something innocuous to her. Let's face it, I'd never been *that* interested in anything Goetzmann had ever had to say.

Watching Bert, though, I'm wondering if I'm the gullible twin, after all. I'd always thought I was a lot more savvy than Bert, especially since Bert had stayed at home for several eons before her divorce thrust her out into the cruel, harsh world. Now, I'm not so sure. Bert does seem to be making it a habit to rush to my rescue. Not that I'm complaining. Hell, I'm just in awe.

I took a long sip of my Coke. I'd almost been killed, yet I was feeling calmer and calmer, even as the caffeine hit my system.

I thought about what I'd been through, trying to get a fix on what I was feeling now. It was pretty obvious I'd jumped into the relationship with Crane a bit too quickly. Maybe next time I'd try for friendship first—that might be a refreshing change.

Even though it might seem odd, I didn't feel any more fearful than I'd been before meeting Crane Morgan. Hey, I had finally come up with the all-time worst dating experience of my life. So from here on in, it could only get better.

In the future, maybe I'd just start listening to Bert a little more closely. She'd certainly had bad vibes about Crane Morgan from the very beginning.

Of course, I don't want to go overboard here. Bert hasn't exactly picked Mr. Right for herself. I glanced at the front door. Unless, of course, she was doing it right now.

I watched Bert's head and Goetzmann's bend closer together as they stood in the open front door. And I knocked on wood as I took a long sip of my Coke, just in case. I watched them some more.

Go on, kiss her, you lunkhead.

Naturally, he didn't.

Chapter 28

●

BERT

My doorbell rang, minutes after I arrived home from work. It was the following Wednesday after all the excitement, and my current assignment—yet another accounting firm— had kept me so busy that I'd missed lunch. Even so, I was thinking about just taking a bubble bath and going on to bed. No dinner, no TV, no nothing.

I peeked through my peep hole.

And quickly opened the door, patting down my hair as I did so.

Hank Goetzmann stood there, looking very big and very uncomfortable, shifting uneasily from one foot to the other.

"Hank?" I opened the door, and he moved past me into my apartment. "Is anything wrong?"

"Nope." Then he just stood there, looking down at me, as if he was thinking about what to say. Great. Now *I* felt uncomfortable. I dropped my eyes, trying to think of something to say to him. Lord, we could stand here all night.

Goodness, what was it about this big teddy bear of a man that made my heart race so? If I didn't know better, I'd actually think I was—

Finishing that little thought made me more uncomfortable than ever, so I didn't finish it. Instead, I turned and closed the door, then followed Hank as he moved into my living room.

"Won't you sit down?" I said, indicating my chair nearest to the fireplace.

Oh God. I sounded so proper. Who was I trying to be— Nancy Reagan?

Hank followed me into the room, sitting down on the sofa, leaving ample room next to him. "I thought you'd want to know, Bert, that we found out who it was that had called Nan at the radio station. The lady Nan called Looney Tunes?"

I perched on a chair as far away from the sofa as possible. Goodness, he made me nervous. "Really? Who was it?"

"Grace Fielding. Marian's mother. She was the one who got Louise Eagleston involved, too. Louise and Grace Fielding attended Daviess County High School together—they'd been good friends back then, before Louise moved to Louisville. Grace called on Louise when she learned Crane had moved to Louisville, too. Grace died the first of this week—from pancreatic cancer—she left a letter explaining everything. Apparently, she felt responsible for Louise's murder."

I shook my head. "That poor woman. It wasn't her fault— it was the Morgan twins." I shifted position in my chair, trying to look more relaxed. "Are they talking?"

Hank shook his head. "But we'll still convict them. We've just about got it all figured out. Those twins had quite a scheme going. When it became obvious that one of the twins was going to be punished for what they both had done, they decided they'd have to give the police someone to blame. A dead someone. They'd fake a suicide."

I grimaced at the thought. "But who?"

"Some homeless guy they found, about their age, their size—he was the guy who took the tumble off the bridge," said Hank. "Hell—pardon my French—they knew after he'd spent some time in the river, nobody would be able to tell that he wasn't Lane. They put Lane's clothes on him and his watch, and then, if that wasn't enough, Crane himself identified the body as Lane. It was a great plan."

"I can hardly believe the man we met was capable of doing such a terrible thing," I said.

"You bet your life he was. After they faked Lane's death," Goetzmann went on, "the two of them began to share one life. They left Owensboro where people might be able to tell the difference, and they avoided any family or old friends. They'd been planning to go into the photography business together before Lane's so-called suicide, and they just kept right on.

"The one thing Lane *has* told us is that the two of them switched places all the time. Even back in high school. They both carried a tape recorder with them some of the time to help the other to remember details. It was just luck that it was Crane who was here when you took the glass with his fingerprints. That's why they killed Marian in the first place."

"What do you mean?"

"According to Grace Fielding's letter, Marian had found out about how they switched all the time—because they did it with her. Marian wasn't this terrible, flirtatious person that Crane Morgan described. Or that his Cousin Edna saw—out with both brothers. Marian didn't know she was dating them both! And she didn't like being the plaything of two brothers when she found out. She tried to break it off with them, but they wouldn't stand for that."

I grimaced. "Both of them. With one girl? How . . . icky." It was all I could think to say.

Hank looked amused.

I changed the subject. "You know, I can't imagine the two brothers being able to pull it off," I said. "I mean, goodness, Nan and I would never share a—I mean, we could never pull such a thing off in a million years—that is, we'd never want to . . ."

"Thank God," said Hank, very low. His eyes were on mine now.

Oh, dear. There was one of those long awkward silences again, and I wondered what on earth to talk about now.

Fortunately, Goetzmann jumped in with still more tales of the twins' and their switching places. I listened to him, but I couldn't help but wonder. Why hadn't Hank just phoned me with this information?

Almost as soon as I'd thought the question, Hank had my answer.

"Bert," he suddenly blurted, "would you go out to dinner with me tonight?"

I stared at him. You might think that, after hearing about Lane and Crane and the way they'd shared every little thing—like a *life*, for example, not to mention, women—the last thing I'd want to do would be to go out with somebody Nan had dated.

But there was a very large difference. Nan has made it abundantly clear that she was no longer the least bit interested in Hank.

And there was something else.

Something had happened as I ran out of the house to tell Hank where Nan was.

Goetzmann had already been getting out of his car.

He had already caught on that he'd been watching me in both apartments. I looked into his hazel eyes. Goodness, he really was cute. "Let me ask you something first, Hank," I said.

Hank frowned. "Why do I think I see a large 'no' coming up?"

I smiled at him, patting his hand. "Not necessarily. Tell me, how did you figure it out? How did you know it was me in both apartments?"

Hank shrugged that careless shrug I like so much. "Hey, it was easy," he said. "I'm looking in those windows; and what do you know, you start picking up Nan's apartment. And loading the dishwasher, folding laundry, and going around the living room, picking things up. And I'm thinking, whoa, *this* can *not* be Nan."

I almost laughed out loud. "Yes, Detective Hank Goetzmann," I said, standing up, "dinner would be very nice."

I went to get my coat.

The way I figure it, if Hank could tell Nan and me apart that well from a distance, the least I could do was give him a chance to discover a few differences close up.